Jonnie Hyde is a PhD psychologist living in SW Washington, where she founded and was executive director of a large community mental health center. After retiring in 2017, she decided to pursue her lifelong goal of writing a novel. And since she has been a close follower of climate science and climate change since reading Paul Ehrlic's *The Population Bomb* in 1970, she decided to bring these two passions together in her novel, *Irrevocable Acts*.

To Meg, for her unwavering faith in me and in this story.

Jonnie Hyde

IRREVOCABLE ACTS

AUSTIN MACAULEY PUBLISHERS™

LONDON * CAMBRIDGE * NEW YORK * SHARJAH

Ordering Information
Quantity sales: Special discounts are available on quantity purchases by corporations, associations, and others. For details, contact the publisher at the address below.

Publisher's Cataloging-in-Publication data
Hyde, Jonnie
Irrevocable Acts

ISBN 9798891550636 (Paperback)
ISBN 9798891550643 (ePub e-book)

Library of Congress Control Number: 2023921638

www.austinmacauley.com/us

First Published 2024
Austin Macauley Publishers LLC
40 Wall Street, 33rd Floor, Suite 3302
New York, NY 10005
USA

mail-usa@austinmacauley.com
+1 (646) 5125767

20240219

I want to thank Linda Stirling of the Publishing Compnay, my wife and my closest friends for reading early drafts, giving me critical feedback, and encouraging me every step of the way. And above all, I want to thank the scientists and environmental activists who selflessly and courageously fight to save our climate and our earth every single day.

Part I
The Shape of Things Familiar

Chapter 1

In her darkened room, Anna pushed back the covers and moved into a sitting position on the edge of her bed, pulling her legs to her chest and wrapping her arms around them. She rested her cheek on her bony knees and watched the clock tick away the last precious moments of normal life. In the deep quiet of the house, every click of the minute hand sounded like a door closing.

At exactly 4:30 a.m., she stood, stepped away from the bed, and let her faded nightgown fall to the floor. Having gathered her gear the day before, it didn't take long to tie back her long, graying hair and dress from head to toe in black: socks, jeans, t-shirt, an oversized hoodie, Merrill slip-on shoes, and a pair of thin glove liners. She slipped a small but powerful flashlight into her pocket, then lifted the stuffed garbage bag from the back of her closet.

If Gracie cried out in a dream, if Kate came downstairs for any reason at all, how in the world would she explain herself? She had tried but failed to come up with a believable lie that would account for the hour, the clothes, and the bulky black bag she slung over her shoulder.

She stepped out of her bedroom and moved quickly and quietly through the shadowy house. Feeling like a teenager breaking curfew, she snuck out of her own back door.

A thick ground fog gave her a sense of invisibility as she walked down the common alley that divided the block lengthwise. She stayed close to the contiguous line of six-foot-high fencing to her right, but her eyes kept darting to the left, to an unbroken expanse of green lawns and leafy deciduous trees that left her feeling exposed. Still, she marveled at the serendipitous preservation of open space on her side of the block, an anachronism from a simpler, more communal time none of her neighbors had yet had the heart to defile.

She heard a rustling noise close by. Already on edge, she stopped in her tracks. She listened, but the only thing she heard was her own blood pulsing in her ears.

It's nothing, she told herself.

A sharp, vicious bark pierced the silence. She screamed—a guttural, broken sound—and started running. The dog raced along the fence between them, growling and snapping its jaws and charging at the wooden panels with enough force to set them swaying.

She made a hard left to escape the alley and the frenzied barking. Halfway across the Ryans' backyard, she triggered their motion-activated security light. Frozen in the sudden glare, with the fat black bag hanging over her shoulder, she thought she must look like a cartoon burglar caught in the act. She tried to resume running, but she couldn't catch her breath. She bent over, put her hands on her knees, and waited for her airway to open.

Finally, after a long wheezing gasp, she could breathe again. She bolted to the Ryans' back porch, reached up and wrapped her gloved fingers around the hot, blinding Halogen bulb, and rotated it counterclockwise. Darkness returned.

She sat down on the cement steps and waited for her heart to stop hammering in her chest, for her breathing to return to normal, for one or both of the Ryans to come stomping downstairs to investigate, for all the other lights in the neighborhood to go on, for the police to arrive with lights flashing and sirens wailing.

A light appeared in the house where the barking dog lived. She heard the back door open, heard a man's voice call the dog inside, and heard the door close.

"No more excitement for you tonight, Cujo," she whispered.

Taking slow, deep breaths to slow her pulse, she waited a full five minutes to see if her fears would materialize. At last, she pulled off her shoes, dug a key out of her pocket, and unlocked the back door. A bright red light pulsed from the security box on the inside wall. She had forty-five seconds to punch in the alarm code Ellie had given her. She pressed the numbered buttons on the keypad and the blinking red light turned a solid green.

In stocking feet, she padded across the mudroom and into the house. She turned on her flashlight and paused to listen for any sounds from upstairs, but other than the elderly couple's loud snores, all was silent. She walked straight to the dining room. Ellie's purse, glasses and keys were sitting on the hutch, exactly where she had expected to find them. Her hand shook as she opened Ellie's wallet, removed her driver's license, and slipped it into her back pocket.

The Ryans would discover the missing license when they checked in for their flight in a few hours, but since a passport was both necessary and sufficient for boarding, she was fairly certain the couple wouldn't panic and abort their longed-for vacation. After all, Ellie was absent-minded and so accustomed to losing things that when something of hers disappeared, she assumed it was she who had misplaced it. She was usually right.

Anna carried the black bag through the kitchen, into the garage. She dropped it to the cement floor, got down on her hands and knees, and shoved it deep under the Ryans' Volvo. Satisfied, she went back through the house, re-armed the alarm, exited the mudroom, and locked the door behind her.

Though Cujo was no longer a threat, she couldn't bring herself to face the alley again, so she walked to the Ryans' side yard to get a view of the street. With the exception of a few pale yellow front porch lights, all of the residences on both sides of the block were dark. She could see two streetlights with down-facing LED bulbs that sparkled like bright crystals, but they cast a narrow beam.

What would happen if someone did look out and catch a glimpse of her dark, cloaked figure? She imagined the watcher's heart might beat a little faster, his eyes might track her, but once she passed, he would gratefully turn away from the shadowy world outside his window. Or maybe no one would see her. Maybe her neighbors were more fortunate than she was and actually slept through the wee hours.

Time to go. She took off, running across the Ryans' front yard until she reached one of the towering sycamores lining the street. She ducked under the dense, green foliage, pausing just long enough to catch her breath, then darted from one tree to the next until she stood beneath a canopy in front of her own home. With the back of one hand, she swiped at the sweat dripping down her neck. Her shoulder blades itched like crazy, so she rubbed her back against the rough tree bark until she found the sweet spot.

Her aging house loomed in the darkness. She didn't need daylight to know the exterior paint, once a comforting sage, was faded and chipped; that moss was breaking down the composite shingles on her roof; that tall weeds had overtaken the once pristine lawn; that the rhododendron bushes around the front walkway were overgrown and spindly from neglect. She didn't need to see the porch, or step onto it, to know that some of the boards were dangerously soft in the middle.

I'm sorry, Kate, she thought. *I didn't mean to let the place go, not like this. It was a beautiful house when we first moved here, but it took so much maintenance. And after you left home, I just threw myself into work and let everything else go. It got away from me. Everything got away from me.*

She looked toward her bedroom's south-facing window. In spring and summer, she often woke early to bright sunlight streaming in through the glass. On such mornings, she would lift the wood framed pane to catch the sweet scent of her neighbor's purple wisteria. She would go into the kitchen to make a pot of coffee and, with mug in hand, return to bed. She would pull the comforter up over her legs and spend hours reading, escaping into whatever supermarket novel had caught her eye, until her daughter and granddaughter roused.

Only yesterday, she and Gracie had slept in that room after going for a walk at Mt. Tabor Park. She remembered curling up next to her sweetly snoring granddaughter, whose right hand clutched a cherished, though battered, doll. She remembered reaching over and touching Gracie's other, empty hand, and being amazed at how, even in sleep, her granddaughter's little fingers responded to touch with touch. She remembered kissing Gracie's palm and holding her own big paw up against it. "Oh my," she had whispered. "Oh my."

In just six hours, she and Gracie would be on their way to the Oregon Zoo of all places, on this day of all days. By nightfall, the old war between her and Kate would likely be raging again.

Fighting back tears, she stepped away from the tree. She re-entered her house through the back porch and stealthily crept into her bedroom. She stripped off her clothes, pulled her nightgown over her head, and climbed back under the covers.

Three weeks earlier, Ellie and her husband, Martin, had come across a last-minute deal on a twenty-one-day European cruise. Their usual house-sitter was already booked, so they asked Anna, their neighbor of some twenty years, if she would be willing to take care of their beautiful and bountiful indoor plants in their absence. She assumed their entreaty was an act of true desperation since the couple had never asked her to housesit before, and were in fact openly critical of her own neglected lawn and weed-infused gardens.

"Sure, I can do that," Anna said. "One of the benefits of retirement."

"That's great," Ellie said. "I'd like to thank you by taking you to lunch at Palermo's tomorrow. We can go over the details then."

Anna loved good food, and Palermo's was one of the finest restaurants in a town that was nationally renowned for exceptional cuisine. Nonetheless, she would have chosen a less expensive, less formal setting, one that accommodated her preference for blue jeans and Birkenstocks.

"Ellie, have you ever eaten at the Haan Ghin food cart, the one outside of the PSU Library? They have delicious citrus-soaked ground chicken, tossed with lemongrass and hot chilli."

Ellie laughed. "That sounds wonderful, Anna, but can you see me, in my Liz Claiborne pantsuit and Cole Hahn shoes, carrying a wobbly plate of steaming food to a picnic bench and eating sticky rice with a plastic fork?"

"No, I can't imagine it," Anna said, also laughing. "Palermo's would be great."

"By the way," Ellie said, "don't feel like you need to dress up for my sake. This is Portland. You can go almost anywhere in jeans."

"Thanks, but for special occasions, I actually can clean up my act."

On the day of their luncheon, Anna pulled a cardboard storage box from under her bed and unearthed a pair of pale green linen pants and a slightly darker green blouse and jacket, remnants of her former working life. She ran an iron over the outfit, adorned her ears with silver loops, and corralled her shoulder-length hair into a rubber-banded ponytail. She met Ellie at the restaurant on time.

Though the two women liked each other, they couldn't have been more different. Anna dressed like an old hippie, Ellie like a fading movie star. Anna was a lefty, Ellie a hardcore Republican, though not of the Tea Party variety. Anna was an agnostic, bordering on atheist, Ellie a practicing Catholic. While it was difficult for them to navigate an entire conversation, they could reliably fall back on two topics: the state of the neighborhood and the tribulations of aging.

About two-thirds of the way through the meal, Ellie brought up the traffic on Hawthorne Boulevard. "The buses are running so late at night that we can't even watch TV without hearing the sound of their brakes screeching. How anybody sleeps through that, I'll never know."

"The noise doesn't bother me," Anna said. "When I was a kid in California, I'd lie in bed at night trying to hear the whistle of the trains in the distance. Now, since I'm often up at all kinds of crazy hours, I listen for the buses. I find them comforting."

"To each her own. Now about your insomnia, I know I've suggested this before, but I'll suggest it again. You really must try Ambien. It puts me into an absolute stupor," Ellie said, as if 'stupor' was a desirable state. "Ask your doctor about it."

"I've never taken sleep medications, though I've often wished I could buy them at the drugstore. I think I'd eat them like Pez."

"Martin and I take one every night. We wouldn't be able to sleep a wink otherwise. We've only had to have the dose raised once in ten years, from five to ten milligrams. They work like magic."

Anna tried to resist bringing up the dark side of Ellie's panacea, but couldn't stop herself. "I've heard a lot of stories about Ambien. Alarming stories, like people doing strange things without knowing it, like getting into their car to drive to work in the middle of the night, or waking up with a half-eaten pie in the bed next to them."

Ellie was not only unscathed by Anna's cautionary tales, she was exuberant.

"Somnambulism can be a side effect," she admitted, in a confidential whisper. "But if I go to bed right after I take one, I'm out cold. Almost nothing can wake me. My brother, Dennis, came by the house late one night, though I can't remember why now. He said he'd been banging on the door and ringing the bell for a full five minutes before Martin heard him. I never did hear him. Believe me, sleep deprivation will kill you faster than sleep walking, so it's worth the risk."

Anna kept nodding to Ellie and smiling, but her thoughts were elsewhere. She had tuned out when she heard the words, 'Nothing can wake me'. She was considering the possibilities when the waiter approached with a tray of pastries.

Ellie tapped her arm. "Anna, these desserts look wonderful. Let's indulge. What do you say?"

"Sounds good," Anna said, trying to sound enthusiastic. She watched as Ellie carefully perused the offerings. At the precise moment, her neighbor selected a banana crème brûlée over a frangipane pear tart, Anna too, made a decision—one that would not be found on any menu in the civilized world.

Unable to fall back asleep after her break-in at the Ryans', Anna didn't need to set her alarm. She got out of bed at 6:15 a.m. on the dot and pulled the curtain back from her window so she could watch the street in front of her house. She didn't have to wait long before the airport van rolled past. Ellie and Martin were on their way.

And so am I, she thought. She tried to avert the onset of a full-blown panic attack by telling herself she still had twenty hours to change her mind.

Chapter 2

"Mom, dinner will be ready soon. It's time for you two to get up."

Anna opened her eyes to see Kate standing in her doorway, leaning with one shoulder against the wall, looking as if she had been there awhile.

"Thank you, sweetie," she said, pushing herself up one elbow. "We were worn out when we got home from the zoo this afternoon. Gracie crashed hard," she said, glancing at her granddaughter's sleeping form on the bed next to her.

She sat up and swung her feet to the floor. "But I didn't mean to sleep so long," she said with a yawn.

"You needed it, Mom. You looked exhausted when you got up this morning. Rough night?"

Anna thought, *'Rough' doesn't even begin to describe my night, or my morning.* "Just the usual insomnia," she said. "I'm used to it."

Kate shrugged. "So, tell me about the zoo. Did you two have a good time today?" Her pained expression belied her light tone, and Anna knew her daughter was steeling herself for bad news.

She thought back to her afternoon with Gracie, walking hand-in-hand together down the descending path to the Pacific Shores exhibit, stepping through the door into a dark underground cavern. Gracie had run up to the viewing window and pressed her palms against the thick glass; Anna had knelt behind her and placed her hands lightly around the little girl's waist. Together they'd watched the sea otters slide into and out of the water from a wide, rocky shelf, again and again.

She could still hear Gracie's intake of breath when one of them rolled onto its back and brought its front paws up to its whiskery chin, as if tucking in for the night.

"Nana, where is his bed?" Gracie had asked.

"He sleeps just like that, sweetie, floating on his back on the ocean."

"Ooh," Gracie whispered, as if trying to imagine such a watery life.

When they emerged from the dark cavern, she lifted Gracie into her arms and carried her to the exit.

They took the light rail into downtown Portland, where they transferred to Tri-Met bus No. 14. Gracie fell asleep and went prone in her seat as they crossed the Willamette River and headed into East Portland. When the doors opened at 16th and Hawthorne, Anna lifted all thirty-two pounds of the little girl's dead weight and carried her down the steps and all the way home.

Kate called out, "Earth to Mom."

Anna, torn from her reverie, looked up and into her daughter's bright green eyes. "Yes, honey. Yes, we had a good time. You were right about the otters. She was mesmerized by them." Anna patted the bed beside her, an invitation.

Kate crossed to the bed and sat down next to her, shoulder to shoulder. "You hated the zoo, didn't you?"

Anna pressed her lips together and gave a slight nod.

"I knew I shouldn't let you take her there," Kate said, shaking her head.

"Let me? You gave me no choice."

"Well, your original plan was to spend the entire day at the Children's Museum. She's sick of that place."

Anna arched an eyebrow. "She told you she was sick of it?"

"No, not exactly. But she did say she wanted to go to the zoo to see the new otter exhibit."

"And how did she know about that?"

"There was an article in *The Oregonian* a few days ago. I showed her the pictures."

"Ah, of course you did."

Kate, cornered, mounted a counter-attack. "You didn't give her the speech, did you? The one about the evils of keeping animals in unnatural, plasticized confines for the viewing pleasure of the public?"

"Ouch," Anna said softly. That was all she needed to say. She knew the quick jab intended to cut her had cut her daughter as well, like a fisted blade.

Kate stared down at her hands as if studying them, but she said nothing for what seemed to Anna a very long time. When she finally spoke, her anger seemed to have vanished. "I'm sorry, Mom. Old tapes, you know? I do trust that you don't tell her all the bad things that go on in your head. You promised me you wouldn't, and I have to admit, I've never heard you do it since. Not once."

"You never heard me do it before, either. Not to Gracie." Kate shrugged off the rebuke.

"You know, we've come a long way, you and I," Anna said.

Kate sighed heavily. "Yeah, I know, but it doesn't seem that way right now."

"We have, though. Most of the time we're able to talk things through and come out the other side, instead of one of us storming off in a huff."

Kate grinned. "That's because you've become so much more reasonable in your old age."

"Ah," Anna said, "and here I thought it was because you finally gave up your oppositional stance to all things parental."

Kate shot Anna a wicked smile, and Anna shook her head in mock dismay.

"A new cut today?" She asked, reaching to touch Kate's hair.

Kate ducked her head and jumped to her feet. She walked over to Anna's dresser. She examined herself in the mirror. "Yeah, a new cut," she said, frowning. "My hair had no shape. Now it does, kind of like the metal spikes when you exit a parking garage. Do not back up over my head: severe tire damage."

"Well, I think it's a cute style. I like that outfit too."

Although it was Sunday, Kate had gone into the office for a brief morning meeting, so she was dressed in an outfit suitable for the burgeoning hi-tech software firm where she worked: tight black running pants, a sleeveless gray t-shirt, a long white over-shirt, and black Converse high-top sneakers. *"You like my outfit?"*

"I do. Why the skepticism?"

"I get nervous when we agree on clothing, Mom, since you believe the invention of blue jeans and Birkenstocks were the crowning achievements of the fashion industry."

"Funny, kid. Very funny," Anna said, lobbing a pillow in her direction. It fell short but the tension crackling between them dissipated, and they both laughed.

"Mommy, I'm awake now."

Kate approached the bed again and lifted Gracie into her arms. "Hello, sleepyhead. So, what did you and nana do today?"

Gracie arched backward so she could get a better look at her mother, and with a dopey delivery and wide smile, said, "We went to the zoo."

"No wonder you smell like an animal cracker. Yummy," Kate said, and buried her face in Gracie's neck.

"Mommy!" The little girl protested between squeals of delight.

Kate nuzzled Gracie's neck one more time, eliciting more giggles, then positioned her daughter on her hip and carried her off toward the downstairs bathroom.

Anna watched them disappear down the hallway.

She meant what she said to Kate—they had come a long way. Their relationship had never been easy, but after Kate left home at seventeen, a chasm opened between them. Anna often imagined her daughter had come across some obscure guidebook on the art of maintaining *de minimus* familial obligations: during occasional perfunctory phone calls or the increasingly rare visit home, she provided her mother with only the sketchiest details of her adult life.

Then, in her late twenties, after being accepted into the University of Michigan's degree program in Information Management, Kate broke off communication altogether.

Then four years ago, late on a summer night, the phone on Anna's bedside table began to ring. She picked up the receiver and croaked out a tentative, "Yes?"

"Mom, it's me."

She could still remember the shock of hearing Kate's voice, the bitter taste of adrenaline on her tongue.

"Mom, I need your help."

"What kind of help?" Anna asked in as neutral a tone as she could manage.

"I'm pregnant, three months, and I'm keeping the baby," Kate said preemptively. "I can't find a job here. I don't have enough money to cover another month's rent. Plus, I'm sick as a dog."

Anna covered the mouthpiece with her hand. "Pregnant," she whispered, and again, 'pregnant', a word familiar but unanchored. Maybe the meaning would sink in if she repeated it a few more times. "What about the father?" She asked.

"He's out of the picture. He's a druggie and an asshole, so no big loss."

"Just a minute," Anna said. She set the phone down on the bed and put her head in her hands. She closed her eyes, massaged her temples, and tried to ignore the muffled crying coming through the speaker.

"Mom, are you still there?"

Anna lifted the handset again. "I'm here."

"I want to come home," Kate whispered.

Tears welled in Anna's eyes. Her daughter was speaking in a voice she barely recognized, a voice she hadn't heard in more years than she could remember. "Where are you?"

"Here, in Oregon. In Gresham."

Anna wanted to ask, 'How goddamned long have you been back in the Northwest without contacting me?', but stopped herself. She opened the drawer of her bedside table and pulled out a pen and notepad. "Give me the address, Kate." It was just that simple in the end.

Anna retrieved half a dozen folded moving boxes from her garage, shoved them into the trunk of her Honda Civic, programmed Kate's address into her cell phone, and started the car. An hour later, she pulled up outside a dirt-streaked, faded, avocado-green duplex in Gresham. The streetlights were burned out, or broken out, but either way, when she turned off the engine, darkness engulfed her.

She left her parking lights on, hoping they wouldn't completely drain the battery, and kept her eyes down as she picked her way across the dirt and weed lawn, past a wreck of a bicycle, a discarded book bag, and a pile of plastic crates.

She knocked at the graffiti-adorned door of Apartment C. She heard a faint "Come in." She recognized Kate's voice, but it sounded tiny, as if coming from a great distance.

Anna stepped inside the dimly lit studio apartment. Almost instantly, her stomach recoiled at the reek of rancid cooking oil mingled with freeway exhaust. One glance was enough to take in the entirety of the barren room: a stained, lumpy mattress on the floor, a disorderly pile of dirty laundry next to it, a legless couch bleeding cotton batting, an open, super-sized bag of cereal on the kitchen counter. She wondered if Kate ate Toasted Oats by the fistful, or if she had milk to pour over them, but she wasn't about to look inside the refrigerator.

Kate, sitting on the couch with her head in her hands, barely looked up when Anna entered. Anna studied her daughter closely: filthy jeans, clavicle bones pressing against the thin fabric of her t-shirt like knife blades, dry, jaggedly cut hair that looked like someone had maliciously taken scissors to it.

Anna sat down on the couch next to Kate, close enough that their legs touched. "I'm here, honey," she said softly. Kate didn't look up or move, so Anna wrapped her arms around her daughter's rigid body and held her. When she felt Kate's muscles give a little, she began to rock her, slowly, gently. When she saw Kate's tears start to fall, she stopped the rocking, and just held her daughter tighter, whispering to her over and over, "There, there, it's okay. It will all be okay, sweetheart."

And it had been okay, until now.

In the living room, Gracie paraded her stuffed animals across the coffee table, while in the adjacent dining room, Kate set out plates and silverware. Anna sat down on the couch, which Gracie took as an invitation to abandon her toys and climb up onto her grandmother's lap. She reached for Anna's ears and tugged. Anna popped her eyes wide. Gracie tugged again, and Anna dropped her jaw open. The third tug made Anna roll her eyes around in circles.

"You are silly, Nana."

"You are an imp," Anna said, mussing her granddaughter's soft hair.

"Read me a story," Gracie commanded, as only a child princess could.

Anna reached for a book from the coffee table, the one she had brought downstairs that morning before they left for the zoo. "Okay, but we can't read for long, just until your mother calls us."

"Okay," Gracie said sweetly, snuggling close.

Anna opened the book to the title page. "Animals of the Wild," she began.

Then the oven timer dinged, and the pungent smells of Kate's cooking permeated the house. Anna closed the book and she and Gracie got up from the couch and took their seats at the table.

Kate brought out the macaroni and cheese casserole she'd made from scratch the night before, and a smaller bowl of steamed broccoli.

Gracie took one look at the vegetable and contorted her face in disgust, turning the corners of her mouth down and pushing her tongue out as if gagging.

Kate ignored Gracie and dished small portions onto her plate.

Gracie escalated to making retching noises.

Kate sat down and, with exaggerated flair, stabbed her fork into a piece of Gracie's hated greens and raised it to her mouth. She dramatically swallowed the broccoli, dropped her fork, clutched at her throat, and crossed her eyes to portray an extreme case of poisoning by vegetable.

Gracie threw her head back and squealed with laughter, her long blond hair flying and her face breaking into a wide, gap-toothed smile.

Anna laughed too, laughed hard, and for that brief moment of ebullient, collective happiness, she could almost forget about the plan she had begun to execute and the damage she would soon inflict.

Kate shepherded Gracie into the downstairs bathroom. Anna cleared the table and loaded the dishwasher, then returned to the living room couch. Through the picture window, she watched a light rain drizzling from the gray sky onto the gray street in front of the house.

Kate returned twenty minutes later and collapsed into the recliner opposite her. "I'm exhausted."

"Is Gracie still in the bathtub?"

"Yes, but I emptied the water, so she won't last long. She's playing with Otto the otter, the plush toy you bought her today."

Anna put her hand on the cushion next to her and patted it twice. Kate shrugged and got up out of her own chair, but she didn't take the seat her mother had proffered. Instead, she perched on the arm of the couch.

"I want to show you something," Anna said, holding up the children's book she'd started to read to Gracie before dinner. "This was yours when you were a child." She ran the tips of her fingers over the faded cover of the Little Golden book, then slowly fanned through the twenty-four illustrated pages, most of which were scribbled on and tattered from Kate's own handling of the book many years ago.

"I remember," Kate said. "That's so cool. I loved that book. Where on earth did you find it?"

"In Gracie's bookcase, under a stack on the bottom shelf. I was looking for animal stories to read to her this morning, as a prelude to the zoo. But we didn't have time, so I started to read it to her tonight, but fortunately, you called us to dinner."

"Fortunately?" Kate asked, sounding suspicious.

Anna nodded. She opened the book and pointed to the illustrations. "Elephant," she said, then turned the page. "Giant Panda." Flip. "Tiger." Flip. "Orangutan." Flip. "Rhino." Flip. "Lion." Flip. She paused and looked up at Kate.

"What? You're trying to make a point, I take it?"

"This was a wonderful book for you when you were a child, but now it reads like a catalogue of environmental disasters. All of these species, and thousands more, will probably be gone from the wild by the time Gracie reaches the age you are now." Anna bit her lower lip and frowned, considering her next step. "At the zoo, so many of the animals we saw were from species on the verge of extinction."

Kate jumped off the arm of the couch and backed away quickly, as if she'd sat on some vicious insect that had taken a bite out of her.

"What's wrong?" Anna asked.

Kate folded her arms across her chest and flattened her hands under her armpits, clamping them down. "What the hell do you think is wrong? God forbid you should come home from spending the day at the zoo with my daughter and tell me, 'Oh the otters were so cute,' they did this, they did that. God forbid you should have a good time. You know, I'd like to make it through one frigging weekend without hearing your doomsday scenarios."

Anna sighed and shook her head. "Kate, you just don't get it."

"Oh, I get it all right. It doesn't matter where you go—the zoo, the park, the grocery store, even kid's movies for Christ's sake. Smurfs are dangerously overweight; Nemo's reef is being destroyed by pollution; and penguins won't have *Happy Feet* for long if the Arctic ice keeps melting. I mean, really, Mom, you always find something to be depressed about, and for some reason, you always feel compelled to share your misery with me."

"No," Anna said.

"Yes," Kate said, insistent. "You haven't changed a bit since I was a kid. You still delight in telling every goddamned detail of every story of paradise lost. Only back then, your obsession was with polluted air, pesticides, and industrial toxins. Now it's global warming, drought, famine, mass extinctions."

"I wasn't obsessed," Anna shot back. "I was paying attention and trying to change things. I volunteered. I marched. I stood vigil. I did everything I could think of to make a difference."

"Oh, I remember exactly what you did, Mom. You stuffed envelopes for a local Earth First group. Big fucking deal. Then you started holding those Friday night potlucks in our living room, and you brought home grubby, longhaired strangers full of stories of a dying earth. I remember them passing around pamphlets with pictures of oil-soaked birds. I remember pictures of kids with sores on their faces from drinking poisoned water. Jesus, I can't stand to think about that even now. Do you have any idea how terrified I was?"

"Kate, I've told you before, told you a hundred times I am sorry. I was so young. I didn't understand what hearing about those things was doing to you. Not then. I had no idea my fears would become the monsters under your bed."

Kate's voice was a dry husk. "You know, sometimes I think about the person I might have become if I'd felt safe in the world. I wonder how different my life would have been."

Gracie came running out of the bathroom, dragging a wet towel behind her and wearing nothing but pink flannel pajama bottoms decorated with drawings of baby bunnies.

"You're going to freeze to death," Kate said, and lifted her up in her arms. "What happened to your top?"

"Otto was cold."

"Otto will live," Kate said, carrying her daughter back down the hall.

Moments later, Gracie returned, fully clothed. She ran as fast as she could toward Anna. "Nana! Nana!"

Anna rose to her feet and opened her arms. "Gracie, Gracie, you are a wild child." She laughed as she lifted the little girl high. She kissed her on the cheek and whispered in her ear, "Goodnight to you, dearest heart, and sweet dreams. Nana loves you more than anything in the whole wide world."

"I love you, Nana," Gracie whispered back.

Anna pulled her a little closer, held her a little tighter. She kissed the top of her head, brushed her cheek against the silky blond hair, breathed in the lingering sweetness of baby shampoo. She closed her eyes tight, trying to imprint the moment on memory. Taking a shuddering breath, she handed her off to Kate one last time.

She was still standing, staring out the window into the darkness, when Kate came back downstairs. Turning around, she noticed Kate raise and drop her shoulders and let her arms hang loose, like a soldier standing down.

"Mom," Kate said. "I don't want to fight tonight. The zoo was my fault. I should never have asked you to take Gracie there in the first place. I knew better. I just—"

"No, honey, you did nothing wrong. You just wanted her to see otters and all of the amazing animals all kids her age delight in."

"So what's upsetting you tonight? You seem off, somehow."

Anna took a deep breath, then softly uttered the sentence she had been rehearsing all day. "Kate, I can't do this anymore."

"Do *what* anymore?"

"This," Anna said, holding out her arms to encompass everything in their shared world. "I can't do this. I try so hard to be upbeat, cheerful, positive, but I can't keep pretending everything is okay all the time."

"All the time? You've got to be kidding. You can't act like things are okay for ten minutes." Kate laughed, as if she hoped to take the sting out of her accusation by cloaking it in a joke.

"Maybe you're right," Anna said wearily.

"This is about climate change again, isn't it?"

"Kate, you don't understand. You believe we will adapt to a warming planet like northerners do to a tropical vacation: take off a few clothes, slather on the sunscreen, turn up the air conditioner."

"Of course I understand," Kate snapped, her temper flaring. "I recycle. I take the bus to work. I don't run the air conditioner until it's practically boiling outside. Christ, I just signed a petition today, outside the grocery store, to keep rail trains from transporting crude oil down the Columbia River. But I am sick to death of you talking about how screwed up things are all the time. Why is that so goddamned hard for you to grasp?"

Anna cried out, "Every time I look at Gracie, I know I'm failing her."

"Gracie is not your responsibility," Kate said, her voice clipped and hard.

"Of course she is," Anna said sharply. What I don't understand is why everyone isn't talking about climate change every single day. What I don't understand is how you, how anyone who has a young child or grandchild, can just take what's happening in stride. I think we all should be screaming as loud as we can, 'the sky is falling, the sky is falling, everybody fucking look, everybody fucking do something, the sky is falling.'"

Kate took a big step backward, then turned and marched into the kitchen. Anna watched her grab a sponge, lean into the counter and start scrubbing the tiles so furiously that it looked like she was trying to take the glaze off. Anna was still watching when Kate threw down the sponge and marched back into the living room. She stopped a foot away from Anna, crossed her arms, and stared at her mother with an angry expression, but her voice conveyed an undertone of compassion—or perhaps pity, Anna thought.

"Look, I love you, Mom, but I will not follow you down this road again. I mean that. You have got to hear me this time. I will not let you make Gracie fear for her future before she even gets a chance to have one. I want her to be grateful for what is in her life, not constantly worried about what isn't. I want her to be emotionally strong enough, and resilient enough to face whatever happens next. But she'll never develop those qualities if I raise her on stories of a coming apocalypse. Believe me, I know that from experience."

Anna opened her mouth as if to say something, but she couldn't find the words, the last words she would ever say to her daughter. She shook her head, and tried again. "Kate, I know I have not been the best of mothers, but I love you with all my heart. I always have. I always will. But right now, I am tired, bone tired, and I must go to bed."

Anna turned away, walked into her bedroom, and closed the door behind her. She pressed her hand over her mouth to stifle a sob as grief washed over her like a tidal wave, carrying away everything and everyone she loved, then surging back again and again to batter her with the detritus of their lives.

Chapter 3

"Thanks for driving all the way up here, son," Jackson said. "I know you'd rather have spent the day climbing some mountain in the middle of nowhere, instead of babysitting me."

"Dry Gulch Ranch *is* in the middle of nowhere," Danny said with a laugh. "And as for babysitting you? That is one terrifying prospect."

Jackson laughed, a deep, gravely sound. "Yeah, I guess it would be. But you know what I mean."

"Bolo and I spent the last two weekends backpacking the Sandia Wilderness, so I'm not exactly feeling deprived. Besides, I don't come here on the anniversary just to comfort you, Jackson. I come to comfort myself as well."

He picked up the bottle of Makers Mark they had been working on all day, pouring the last trickle of whiskey into Jackson's tumbler. "That's all there is and a good thing too. You can barely keep your eyes open."

Jackson downed the drink in one gulp. "You know damn well I would have drunk you under the table if you hadn't switched to those washy drinks."

Danny laughed. "Washy, huh? You're dating yourself, old man. I believe I kept pace with you for quite a long time. In fact, I would have beaten you hands down if I hadn't had to sober up enough to drive home tonight."

"Ha!" Jackson said, in a tone of prosecutorial triumph. "So you admit it was not an even match?"

"Okay, okay, you're right, it was not an even match," Danny said with a grin.

"Damned right," Jackson said. He set his glass down and picked up the bottle. He held it upside down over his open hand. "Bone dry, like everything else in this godforsaken land." Then his eyes closed, his body slumped, and the bottle tumbled to the carpeted floor.

Danny gave him a moment to see if he'd wake. When he didn't, he reached over and patted his arm. "Hey, buddy, you nodded off. You need to get to bed, and I need to get on the road."

He watched Jackson lift his big head, clench his hands on the arms of the high-backed leather chair, and try to heave himself upright. *He looks like a wounded buffalo*, Danny thought. Jackson, unable to raise his two hundred and thirty-pound frame, fell heavily back and passed out cold.

Reaching into the pocket of his blue work shirt, Danny pulled out an elastic band and gathered his long, gray, and ash blond hair into a ponytail. He got to his feet, wrapped both arms around the seventy-nine-year-old man, and half-carried, half-dragged, him to the couch a few feet away. After easing him down into a prone position, Danny lifted Jackson's legs up onto the cushions, removed his cowboy boots, and pushed a pillow under his head.

Looking down at his old friend's disheveled white hair, his grizzled face, his rumpled clothes, Danny was taken aback by how oddly small and plucked the old man looked. "Sorry, buddy," he whispered. "You're going to wake up in the middle of the night with one ferocious headache. You know, I sometimes forget how goddamned old we are."

In the kitchen, he filled a glass with tap water and looked out the window. It was almost dark. He had a three-hour drive in front of him and needed to get on the road, but he couldn't risk failing a breathalyzer test, not in Bernalillo County, not when the Albuquerque cops were tracking Jackson's every move. Over the past few years, the police had repeatedly used the flimsiest of traffic violations to pull the old man over and search his car.

Lately, the surveillance had reached a new level: more than once, Jackson had seen a shiny black van parked on the ranch access road, and a few weeks ago they had both heard a clicking sound on the landline when Danny called to say he was coming to visit.

Danny emptied the water glass and rapped his knuckles on the counter to wake his dog. Bolo looked up from her bed under the table, opening one bleary eye, then the other. She slowly got to her feet and walked over to him, her tail and rump wagging.

"Hey, girl," he said, rubbing her all over while she pressed up against him. "Let's go for a walk, get some fresh air."

As soon as he stepped outside, Jackson's dogs barked sharp warnings that shattered the silence. Danny called out to them. "Hush, boys, it's just me."

At the sound of his familiar voice, they settled back down with a few guttural 'woofs' for good measure. The desert was not hospitable to dogs and Jackson had lost a number of them during the years Danny had known him. A coyote carried off one, and another, its face blown up like a balloon, died of a rattlesnake bite. The last one to survive, some kind of pit bull mix, was fourteen years old and still alive, but barely, and the other two were young hounds. They stayed in a big outdoor kennel at night, or in the barn when the weather was bad, but in the daytime, they were free to run.

When anyone drove up to the property, they charged out, barking and threatening with bared teeth and subterranean growls, but the minute they heard Jackson's whistle, they stood down. The old man never invited his dogs into the house, coddled them, or made them a substitute for a human family, as so many Americans did, and as Danny did with Bolo. But he did respect them and was conscientious about their care.

Danny let Bolo run with the pack during the day, but at night, he made her come inside. Jackson teased him about being a sentimentalist, but the old man had grown fond of the cheerful little Labrador, and the bed of blankets under the kitchen table had been his idea.

Danny walked down the dirt road, keeping an eye on Bolo, who was racing around in wide circles with her nose to the ground. After a few hundred yards, he turned around to head back. On the western horizon, he saw the sun sink into a low bank of clouds. Shafts of yellow light streamed across the cerulean sky and lit the whitewashed walls of the hacienda, making it shine like a luminaria burning in the darkness.

Danny thought back to his first visit to the stately, two-story adobe some eighteen years before. In those days, he had been driving an old Ford pickup, its bed laden with tools: shovels, pickaxes, hoses, a chainsaw, and a jackhammer. The truck bounced up and slammed down hard as he maneuvered around deep ruts in the eroded dirt road that led to Dry Gulch Ranch.

He remembered stepping onto the patio, under its canopy of loosely woven, living ocotillo branches and watching the last slivers of sunlight slip through the leaves, then sparkle and scatter, like a fall of fireflies.

He crossed to the front door, lifted the heavy, hand-forged iron knocker and let it fall. A woman appeared, wearing a colorful, full-length, hand-embroidered Puebla dress. She was thin, with long, straight gray hair that fell to the middle of her back, and pale beneath her brown skin, as if she'd been ill.

Her face was not beautiful exactly, in fact her features were unremarkable. But something about her, a presence, a sense of self-possession perhaps, held his attention.

"Hello. I'm Dan Shepard, from Pinyon Landscaping."

"Yes," she said, looking deep into his blue eyes as if to see who was behind them.

She gestured for him to follow. Moving slowly, stiffly, she led him down the hall to an arched opening. "This is the sitting room. In front of the couch, you'll find a tray with iced tea. Please make yourself at home. Jackson will be back soon." Her smile was both a bow and a dismissal. She stepped into the hallway and was gone. To his surprise, he felt a pang of sadness when she left.

The walls of the room were decorated with oil and acrylic paintings of desert scenery, prints of Southwestern wildlife and flora, photographs of lightning storms, a weaving from Peru, a handmade quilt. The furniture, a Trastero hutch, a handcrafted mesquite table, a hand-painted pine bench, and wall-to-ceiling bookcases filled with volumes in both Spanish and English, provided surfaces, and every surface that could hold an object had an object to hold: a devil's claw pod from a unicorn plant; a perfectly round river rock; a Zuni bear fetish; a wide, hand-woven basket; a small cast-iron bell.

He noticed four framed photographs on a corner shelf and walked over for a closer look. He picked up what appeared to be the oldest of the prints—a small, black-and-white studio portrait of a tall boy with wide eyes and thick dark hair who looked much too young for his U.S. Army uniform. Next to him was a Hispanic girl in braids, wearing a white Mexican wedding dress and holding a bouquet of flowers. This was the woman who had shown him into the house.

Behind him, a deep male voice boomed, "El Paso, 1955."

Danny, feeling like a shoplifter caught in the act, cringed. He turned around to find himself looking up at a giant of a man, a good three inches taller than his own six feet two inches, muscular and broad-shouldered, without an ounce of fat on him. He had a full head of white hair and a darkly tanned face. His blue jeans and pearl-button cowboy shirt seemed relatively new, but his intricately tooled cowboy boots were scuffed and worn.

"Jackson," the man said gruffly. "Jewell Thomas Jackson."

Danny handed him the picture, and Jackson set it back on the shelf.

"Danny," he said, swallowing hard. "Danny Shepard. Good to meet you, Sir."

Jackson grabbed Danny's right hand with his two hands and gave it a shake. "Welcome, son. We're mighty pleased to have you. There are no 'sirs' here," he added with a wink. "You've already met Estrella, my wife," he said, nodding at the photograph. "This," he said, "is her room. Her sanctuary, as she calls it, though I think it's also a shrine."

"It's an amazing room," Danny said.

"She's an amazing woman," Jackson said. Then his hands went into his pockets and his exuberance gave way to apprehension. "She's ill, and damned if she'll see a doctor. Hell, she wouldn't let one treat her anyway, so I've given up fighting her about it. Anyway, she stays upstairs in our room most of the time now, and I take her meals up to her, so I doubt you'll see much of each other. She shouldn't have come down today, but I was late getting back."

Danny nodded and looked down at the floor.

"Let's get you settled in," Jackson said, his warm smile returning. "After dinner, we'll take a walk around the grounds. You've got your work cut out for you."

Danny's temporary quarters weren't in the barn, as he'd expected them to be, but in a furnished guest room at the back of the house, with a private entrance and bath. Dinner had already been set out in the kitchen, and Danny took a seat at the table when Jackson beckoned. Over a meal of chili and cornbread, Jackson explained that Dry Gulch was a ranch in name only; years of drought had forced him to sell off his herd and let go of his wranglers and ranch hands.

After his two grown sons, Roberto and Jake, left to pursue opportunities far from the parched plains of New Mexico, Jackson turned his full attention to landscaping the hacienda: the gardens were a gift for Estrella, intended to lift her spirits and heal her body.

Danny worked the land for the next two months, laboring in the blistering heat every day, tilling the hard ground, breaking up and removing the calcified layers of caliche, enriching the soil with fertilizer and mulch, planting heat and drought-tolerant shrubs, native perennials, and cacti. Every night, as if he were an old friend instead of a hired hand, he joined Jackson for dinner. A housekeeper came twice a week and an elderly cook came for a few hours every afternoon to prepare meals. Jackson took a tray up to Estrella at mid-morning and in the evening, checking on her many times in between.

Just before the dog days of summer began to bear down in earnest, Danny finished his job of rehabilitating and restoring life to the barren grounds. He explained to Jackson that he had grafted a wide swathe of desert life onto the denuded plain, and with a little time and some water, the transplanted acacias, creosote bushes, barrel cacti, and ocotillos would flourish and bloom.

On the day of his departure, Jackson came outside to see him off. "You're welcome here anytime, son. I'm sorry you didn't have a chance to get to know Estrella, but she asked me to give you this." He reached into his pants' pocket and removed a small leather bag that was tied shut with a long, thin leather strip, and placed it in the palm of Danny's hand.

Danny stared at it, puzzled. He hadn't seen or talked to Estrella since the day she opened the door to him.

"Go ahead, take a look inside. It's yours now."

Danny rubbed the soft, worn leather between his fingers. He carefully tugged at the drawstring to loosen it, then turned the pouch upside down and dropped a hard object onto the palm of his hand. It was a small, polished white stone carving in the shape of a bear, with an onyx arrowhead inlaid on its back.

"It's a Zuni fetish," Jackson said. "According to one version of Zuni cosmology, the creator sent his sons, known as Bow Priests, to lead the people out of darkness. This carving of a great white bear is a Prey God of the Priesthood of the Bow. It's supposed to help ceremonial priests avoid being captured by enemies. The arrowhead on his back increases his power and prevents surprise attacks."

"You should feed it cornmeal once in a while, and keep it inside the pouch. If you need to call on it, take it out, hold it against your lips, breathe onto it, and breathe in its spirit."

"Please thank her," Danny said. To his dismay, he felt himself blushing like a fifteen-year-old boy after a first kiss. He closed his fingers over the smooth stone. "I don't understand. I mean, it's beautiful, and I'm touched that she wants me to have it. But why does she? And why this? I'm no warrior. Far from one, in fact."

Jackson nodded. "She could see you from the second-story windows while you worked. She probably heard some of what we said over dinner since our bedroom is right above the kitchen. And Estrella, well, she just knows things. She always has."

Danny shrugged. "Well, please tell her how grateful I am. I mean, really, Jackson. I'm honored."

"I'll tell her."

Danny placed the small carving back in its pouch, cinched it shut, and tucked it into the breast pocket of his shirt. He climbed into the truck and started the engine.

Suddenly, Jackson moved in close and clamped his hands on the driver's side sill. "Do you shoot?"

"Like deer?"

"Shoot, not hunt. Target shooting."

Danny relaxed his grip on the wheel. "My dad was in the military when I was a kid and he taught me to shoot. I haven't touched a rifle in many years but I know the basics."

"Good man," Jackson said, "good man." With that, he stepped away from the truck and shoved his hands into his back pockets, which was how he remained until Danny lost sight of him in the rearview mirror.

Five weeks later, Jackson called him at work to tell him, in a voice that had flatlined, that Estrella had passed in the night. He hadn't been able to reach his sons yet, and he wanted to know if he could hire Danny to come up and help him arrange the burial. Danny refused the offer of financial compensation but agreed to drive up that night after work.

Jackson's sons didn't make it home in time for the funeral. Jackson had declined the services of a preacher, so Danny, the old Mexican woman who did the cooking after Estrella took ill, two men from the mortuary, and a rough-hewn man from a neighboring ranch, Mike Hansen, were the only mourners standing at the graveside with the grieving widower. Estrella had chosen the burial site herself, a remote corner of the ranch at the foot of pale green, low-lying hills where a spring creek still ran and a small stand of cottonwoods grew.

Jackson, his thick white hair greased down and neatly combed, his dark gray suit a little short in the sleeves and his new black leather shoes a little too shiny, stood in front of the hole in the ground with his hands folded.

The men from the mortuary lowered the casket. A warm breeze rustled through the trees, dappling the leaves with sunlight and shadow. Jackson began to speak.

"I met and married Estrella when I was in the army. I was seventeen years old. She was eighteen. I had never known a woman before her, much less loved one, and I have never since, and never will again. She was elusive, a mystery even to herself, I think. She was wild, not crazy like people can get, but wild like this country used to be before we cultivated the life out of it. In time, I came to understand that she belonged more to the land than to its people. Sometimes she was a cactus flower, sometimes a river, sometimes a stone."

"She had such a small footprint that her tracks were almost invisible, like a deer stepping lightly on hard ground. But every place and everything she loved impressed itself on her, and she brought home totems, images of the sky, carvings of sacred animals, seedpods picked up off the ground. She told me they helped her find her way, and would help her even after death if she got lost in the darkness. She told me, with the greatest kindness, and a touch of pity, that they could guide me home as well. My wife was the best of me. Today, I am a lesser man, and adrift."

He nodded, as if satisfied that he'd said what he'd wanted to say. He pulled a handkerchief out of his pants' pocket and wiped his eyes, blew his nose, then turned away from the grave.

After Jackson's sons arrived the following day, Danny returned home. He called the ranch a few weeks later to see how things were going and was saddened to hear that Roberto had already departed for St. Louis, and Jake for Los Angeles. Worried about the old man being left alone with his grief, Danny decided to drive north again.

The two men shared a passion for good whiskey, target shooting, and conversations that rambled on into the wee hours of the morning. They spent many full-moon nights sitting on the tailgate of a truck in the middle of the desert, shooting at tin cans intermittently, but always drinking, talking, and listening to coyotes howl.

Danny loved hearing Jackson's stories about growing up in a small Texas farming community which he escaped from at the age of sixteen by lying about his age and enlisting in the army. Jackson had made it to Korea for the second battle of Pork Chop Hill, and taken a bullet in his shoulder. The war ended with an armistice agreement three weeks later, so Jackson returned to the States. While on leave in El Paso, he met and married Estrella. He asked to be discharged from the military not long after.

The couple's early years were spent on a cattle ranch, where she worked as a cook and he worked as a wrangler while attending night classes at Texas A&M University, courtesy of the G. I. Bill. When he told Danny he'd graduated with a bachelor's degree, with majors in both Animal Husbandry and Humanities, Danny tried to hide his surprise and his envy.

Danny, as reticent as Jackson was loquacious, said little about his own past. Over the years, Jackson let the questions go. Their loose bond of friendship held fast.

Danny didn't pass a single police car on the drive home. He exited the freeway just south of Las Cruces, and drove past strip malls, an industrial park, and a long stretch of undeveloped land.

Nearing home, he slowed down as he drove through an old old barrio, a poor Mexican neighborhood with block after block of one and two-bedroom adobe houses on lots the size of postage stamps.

In the daytime, he often saw old men and women sitting out front on their porches or working on their small plots of sand and succulents. They swept the stepping stones, bent down to pick up fallen leaves, and scored the sand with wooden rakes, like Buddhist monks tending Zen gardens.

As soon as he turned into his drive, cut the engine, and opened the truck door, Bolo leaped out. She raced in stops and starts with her nose to the ground, following one scent after another in search of creatures that might have trespassed in her absence.

Ravenous after consuming nothing but whiskey all afternoon, he made a beeline for the kitchen, or what passed as one: a sink, a stove and a single-sided refrigerator, all lined up against one wall. He poured a little oil into a frying pan and cooked a dinner of pinto beans, onions, and corn tortillas folded over slices of melted cheese.

He carried the plate to his desk, a wooden monstrosity he'd bought at an open-air flea market, sat down, and turned on his laptop. He scanned the Internet to see if civilization had fallen off the flat edge of the world yet, which he fully expected it to someday.

He always hoped to discover something good had happened while he wasn't looking, but it was almost always more of the same: occasional tales of human decency, even heroics, but no end of stories about intolerance and cruelty and human suffering, pathetically ineffective and egregiously autocratic governments, interminable wars, and portentous weather reports of floods, droughts, wildfires, and other harbingers of a warming planet. Politicians promised voters that when they took office, they would eagerly begin to implement whatever campaign promises they had made, but the covenants they made with their corporate sponsors were more binding.

Voters usually re-elected them anyway. "Democracy at its worst," he grumbled. "So what else is new?" He muttered, shutting down his computer.

Bolo scratched at the door and Danny got up to let her inside. He washed his plate and silverware and wiped out the cast-iron frying pan, then sat back down. As he did on most evenings, he put his feet on the desk and leaned back, clasping his hands behind his head. He stared out of the west-facing picture window, the only window in his adobe.

The horizon was a black hole, but the sky above shone bright with stars, and in the far distance, he saw lighting strikes split the sky with jagged shards of white light. He listened to crickets chirping outside, checked the dusty spider web in the corner for signs of life, and smiled at his dog's twitchy dreaming as she slept on the cool paver floor.

His eyes grew heavy. He walked the ten paces to his bed, hung his shirt and pants on the clothing hooks that held his wardrobe, such as it was, and stretched out on the cool sheets.

Bolo woke and followed him to bed. She stretched, extending her front and back legs and pushing out her chest before hopping up to curl in a tight ball next to him. Danny freed his hair from the band he'd tied around it at Jackson's, letting it fan out against the dog's dusty black coat. He buried his face in the thick fur of her neck and rubbed her shorthaired belly.

He would have to get up at 5 a.m. Tuesday morning to be at the office by 6 a.m., but he didn't mind. Twenty years ago, when he wandered into Las Cruces in search of shelter and a job, the landscaping position with Pinyon hadn't interested him at all, but manual labor was the only option available to a forty-five-year-old man with no references, degree, or marketable skills. He didn't appreciate his good fortune until he discovered that hauling rock and heavy cacti and digging down through caliche-layered soil left him physically and mentally spent at the end of each day—a blessing for a man who could not sleep.

After a full year of steady employment, Danny decided that two decades adrift was enough—it was time to set down roots. He bought a half-acre of land adjacent to the barrio and began working every weekend to build his seven-hundred-square-foot, two-room adobe. He dug the footing trench, set the rebar in place, and poured the concrete floor. He mixed truckloads of red, loamy soil with water, one wheelbarrow at a time, then packed the thick mud into molds to be baked dry by the sun.

He layered the bricks to build the walls, and framed the doors and windows. Then, in order to finish before the summer monsoons arrived, he contracted with a roofing firm, an electrician, and a plumber to help him with the rest.

With the house built and his weekends free, he began exploring the high desert and the rugged mountains of Arizona, New Mexico, and Utah. In temperatures as low as twenty degrees, and as high as a hundred and five, he hiked with the same intention he brought to his job: to labor so hard and so long that he would wear himself down until emptied of wants or needs. Whenever he bedded down under a borderless sky, his body numb with exhaustion, his head filled with visions of blowing sand and desert sage, he felt himself disappear into the landscape.

Chapter 4

Awakened by the sound of Kate's alarm going off upstairs, Anna curled deeper beneath the covers. She listened to the sound of footsteps coming down the stairs, then water running, then the refrigerator door opening. She heard Kate talking on the phone, arranging for daycare. Of course, she was making other plans. When their conversation went sideways last night, her daughter's old resentments had erupted, thick and acrid as chemical smoke.

She heard Kate call out to Gracie, "Stop dawdling, we're running late," followed by, "No, honey, she's sleeping. Don't bother her."

Anna closed her eyes and pretended her little family was still intact, that this was a morning like any other. Any moment, she imagined, Kate would save her from her own folly by entering the bedroom with a steaming cup of coffee in hand. Gracie, close behind, would jump on the bed and cuddle up next to her, and she would begin to plan their day.

Normally, the storm that had blown up would have dissipated by dinnertime, and they would all be sitting down at a meal together. Their emotions would be heightened for a few days, but in time, they would return to baseline—and their baseline was a pretty sane place.

She heard the front door open, then close. She got out of bed and walked to her window. When she had first conceived of the journey she was about to take, she had tried to be brutally honest with herself about the costs. But there is knowing, and then there is *knowing*. She watched her daughter and granddaughter, hand in hand, walk down the sidewalk toward the bus stop. Only Gracie stole a quick look back.

Anna poked her head out of her covers like a mole burrowing up through the ground. Through her bedroom window, she saw a dirty gray sky. She hated the Northwest at that moment: the clouds shrouding everything, the steady drizzle of rain, the sopping wet earth. She checked the time: three in the afternoon. It was late, but not too late, and she had needed the sleep.

A shower, a hot cup of coffee and a piece of toast brought her back to life. There wasn't much left to do. She had already gassed up the car, loaded her backpack into the trunk, and written the note. But she couldn't stop perseverating about her computer's hard drive. She worried that reformatting hadn't wiped it clean.

She turned on the oven, set it to four hundred degrees, and left it to preheat while she returned to her desk. That morning, she had gone through the agony of shredding her old journals, letters, and photos. All that remained was a single drawer of manila file folders, their contents neatly labeled: Homeowner Policy, Cable Contract, Utilities, Repairs, and in front of these, where it would not be missed, a bright orange folder labeled Legal/Financial.

She tipped over her desktop computer and removed the screws that held the cover in place. She pulled out the hard drive and memory strips, then put the case back together so it would look intact. She carried the hardware into the kitchen, spread it out on a non-stick baking tray, turned on the exhaust fan, and slid the pan into the oven. Overkill, she suspected, but she had heard too many stories about the government retrieving digitally stored information that others had gone to great lengths to destroy.

Twenty minutes later, she removed the cookie sheet. The melted pieces of plastic and the deformed metal were too hot to touch, so she left them to cool while she retrieved her garbage bag of shredded memories from the garage. She topped off the confetti with food and wet coffee grounds from a compost pail in the kitchen, then dumped the baked innards of the computer into the mix.

She carried the whole mess outside to the curb and buried it under the other bags of garbage already deposited in their thirty-two-gallon trashcan, which would be picked up tomorrow.

There was nothing left to do but get dressed, and she had plenty of time for that before Kate and Gracie returned home. She opened a bottle of cabernet, poured a glass of wine, and turned on the weather channel. The powerful storm approaching the Olympic Peninsula was expected to pound the coastal mountains with gale-force winds and heavy rain, and bring rapidly dropping temperatures to the region.

She drank a second glass of wine.

She walked through the entire house one last time, upstairs and down, room to room. She felt tipsy and leaden at the same time, like an inflated Bobo doll. She moved slowly, running her fingers over everything she passed, the door frames, the walls, the furniture, the collection of stuffed animals in Gracie's bedroom, the perfumed nightshirt hanging on Kate's open door. Her touch was light but lingering as she tried to memorize the shape of things familiar.

Darkness finally descended. Anna undressed in her bedroom. At five feet five inches tall and a hundred and twenty-five pounds, she was no match for the tempest up north. She dug through her dresser and closet for winter clothes and pulled on layer after layer of warmth: a thermal undershirt, a long-sleeved cotton shirt, a heavy flannel shirt, and a thick fleece jacket. She pulled thermal tights and jeans over her thin legs, followed by a pair of Gortex ski pants.

She topped off the outfit with a puffy, purple down coat, making a mental note to find and pack its waterproof shell. All the padding made it hard but not impossible, for her to bend over and lace up her short brown hiking boots. She stuffed a black fleece cap, a pair of down gloves, and a miniature flashlight into her pants' pockets. Fully dressed, she waddled into the bathroom and positioned herself in front of the full-length mirror. She took one look and burst out laughing. She couldn't decide whom she most resembled: a short, fat Paul Bunyan, or a colorful Stay Puft Marshmallow Man.

She stopped giggling when her anxiety began to morph into terror.

Outside, the streetlights flickered on. Kate wouldn't get home with Gracie until at least 7:30 p.m., but there was no reason to risk a chance encounter. Anna posted her neatly printed note on the refrigerator door with a Multnomah Falls souvenir magnet.

Kate, I'm sorry I missed you. I couldn't sleep last night yet again, and I've had a fierce headache all day today, so I'm going to bed early. I hope you both had a good day. I may see you in the morning before you leave for work, but if I'm still sleeping, please don't wake me. I love you, both of you, to the bottom of my heart. Mom.

Her day in purgatory would soon be over; it was almost time to cast herself into the fire. But for now, there was nothing else to do but strip off the outer layers of her swaddling clothes, remain hidden in the bedroom with the lights out, and wait. Wait for Kate to come home with Gracie in tow. Wait for the smell of dinner being served, and the sound of the dishwasher starting. Wait for the bright crack under her door to go dark. Wait for the ticking hands on the clock to turn. Wait to see if she would have the courage to do the unthinkable, the unforgivable.

Kate and Gracie were sleeping peacefully in their beds when Anna snuck out of the house for the second time in less than forty-eight hours. She left through the front door, climbed into her old Honda Civic, shifted the clutch into neutral and let the car roll down the driveway and onto the street before starting the engine.

The drive to the Olympic Peninsula took four interminable hours of hunching over the steering wheel and staring fixedly at the white lines that seemed to speed past her. It was the only way she could navigate in the sheeting rain on a moonless night. At long last, she exited the state highway and turned onto a two-lane county road. After following it for 3.6 miles, she slowed the car to a crawl. Squinting into the darkness, she located the rectangular, white-on-brown sign that read Forest Road 2937. She drove up the old logging road for maybe a hundred yards before she brought the car to a stop.

Reaching into the back seat for her parka, her fingers brushed the silky outer lining. "Goddamn it all to hell," she cried. She had forgotten to pack the coat's waterproof shell.

Bracing herself for the pelting rain, she threw open the car door and hurried around to the trunk. She lifted out the heavy backpack she'd placed in the car the day before and deposited it behind a thicket of blackberry bushes.

She drove another two-tenths of a mile uphill, then made a right turn into a barely visible opening in the undergrowth. She drove slowly up a narrow, rutted path that dead-ended on a wide, flat rock ledge forty feet above the roiling waters of Puget Sound.

With the parking brake on, the gearshift in neutral, and the engine running, she sat there in full body armor and listened to the storm rage. The sound of thunder boomed from the sky above her and she heard the crashing of waves against the rocky cliffs below. Rain, as hard as buckshot, pinged the roof of her car. Without warning, a sudden gust of wind slammed her from behind and pitched the two thousand-pound piece of machinery forward on its axis.

She held her breath and clenched the steering wheel so tight, her nails left half-moons on the flesh of her palms. The unseen hand finally released her, and the car bounced and swayed from side to side as it settled back in place. *So this is the culmination of all my planning,* she thought. *Riding a rocking horse on the edge of an abyss.*

Time to prepare for flight. She put the car in reverse and backed up, leaving maybe six yards between it and the cliff's edge. She shifted into neutral, lowered all four windows, and grabbed a pre-cut stick of dried bamboo from the passenger seat. She opened her door, praying the wind wouldn't catch it, and backed out of the car. Kneeling on the ground next to the driver's seat, she leaned in again.

With one hand, she pushed the accelerator pedal all the way to the floor, and with the other, she wedged the stick between the underside of the dash and the top of the pedal. The bamboo, brittle enough to shatter on impact, light enough to float away on the current, held fast. At full throttle, the roar of the engine drowned out all other sounds.

Then everything stopped, and the next few seconds stretched out like an interminable silent scream. There was no roaring engine, no waves crashing against the craggy outcropping, no wind tearing at her clothes, no rain soaking them. All that existed for Anna in that moment was the perfectly clear, terrifying realization that every step she'd taken before this moment had been mere fantasy: her next act would take her to an entirely different plane of commitment. *What if I change my mind after? What circle of hell will I be in then?*

The wind walloped the car again and made it groan. Anna felt fear course through her like an electric shock. She reached across to the passenger seat again, this time to retrieve the cane she'd bought at a drugstore a few days earlier. Holding its rubber tip in her left hand, she grabbed the car door with her right hand and pulled herself to a standing position. She centered the T-shaped handle against the gearshift.

She thought she should say some incantation, thought the cane should glow like a hero's sword that burns with a fiery white light when raised to slay the dragon. *But I am no hero*, she told herself, *and I do not live in a time of magic.*

She shoved the cane hard, shifting the Honda into drive. The car shot across and over the bluff, and for a dazzling, improbable moment it hovered above the ocean, buoyed by the wind. Then it plummeted straight down and into the turbulent waters below.

She walked to the edge of the cliff and peered down. She expected to see the car pop back up to the surface, bobbing like a fisherman's cork, but there was no sign of it. She waited a little longer, watching the water churn, until the muscles in her legs began to quiver and threatened to give out. She stumbled to a smooth, mossy boulder and sat down hard. Soaking wet and chilled to the bone, she pulled her feet up and brought her knees to her chest.

The hard rain bit into her skin, and the wind whipped through the creaking cedars. Their long boughs seesawed in wide arcs above her and the smell of salt and evergreen infused the air.

Without warning, she was suddenly flooded with images of the life she was leaving—the life that, at that very moment, was being entombed. Laughing and crying simultaneously, on the verge of hysteria, she got to her feet and, keeping one hand on the boulder, attempted a deep knee bend to make sure her legs could carry her. Satisfied, she pulled the flashlight from her pocket and began to follow its narrow beam.

She crossed the bluff and started down the dirt road, paying attention to the simple act of putting one foot in front of the other. She coached herself silently: *breath in, step down, breath out, step down.* For the next twenty minutes, all thought, all memory, all remorse evaporated as she descended the muddy, treacherous path.

Stepping onto the graveled surface of the logging road, she pumped her fist in the air and cried, "Yes." It didn't take her long to locate the bag she had tossed into the bushes earlier. She opened it, dumped her backpack out, slipped her arms through the padded straps, and began walking downhill. After reaching the paved county road, she turned right for another few hundred yards until she saw the wide pullout she'd noticed on the drive-in. She walked across the clearing, past a makeshift fire pit littered with burned beer cans and empty shotgun shells, and into the forest.

In the shelter of a stand of cedars, she pulled a tarp, a one-person tent and a sleeping bag out of her pack, and set up camp. Inside the tiny, domed shelter, she stripped off her boots and Gortex pants. Much to her relief, her socks, jeans, and thermal pants were still dry. Her down coat, however, was so soggy she had to lean out of the tent and wring the water out before stringing it up with a ceiling tie. Her thick fleece jacket was wet on the outside, but only damp on the inside; she hung it up as well.

She rolled up her jeans to use as a pillow and crawled into the soft cocoon of her sleeping bag. Shivering, teeth chattering, she curled into a tight ball. As soon as she closed her eyes, waves of fatigue and nausea washed over her. She fell asleep to the cadence of her fears whispering dark warnings. 'Anna, you are too damned old to pull this off. Anna, you have lost too much, and all that you have loved will weaken you.'

She woke to the sound of the tent sides flapping in the wind. "Oh, oh, oh," she moaned. Her body was a pain map of last night's journey: her hands ached from gripping the steering wheel, her shoulders from hunching over it, her hips from sleeping on the hard ground. The rain was still beating down, and dark clouds shrouded the sky, so she curled deeper into the warm down bag to escape the misery of it all.

She woke a second time. The sky, now a watercolor smear of blues and blacks, appeared to be clearing, and the rain had slowed to a drizzle. She checked her watch: almost noon. The sound of an approaching car reached her. Terrified the driver would see her and stop, she peeked outside to get a view of the road to get a view of the road. A blue sedan drove past without slowing. *Give me twenty-four hours, just twenty-four hours,* she prayed.

She doubted the prayer would do any good, since she didn't really believe there was a God, much less a merciful one. Still, she prayed. *Give me twenty-four hours before they find the car. That's all I need.*

She dressed and took down the tent. She stuffed everything she'd brought with her into the backpack: Using the cane for leverage, she pushed herself up, lifting the pack with a groan, the tent, the tarp, the bedding, and the still soggy down coat surprised by how much weight the water added. Cinching it around her waist, she walked out of the forest, across the clearing, and onto the narrow shoulder of the county road.

Several cars passed by, ignoring her outstretched thumb, and she wondered how long she'd have to wait until someone came along who was kind enough, or foolish enough, to give a ride to a worn-out old woman standing in the rain with a towering backpack, dressed in wet, muddy clothes, wearing the furtive expression of an escaped convict.

Minutes later, an Isuzu Ranger pulled over a few yards in front of her. She lumbered toward the car and saw the driver had lowered the passenger-side window halfway.

"Hi," she said, looking in through the narrow opening at a balding, bearded man who was dressed like a construction worker. "Thanks for stopping. I'm trying to get to Seattle via the Bremerton Ferry."

"So am I," he said. "So is everybody on this road right now, I expect." He glanced at the seat next to him, laden with a large metal toolbox, a carpenter's belt, a lunch box, and a hard hat, and frowned. "Go ahead and get in back. There's a towel you can sit on."

She spread out the grease-stained towel and clambered into the car, propping her backpack on her lap so she could hide behind it. If the driver identified her to the police, her efforts would have been for nothing.

When they reached the ferry landing, three lanes of cars were waiting to board. A long pedestrian line had formed as well. The Isuzu pulled into the shortest lane and came to a stop behind a Mercedes. She thanked the driver again and got out in a hurry.

Pulling a small roll of twenty-dollar bills from her jeans' pocket, she purchased a ticket. She wanted badly to stand beneath one of the heating vents in the enclosed passenger seating area, but instead she carried her gear to the exposed upper-level deck. The ferry pulled away from the dock, and Anna sat down with her back against a wall and the pack in front of her to block the wind and mask her face. She periodically peeked around the pack at the open water for signs of life, for the tail of a killer whale, or the fin of a spinner dolphin, but only gulls blessed her crossing.

The ship landed at Seattle's Ferry Terminal. Anna put her arms through the pack and hoisted it one more time. Ignoring the still drizzling rain, she climbed the steep stairs from Pier 52 up to Second Avenue. She kept going south to

King Street Station, where she bought a ticket for the 5:16 p.m. southbound train to Portland.

Four hours later, she woke to the voice of the Amtrak conductor calling, "Portland, Oregon, twenty-minute stop." She lugged her backpack down the metal train steps to the platform, walked far enough to find a wall to lean against, and burst into tears. She was hungry, tired, wet and cold. All she wanted was to go home, kiss her daughter and granddaughter, take a scalding hot shower, and crawl into her own bed. The finality of her disappearing act hit her again, hit her so hard it took her breath away, and the specter of an irreversible, unbearable mistake threatened to engulf her.

"You can't go there," she warned herself, roughly swiping her eyes with her sleeve.

In the women's bathroom, she left her coat, which when dry had been a toasty warm coat, on the counter. On her way to the Salmon Street light rail stop, she handed her sleeping bag to a homeless man, and a few blocks later, deposited the backpack containing her tent in a doorway. She continued walking, having let her belongings fall like pennies from a hole in her pocket for someone else to find and spend.

Chapter 5

At 9:00 a.m. Monday morning, on the top floor of his uptown row house in Madison, Wisconsin, Mac woke to the driving beat of the Rolling Stones singing *I Can't Get No Satisfaction*. He could have sworn he'd set the alarm for 10 a.m. He reached over to the bedside stand, found the button, and silenced the damn thing.

Half an hour later, he woke again, untangled his arms and legs from the sheets, and with a deep groan, sat up on the side of the bed. He glanced back at Patricia's lovely, lean, naked body. She didn't appear to have moved since they'd fallen asleep at three in the morning. He put one chubby hand on her carotid artery. Still breathing.

He had grown tired of waking up next to her. Over the past year, they'd told each other all the stories they were willing to tell, discussed most of the subjects that interested them, and had sex so often, it had become perfunctory. Now they were just killing time until the end of the semester, when she would move to Nashville for a tenure-eligible teaching position. They would part friends, of course. He had perfected serial monogamy and the art of pleasant endings with all his exes.

He stood up, pulled on the t-shirt he'd worn the day before, and padded into the bathroom. He stared at his pudgy belly in the mirror with such familiar resignation, it didn't even provoke a sigh. He ran one hand through his white, thinning, shoulder-length hair, stroked his droopy mustache, and rubbed his puffy eyes. No half-assed attempt at grooming was going to redress the damage done to a sixty-five-year-old man by two days of cocaine-fueled partying.

"Finals week is not for the faint of heart," he said to his reflection.

He poured a cup of yesterday's coffee and drank it cold. He showered and dressed in a clean pair of Dockers, a plaid shirt and a tweed coat. Grabbing his briefcase in one hand and a bagel in the other, he left the house. At least he wasn't running late, so he wouldn't have to make his usual humiliating jog to the Meteorology and Space Sciences Tower. He could take a leisurely stroll across campus.

The day was humid, but not yet hot enough to make his clothes stick to him like wet tissue paper. Though he had grown up in California, he had lived in the Midwest for most of his adult life. He was willing to put up with the bitterly cold winters and the sweltering summers because he wasn't about to give up full tenure—not for a more temperate climate anyway. And he did love the university: the mishmash of its architectural styles, the sparkle of its lakeshore, the diversity of its student body, and the generally affable culture of learning.

And, he thought, next week will be the best week of the year on campus. The students will complete their final papers and take their last exams. For a brief moment in time, their burdens will be lifted, and they will open their eyes to the world as if it was made fresh that morning. Their feet will barely touch the ground, and every sensory neuron will become ravenous for air, taste, and touch. They will drink cold beers on the patio of the Student Union and gaze out at the sparkling waters of Lake Mendota.

They will kick off shoes, unbutton shirts, and pull on bathing suits or shorts. On the quad, or in their yards, or on the roofs of their apartment buildings, they will set out blankets or lawn chairs. They will stretch luxuriously, open their arms, and bare their bodies to the healing heat of the early summer sun.

He arrived at the small amphitheater at the stroke of 11 a.m. The room hadn't filled up yet but it would soon. He took his place at the podium at the front of the lecture hall and looked pointedly at the huge wall clock at the back of the room. He knew the stragglers weren't the least bit intimidated, since this was the first time all year he had even come close to starting the class on time. They slowly shuffled in and gravitated to their usual seats. Most of them had been preparing for finals all weekend and many looked as ragged as Mac felt.

"Good morning, class," he said in his practiced Mister Rogers imitation.

"Good morning, Dr. Caffrey," they recited in unison.

"Were you good boys and girls over the weekend?"

"Yes, Dr. Caffrey," they responded, laughter rippling through the room.

Mac grinned. "I'm sorry to disappoint you but I forgot my cardigan today. Rest assured, though, we will carry on."

Switching gears, he straightened his back, puffed out his chest and announced, in his best drill instructor voice, "Show up here tomorrow at 9:00 a.m., on the dot, for your final exam. No one will be allowed in after 9:10, and I mean no one. Do not bring your notes, phones, iPads or tablets. The TAs will hand out the test, pencils and blue books. You may bring a pen if you'd prefer. Grades will be posted next Tuesday. Your scored essays may be picked up the following week."

He dropped the act and spoke as his own weary, professorial self. "You will have an hour and a half to answer three questions, each more complex than it appears at first blush. So, think before you write. I'm certain your penmanship is impeccable…" He paused, waiting for the laughter to subside.

"Even so, there are seventy-three of you in this class, and it will be a challenge to give each of your answers a fair reading in time to meet the Monday deadline for turning in final grades. While that is a challenge I assure you I will meet, be advised I will not have time to write highly detailed comments in your blue books, if I write any at all."

He heard an outbreak of skittish chatter in the background. The colts were eager to get out of the paddock and just run the damned race.

When the room quieted, he resumed. "Well, here we are, our last class together, and a fine class it has been. Yes, I will let you out of here early, exactly thirty minutes early, which means you will be in my custody for only another few thousand seconds, a mere wisp of time."

"Now, as you may have heard, I like to end the last class of each year with an open mic, not so you can finagle me into giving you clues to the exam, but so you can bring up any burning questions remaining after a full semester of discussing the physics behind meteorology in general, and climate change in particular. It is up to you to determine where this discussion goes."

Mac put his elbows on the lectern, leaned forward, and waited.

The young men and women looked around the room at each other, each waiting for someone else to throw the first pitch.

A boy on the right side of the room finally asked exactly how the exam would be scored. Mac summarily dismissed him. "The same way I score every test—on merit. If you don't understand the material, talk to your assigned teaching assistant. If you don't understand a score when you get your finals back, talk to your assigned teaching assistant. If the problem isn't resolved, your TA will let me know, and we'll arrange a meeting."

In the front row, a handsome kid wearing a white button-up shirt and bleached-out blue denim pants stood with his hand raised high.

"Yes, Mike?"

"Doc, there are so many things that could go wrong if the planet warms too much, it's pretty overwhelming. I mean, it's hard for people not to just think it's unfixable, so screw it, let's just party." Other students rewarded Mike with laughter and the boy flashed a winning grin.

"And your question is…" said Mac, waiting for the boy to continue.

"Why is it the public, and politicians, don't seem to understand the urgency? And what trends are you seeing in the climate data that scare you the most?"

Mac stroked his mustache and rubbed his chin, considering the questions. "Anybody else want to hear the down and dirty?"

Affirmation wasn't unanimous but there was a sufficient show of hands for him to proceed.

"Okay, Mike. Those are good questions, and I'll do my best to answer them. So first, why doesn't everyone understand the urgency of what we're facing? My knee-jerk reaction is that we regularly educate people about the need for immediate action. We inform them through research journals, newspaper articles, documentaries, nightly news shows, lectures, TED talks, movies, blogs, tweets. Oh, I almost forgot, and through textbooks, such as the one for this class, which I'm sure you've all read cover to cover."

Scanning his audience, he was surprised, and pleased, to see only a few embarrassed faces.

"The public, if they are paying any attention at all, should know by now that in the history of our species, land and ocean temperatures have never been as hot, glaciers have never been as diminished, sea levels as high, droughts as long, storms as intense, and fires as destructive. But even with that knowledge, too many people fail to fully grasp the impending threat to our civilization."

Mac always carried a one-quart, neoprene water bottle with him to class. He reached for it now and took a long, slow drink before he continued.

"Imagine this classroom is your town, or your state, or your continent. Imagine you are just one among many, many people without access to water," he said, sweeping his arm from one side of the room to the other. "You are parched, weak from thirst, dying from thirst, and so is everyone else around you. Worse yet, you are a father, or a mother, and you are holding a young child in your arms." Her tongue is so swollen from dehydration, she can barely breathe.

"Now look at the man or woman sitting next to you. He or she is also holding a suffering infant. Now imagine learning that in the next town over, or state, or continent, a river still runs. And if you had just one flask of water, like the one I am holding, you would be able to make it to that place of refuge. Just to make this scenario really wild and crazy, let's say that not only do you survive long enough to get that far, but when you reach that idyllic place, its citizens actually welcome you with open arms."

He heard snatches of laughter and hoped his cynicism hadn't ruined the moment. He took the bottle with him to the edge of the stage. He looked out at the young faces waiting expectantly in perfect silence.

"Which of us has a right to the water in this bottle? Which of us owns it? Which of us deserves it? Which of us needs it the most? Those are the ethical questions every civilized society must weigh when faced with limited resources. How are you going to answer those questions when climate change, aided and abetted by out-of-control population growth, leads to catastrophic shortages of food, drinking water, and land?"

"Personally, my greatest fear is that a desperate humanity will abandon moral deliberations altogether. If that happens, the fate of this water bottle will be determined by the answer to one simple question: Which of us has the power to take it?"

He stepped back behind the podium and took another long, slow drink.

"But I have digressed. This is a physics class, not a course in the humanities. Mike asked what climate trends scare me the most. That's an easy one. More hot days, fewer cold nights. So, why does that matter?"

Hands went up around the room, and a few people called out, "Equilibrium."

"Yes," Mac said. "You are absolutely right. The biggest physics problem we face is not that hot is getting hotter. It's that cold is getting hotter too. People who live in Boston may disagree with me after the extreme winters they've experienced for the last few years, but when you look at the big picture, it's an indisputable fact. And the closer we get to a state of temperature equilibrium, the closer we are to the day when the climate we know and love will become not only unrecognizable, but unrecoverable."

"Disequilibrium is the magic that creates the weather and cools the earth. If temperatures get too close to stasis, the Jet Stream will disappear, the Gulf Stream will shut down, the Hadley cells won't circulate, the trade winds won't blow, and the whole bloody thing will come to a standstill. And we are this close," he said, holding his thumb and forefinger an inch apart, "this close to that future becoming an inevitability."

A few nervous giggles, then silence again.

He stopped talking. He thought about how tired he was of his own voice, of hearing himself speak the words of a disillusioned, aging man who has told the tragic tale too many times and is sickened by having to repeat it.

A girl in the back row raised her hand. He recognized her straight black hair, purple lipstick, tight black pants and black shirt with a slogan written on it in Chinese characters. 'Anarcho punk' was the term he'd heard used to describe her choice of clothing. He nodded to her, "Yes, Cynthia?"

"Why don't other scientists say it that directly? Are they afraid of being wrong? I think you're right, by the way, about how terrible it's going to get."

Mac laughed. "Well, thank you for the vote of confidence, Cynthia. I don't think scientists have feared being wrong as much as they have feared being right. If they've seemed reluctant to engage in prognostications of doom, or to paint the whole bloody picture in living color, I think it was for one reason only: they still had hope that if others had hope, actions would be taken and disaster would be averted. But in the last few years, I've seen scientists pleading, weeping, begging to be heard before all hope is lost."

"Our fate may well hang on if-then constructs. If people don't believe we are heating up the planet or believe that even if we are heating up the planet, no terrible consequences will ensue, then they tend to make little or no effort to stop emissions. If, on the other hand, people understand we are heating the planet to the point where our economy, our way of life, and our very survival as a species is threatened, then they will, at least in theory, take any and every action needed to stop emissions."

"But what if people believe global warming has already progressed so far that cataclysmic consequences are both inevitable and irreversible? Well, then it becomes tough to predict what will happen. Heroic efforts to save Mother Earth? Global warfare to claim what's left? Hedonistic nihilism?"

He dropped his hands to his sides and looked out at his audience. The students were mutely staring at him, waiting, he thought, for him to redeem the moment. Maybe he had gone too far. He heard the theme to *Jaws* playing in his head as his depression circled, moving in for the kill.

"That should leave you with something to think about over the summer. Or not," he said, unable to muster any semblance of enthusiasm. "We're out of time, folks, literally out of time." He hurriedly stuffed his notes and his water bottle back into his briefcase and turned to leave. At the exit door, he stopped just long enough to turn and bow slightly. The students were giving him a standing ovation.

He left the lecture hall and went straight to his office to begin catching up on paperwork.

Three and a half hours into it, he had barely made a dent in the stack that had been accumulating on his desk for the past few months. The end of finals week might mean shore liberty for the students, but for him, it was the time of year when the demands of his job intensified in proportion to his longing to escape them.

He got home in the late afternoon to find that Patricia had piled his mail on the counter and chalked one word on the refrigerator blackboard, 'Thursday?' Mac wiped off the message with the side of his hand. He grabbed a bag of potato chips, opened a beer, and took his armful of mail to the kitchen table. He thought about getting wasted but instead began sorting the stack in front of him.

About halfway through, he picked up a single white envelope with a Portland postmark. The familiar handwriting seemed to throb, black letters pulsing against the white background. Holding his breath, he ripped off one end and pulled out the single page enclosure.

He read the contents and felt his stomach clutch. Shoving the letter into his jacket pocket, he left the house. He walked six blocks to the Laughing Bear, a seedy neighborhood tavern where he rarely ran into students, other professors, or ex-girlfriends. The place had a serviceable menu and great brews. At the bar, he ordered a pitcher of dark beer and chicken wings with fries, then retreated to a corner booth. He pulled the letter from his coat pocket and read it again. "Crazy shit," he said, shaking his head.

From his wallet, he pulled out a worn, two-inch by two-inch black-and-white picture he had tucked between an expired Costco card and an expired movie discount card. He ran his thumb over it several times, touching it lightly, tenderly. The photo was a single frame cut from a strip of four that had been taken in a shopping mall photo booth. He hadn't looked at it in a year or more, but like every other time he looked, he was struck by how young they had been.

There was Anna, her hair long and wild, her expression defiant. Danny, next to her, looked like a straight arrow, with his short hair and suit coat and skinny tie, his lips pressed firmly together to hide his retainer. Erin was on the right, flashing a peace sign and an easy smile, but there was no hiding the intensity in his eyes. Then there was his own face, much thinner in his youth, with a drooping mustache and long, dark hair, grinning in stoned bliss.

Ah, Anna, what is going to happen now? We have been bound by love and grief, conditioned by allegiance, by memory, by history, to hop on this bus if it ever pulled up outside our doors. Where will it take us if we board?

With great care, he tucked the picture back in his wallet. He poured another beer. Tomorrow he would need a clear head, but tonight he was in pursuit of oblivion.

Chapter 6

Kate, with Gracie in tow, arrived home Tuesday night to find the porch light on and the house dark. She unlocked the front door and was reaching inside to turn on the overhead light when Gracie squeezed past her and ran into the living room, announcing, "Nana? Nana, I'm home."

Kate caught up with her from behind. She put her free arm around Gracie's waist and lifted her over one shoulder in a fireman's carry. "Come on, little munchkin," she said, heading for the bathroom.

"But nana," Gracie said, squirming to be put down.

"No buts. Nana does not want to be disturbed. I'll have dinner ready in a few minutes. Don't forget to wash your hands."

Kate served grilled cheese sandwiches with baby carrots and cherry tomatoes on the side. After they ate, she gave Gracie a bath and got her ready for bed. After tucking her in, Kate opened a book to read her a story.

"Where's nana?" Gracie asked in a plaintive voice.

"I told you, honey, she hasn't been feeling well for the past few days, and she needs her sleep."

"But where is she?" Gracie's face started to crumple, a precursor to tears.

"Where's nana?" Kate said enthusiastically. "Where's Waldo?"

"Where's Waldo?" Gracie repeated. She sounded puzzled but intrigued.

"Yeah, where the devil is Waldo?"

"Yeah," Gracie giggled. "Where the devil is he?"

Kate spoke in a conspiratorial, hypnotic whisper. "I'll tell you what. After I read you a story, and your big eyes get that dopey look in them I love so much, and you start to slip off to sleep, and I hear you making those sweet little snoring sounds—"

"I don't snore," Gracie protested softly, already going under.

Kate lowered her voice even more. "Then, when I go to sleep, I'll meet you in dreamland so we can look for Waldo together. I think he might have gone to the beach."

"The beach," Gracie murmured.

Kate turned out the lights.

Downstairs, she poured herself a glass of wine and turned on the television. She flipped through half a dozen channels but couldn't find anything to hold her attention. Why was her mother still holed up in her bedroom? It had been forty-eight hours since their fight, more than enough time to stop sulking. The note on the refrigerator last night had seemed like an apology of sorts, but this morning, she hadn't even bothered to get out of bed to see them off. Now even Gracie was starting to worry.

"That's enough," Kate said irritably. She walked over to Anna's door and knocked. "Mom," she said loudly, "we have to talk."

Hearing no reply, she turned the knob, pushed the door open, and flipped on the overhead light. "You've got to be kidding me." The bed was not only empty, it was neatly made with the sheets tucked in and the bedspread pulled up as if it hadn't been slept in at all. There was no new note, no indication of where she might have gone or when she would return. Kate frowned suddenly, realizing her mother's Honda Civic hadn't been in the driveway when they arrived home.

She abruptly exited the bedroom, marched across the living room to the kitchen, and yanked open the door to the garage. The car was gone.

Anna unlocked the Ryans' back door just as she had Sunday morning. This time she didn't take her shoes off. This time she locked the door behind her. She found a set of car keys hanging from a hook in the kitchen. In the garage, she retrieved the black garbage bag she'd pushed under the Volvo during her Sunday morning break-in. She reached into it and removed a small zippered gym bag, which she hid in the car's wheel well.

The rest of the contents—a few changes of clothing, a pillow, a blanket, and a burn phone—she left in the bag, which she tossed onto the back seat. The car started without so much as a sputter. After backing it down the driveway, she pushed the remote to close the garage door.

She wondered what the Ryans would think when they returned. She hoped they wouldn't realize she was the one who had robbed them, like a common thief. But even if they never suspected her as the culprit, she was certain they wouldn't forgive her for leaving their beloved plants to wither and die. For that matter, she didn't think she could forgive herself for such a dereliction.

A little before midnight, she merged onto Interstate 84 heading east. The storm that had battered her on the Olympic Peninsula had moved south. The heavy rain pounded against the windshield, obscuring an already black night. Though she couldn't see her surroundings, she knew this section of the Interstate by heart. The Columbia River was on her left, and on her right, fantastical, fine-grained basalt cliffs rose six hundred feet high.

She couldn't see the waterfalls—Horsetail, Wahkeenah, Multnomah—but she knew they were there, twisting, turning, roaring down steep rock faces, ending in deep terminus bowls bored into the ground over millennia. When she hiked the gorge on hot summer days, she often stopped to cool her feet at the edges of the pools. She loved watching the turbulent waters lift fallen trees and toss them about like pickup sticks.

The adrenaline rushes of the past seventy-two hours were spent and fatigue threatened to pull her under. She hunched over the wheel, clenched her hands, and stared hard, trying to penetrate the darkness. She felt her eyes grow heavy.

The thumping vibration of rumble strips startled her awake. She straightened out the wheels, barely in time to keep from going into a ditch, only to discover bright red and blue strobe lights pulsing around her. Just twenty-five miles from Portland, she pulled over on the right shoulder and came to a stop. The highway patrol car pulled in behind her.

While waiting for the officer to appear, she pulled a driver's license from her shirt pocket, and the car registration and insurance card from the visor. All were printed with the name and address of Ellie Ryan, age sixty-six. Ellie was roughly her same height and weight, and both had brown eyes, so Anna was pretty sure the cop wouldn't be tipped off by the license's biometric data. Plus, at a quick glance, she did bear a passable resemblance to Ellie's tiny Department of Licensing photo.

The only problem was Ellie's hair: thin, short, white and straight. Anna's wild mane was thick, shoulder-length, and though graying, still auburn at first glance. Before she left the Ryans' house, she had cinched her hair back with a rubber band, pinned it down, and tied a red bandanna over it. She prayed the disguise would pass scrutiny.

A female highway patrol officer appeared at her window in a thick yellow raincoat. *Just like the girl from the Morton Salt box*, Anna thought. She remembered her first day of second grade, the rain coming down and her mother waving from the front porch as she splashed to the bus stop in a shiny new yellow slicker with matching hood and calf-high rubber boots. But the woman standing by her car looked grim. Anna couldn't imagine her ever jumping into a puddle for the simple joy of the mess it would make.

The officer made a rolling motion with her hands and Anna lowered the window halfway. She noticed the raindrops made plopping sounds as they hit and bounced off the hard, flat rim of the patrol hat.

"Did you know you were drifting in and out of your lane, Ms. Ryan?" The officer asked after a quick glance at the papers Anna handed her.

Anna pleaded her case. "I did, and I feel terrible about it. See, my daughter just gave birth tonight in The Dalles," she explained, referencing the small town about sixty miles to the east. "She had a girl, my first grandbaby," Anna said proudly. "But my car battery was dead and I had to find someone to jump it, and then I had to pack everything and time just flew by, you know? And the weather is so bad. Before I got on the road, I called her to see if I should wait until tomorrow, but she begged me to come."

The officer turned the flashlight on her face. "Have you been drinking tonight?"

"No, no, ma'am. Only coffee," she said, holding up an empty Starbucks' cup Ellie had left in the drink holder. "It didn't do me much good, I guess," she added, trying to sound penitent. "I'm a good driver normally. It's just this godawful rain."

Without a word, the officer walked back to her patrol car, documents in hand.

Anna closed her eyes and tried to remain calm. The Volvo couldn't have been reported stolen, not yet. *Cops don't check out alibis during a traffic stop,* she thought. *Of course, they don't. Maybe she'll take pity on me, a tired, babbling, haggard old woman, a fledgling grandmother, trying to make it to The Dalles for a truly once-in-a-lifetime occasion.*

She waited for what seemed like a terrifyingly long time. Finally, the officer returned and handed the papers back, followed by a brief lecture about the dangers of driving when fatigued, and ending with, "If you begin to feel sleepy again, pull over immediately." Then she turned and walked back toward her cruiser without handing Anna either a ticket or a written warning.

Heart racing and hands trembling, Anna wrapped her arms over the steering wheel and rested her forehead against it. She said a prayer of thanks for Ellie, whose driving record must have been unblemished for the cop to let her impersonator off so lightly. Looking in the rearview mirror as she pulled onto the freeway, she saw the officer's head bent down. She imagined the woman writing up her report, working a crossword puzzle, or reading the last chapter of a detective novel—whatever highway patrol cops did to pass the time on late-night shifts.

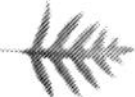

Anna tuned the radio to a rock station and cranked up the volume. She straightened her back, flexed her shoulders, stretched her neck muscles. She could do this. She had driven twenty-four hours at a stretch more times than she could remember, and it would only take nineteen hours to reach Farmington.

Less than an hour later, the sirens of fatigue called to her in the drumming rain, *Close your eyes for just a second or two...there, there, just for a second.* She nodded off again, and again was wakened by the sound of rumble strips. "Goddamn it," she cried, swerving back into her lane. She rolled her window all the way down and leaned her head out. The cold, biting rain was her only hope.

She pulled off at a rest stop in Boardman, Oregon. She saw one car parked at the far end of the lot and three eighteen-wheelers in the truck area, but every engine had been turned off, every interior dark. She used the facilities, washed her face in cold tap water, and frowned at the deep circles under her eyes. The towel dispenser was empty, so she dried her hands on her t-shirt. She itched to run a brush through her hair but thought better of removing the bobby pins and bandanna.

She climbed into the back seat of the Volvo. After retrieving her ancient Pendleton blanket and her pillow, she shoved the black bag on the floor so she'd have room to bed down for a few hours. She tried all her old tricks to shut down the chatter running in her head: counting breaths *one in, one out;*

two in, two out, silently singing *Ninety-Nine Bottles of Beer on the Wall*; consciously tensing, then relaxing her muscles. Big raindrops hit the roof of the car like pebbles thrown into a still pond and she imagined the ripples rocking her gently, wave after wave.

She started to drift. In the liminal state between sleep and waking, she saw Erin standing on a wooded trail. He wore patched jeans, a blue work shirt, and hiking boots. A red bandanna, tied around his forehead, kept his beautiful, long brown hair away from his face. She saw herself standing in front of him, looking up into his green eyes.

"You were so wild, so impulsive," she said.

"I carried the wildness for both of us," he said with a tender smile. Then he was gone.

Anna wiped her eyes with her shirtsleeve, not memory or dream, just the sad old woman she was now, crying in a car in the rain.

Part II
Conjuring Ghosts

Chapter 7

Danny walked into the office Wednesday morning and saw Renata, Pinyon's cheerful, gregarious, twenty-something receptionist, waving him over to the counter.

"*Hola*, Danny boy," she said.

"Hey, wasn't your hair green yesterday?" He asked with a grin. "Is blue trending now?"

She smiled wickedly. "*Todos los colores* are in play, my friend. Just wait till you see what I have planned next."

"So what's up?" He asked.

"A call came in for you last night. *Un tipo* named Mac."

"Mac? Did he give you a last name?"

"No. Said he was *tu amigo*. I told him you would be in today at 6:00 a.m. He asked for your home number—*por supesto* I didn't give it up. I called you at home a little after seven, *pero no contestaste*."

"Didn't hear it ring," Danny said. "I was probably outside. Did he leave his number?"

"No. He seemed to think you knew it, knew him," she said. "Hey, you okay? You look funny. Upset kinda funny."

"I'm fine," he said, attempting a smile. "You did the right thing. I'm pretty sure I do know who it is, and I have his number at home. Not to worry."

Renata picked up an incoming call. After her rote, 'Pinyon Landscaping. May I help you?', she switched to her native language. Her bilingual skills were invaluable in a community where a third of the population spoke Spanish.

Danny sat down at his desk and tried to focus on his job. His crew would be ready to head out soon, but first, he had to arrange deliveries for the new housing development they were landscaping. He called a wholesale nursery and ordered twelve more Elderica pines and an equal number of Chinaberry trees. He called a local quarry and ordered more yard rock.

"Danny," Renata called from across the room. "Another weird one. *Esta vez, una mujer*. She insists on talking to you but won't give her name. Line two."

With a shrug, Danny picked up the call. "Hello?"

"Hello, Danny."

Every muscle in his body felt tight. "Well, well, what do you know? It's been a long time. What, fifteen years?"

"More like nineteen," Anna said, "but who's counting?"

"Where are you calling from?" He asked, trying to sound nonchalant.

There was a moment of silence before she answered, "I'm still in Oregon."

He breathed a quiet sigh of relief. "So, how are you?"

"I'm okay," she said. "Pretty much as usual, good times interspersed with bad times and bouts of deep depression. And you, my young friend?" Anna was one month and one day older than him, and this had been a long-standing joke.

"The same. Working hard, hiking whenever I get the chance. Keeping those bouts of depression at bay."

"Well, aren't we the pair?"

"So, what's new, Anna?"

"Well, let's see. I retired three years ago."

"You're kidding. I thought your consulting work was your passion, your life's calling."

"It used to be when environmental impact assessments actually carried weight. These days, most development projects have so much money behind them, and so many political futures riding on them, they're done deals before we ever get to weigh in on the environmental or human impact. Now and then, developers will agree to tweak things a little, but getting them to change course? You might as well try to stop a juggernaut by holding up a stop sign."

"Big money, crooked politics, it's the way of the world," Danny said, leaning back in his chair.

"How are your folks, Danny? Did you ever make peace with your dad?"

"Both deceased. They died a long time ago," he said. "And yours?"

"My dad passed eight years ago—congestive heart failure."

"Ah man, I'm really sorry to hear that. I know how close you two were. What about your mom?"

"Two years after my dad died, she fell in love with a man from Australia. She's been living with him in Sydney for years. I've visited her there a few times but she won't come back to the States again. She's too frail."

"And Kate? Are you two on speaking terms?"

"That's a long story but the gist is she lives with me now, she and Gracie, my adorable, infinitely lovable granddaughter."

"Wow, I never saw that coming."

"Me either." She laughed.

"It's cool, though," he said. "Very cool. So, Anna, now that we're all caught up with current events, why exactly are you calling?"

Anna didn't answer, so he rephrased the question. "What are you up to?"

"Didn't you get my letter?"

"Not that I know of," he said. He pictured the daunting stacks of mail accumulating on his desk at home, on the floor next to his desk, and on top of his refrigerator. He rarely received any correspondence that interested him; most he just tossed into a pile, unopened. When the bulk was sufficient to justify the fuel it took him to get to the recycling center, he'd cart it all away. "So what did you say in this letter?"

"Are you still living on West Placita?" She asked.

"Yep."

"You should have received it by now," she said, sounding worried. "Have you been in touch with Mac?"

"Not since the last time we all met."

"I sent him the same letter," she said. "I tried to call him too, but no one answered and no answering machine picked up. Maybe he's moved?"

"I wouldn't know," Danny said. He glanced over at Renata, who was simultaneously typing and talking on the phone she had wedged between her chin and shoulder. "I used to see his name on journal articles once in a while, but not for the past few years. I'm pretty sure he's still at the University of Wisconsin." He lowered his voice to a whisper. "What's this about, Anna? What the hell is going on?"

"Danny, I know it's been a lot of years, but all the times you, Mac and I met and tried to talk things through, we never really…said anything, you know?"

"Yeah, I know."

"Why is that?"

"Ah, come on, Anna, you know why."

"Danny, if I needed to talk about things, I mean, really talk, would you?"

His deep intake of breath was audible. "I don't know. I'd have to think about it."

"And Mac?" She asked. "Do you think he would?"

"Are you sure you want to put him through that?"

"Not want, but—"

"Anna, we all coped in our own way. Mac, he just kept on pretending like nothing happened. My guess is that's how he still wants it." He hesitated for a moment. "And that's how I want it too." He heard a scuffing sound, as if she had placed her hand over the mouthpiece, followed by muffled crying.

When Anna finally spoke again, she sounded resolutely apologetic. "I am so sorry, Danny. If you find the stupid letter, please just toss it. This was all a terrible mistake. I shouldn't have called you." He heard a click. She was gone.

A feeling of dread blossomed in Danny's gut. He told himself he should just forget about her call, and the call from Mac, but as the day wore on, he couldn't stop thinking about them. As soon as he got home from work, he placed an open paper grocery bag in the middle of the room and began to winnow through his piles of mail. One by one, he tossed out coupon books, life insurance offers, one page flyers, newsletters, advertising circulars, penny papers, and scores of letters sent by political and environmental groups in search of donations.

He filled the first bag, opened another one. He lifted the last stack of mail from the top of the refrigerator and lowered it to the floor for sorting. A third of the way through, he saw a single white envelope, face down. He knew it was Anna's letter even before he flipped it over and saw the Portland postmark and recognized the familiar handwriting. He carried it to his desk and held it up to the lamp but he couldn't see inside. He considered putting a match to it but instead, he dropped the envelope into the paper bag and quickly backed away.

Bolo had been scratching to come inside for some time but Danny had ignored her. Now she let out two piercingly sharp barks. He stomped over to the door and yanked it open. "Can't you wait just a goddamned minute?" He shouted. Bolo cowered. Danny stared at her, horrified. She had been his closest companion for the past eight years and he had never before given her reason to fear him. He knelt down and tried to soothe her. "I'm so sorry, you beautiful girl. I would never hurt you."

He reached out to her. She inched forward on her belly, trembling. He gently stroked her muzzle. She pressed her face against his hand. He stroked her head. She slowly rolled over on her back. He leaned in close, rubbed her belly and whispered into her ear, "Thank you, Bolo. If all my sins could be so easily forgiven, I would be a happy man."

She got to her feet with her tail wagging and went straight to bed, but he wasn't quite ready to turn in. He started pacing, slowly at first, then faster, back and forth, wall to wall. He needed to move, but the room was so small, he felt like a caged animal. Bolo, unnerved by his restlessness, whined sharply.

He stopped pacing, walked over to the paper bag and retrieved the envelope. He ripped it open and read the single page insert. He went to his desk, turned on his laptop, opened the browser and picked up his phone.

"Who the fuck is this, and why are you calling me at this ungodly hour?" Mac snarled. Two pitchers of beer at the Laughing Bear had put him under, and when the ringing woke him, a Class III headache began to pound the back of his skull.

"Mac?"

"Who the hell is asking?"

"Mac, it's Danny."

"Danny, what the fuck?"

"How about a 'Hello, Danny?', or a 'How are you?', or a 'Good to hear from you, buddy?' You called me, remember?"

"Hello, Danny. How are you? Good to hear from you," Mac said, making no effort to hide his sarcasm. "Lighten up, man. You woke me the fuck up."

"It's not even midnight, Mac. I thought for sure you'd be out partying."

"This is finals week. I work for a living."

"Good for you, Mac. I'm impressed."

"Fuck you," Mac said. "How did you find me?"

"You mean since you didn't bother to leave a number when you called my office? I used a website that sells access to unlisted phone numbers. While I was at it, I checked out the UW staff directory. Mac Caffrey, PhD, and Department Chair to boot. Impressive."

"Somehow that doesn't sound like a compliment."

"Nice picture, by the way. I mean, the mustache still looks great, Mac, but what the hell happened to your hair?"

Mac turned on the lamp next to his bed and sat up straight. He checked out his image in his dresser mirror. He didn't think he looked much different than he had at twenty, or forty for that matter, except for normal wear and tear. Yes, his hair was white and receding, and his cheeks were rounder. But otherwise, he was still the spitting image of the brilliant but absentminded professor who had once dropped too much acid and who now drank too much booze.

"Screw you, Danny. When you get tired of insulting me, let me know."

"Mac, I'm sitting at my desk staring at a letter from Portland, Oregon. Sound familiar?"

"Did you read it?" Mac asked, picking up his own copy from the bedside table.

"Yep."

"'Calling all angels? Help me go forward by going back? One quiet week?'."

"That's the one," Danny said.

"Then there's a ten-digit number, a four-digit extension, and a date. Have you deciphered it?"

"I have."

"So where's the meet?"

"You think I'm going to announce it over the phone? Figure it out yourself, Professor."

"Sounds like you're getting a little paranoid. That can happen with old age," Mac said.

"I'm not paranoid, Mac, just not reckless. But I have to admit, if anyone bothered, which I can't imagine anyone would at this point, they could crack this code in a split second."

"Yeah, I know," Mac said. "I'm actually embarrassed to admit I had any part in creating it. It's so cheesy it could have come from a Cracker Jacks' box. Our whole 'quiet' strategy is totally outdated. I mean, no one can go undetected anymore just by avoiding the use of credit cards or staying in dives. With NSA computers and drones and GPS trackers and cameras on every street corner, and every pedestrian armed with a photo-snapping cell phone, amateurs are busted before they even have time to do the crime. Avoiding surveillance has become a high-level science, not a sleight of hand by artful dodgers."

"Okay, okay, I get it," Danny said. "We weren't sophisticated."

"I did figure out the date is this coming Saturday," Mac said. "She has some nerve trying to arrange a meet at the last minute. And she wants us to stay for a week? Six hours is the longest we've ever lasted. Usually less."

"Mac, seriously, her missive worries me, especially the angel part, and the going back part."

"Yeah, both are a little disconcerting, though I don't mind being seen as a winged cherub," Mac said. "Ah, I don't know, man. Maybe she's found religion. Or maybe she's having some kind of mid-life crisis."

"We're too old for mid-life crises," Danny replied.

Mac laughed out loud in spite of himself. "At any rate, there's no way I'm going to do what she's asking," he said. "I haven't talked to her in what, sixteen years?"

"More like nineteen. At least that's what she said when she called me at work this morning."

"She called you? You've got to be kidding."

"No joke."

"How did she find you?"

"I'm listed."

"Huh. I'm so used to students who only own cell phones, it never occurred to me to look you up in the phone book. What did she say?"

"Just banter at first. She's retired, and Kate has a kid, a little girl. They're both living with her. It's weird to think of her as a grandmother."

"Very weird," Mac said in a hushed voice. "It's hard to believe she's old enough. It's even harder to believe you and I are that old. What did she want?"

"I'm not entirely sure. She asked me why the three of us had never 'really talked'. She asked if we'd be willing to."

"Talk about what? Like the past?"

"I'm pretty sure that's what she meant."

"Now you've got me worried," Mac said. "I'm suddenly getting a vision of Pandora riding in on a dark horse, her hair streaming behind, her hands full of secrets she's scattering to the wind, the bearer of unbearable memories."

"Wow, what an image. I was already freaked out enough without your help."

"Danny, you have to know, man, back is not a place I'm willing to go. And why in God's name does she want to? What's she up to?"

"I have no idea. She ended the call by telling me to toss the letter. She said it was all a mistake, never mind, and thank you very much."

"Well, that's a relief. We can just let it go."

"I guess so. But, Mac, she has never once, not in forty-three years, asked us for anything."

"So?"

"So maybe she's in trouble. Maybe she needs us."

"Danny," Mac said, pleading. "She said never mind."

"Yes, she said it to me but she hasn't been able to reach you by phone. What if she still goes to the meet on the off chance you'll show?"

"Goddamn it, Danny. You are talking about Anna Sanders, right? Of course, she'll be there. But she gave us an out, man. We should take it."

"I don't see it that way, Mac. If I ever get a good night's sleep again, maybe I'll feel differently, but for now, my instinct is to go to the meet. Something's gone wrong. I want to know what."

Mac, holding his phone out at arm's length, spit out every choice expletive he could think of before bringing the phone to his ear again. "Fuck you, man. If you go, I should probably go too, for my own protection. But this coming Saturday? Is the meet anywhere close to Madison?"

"I'd guess about twelve or thirteen hundred miles."

Mac groaned. "I gave my last lecture Monday but I have finals to grade. I can't just walk away from everything on the drop of a dime." Danny said nothing.

Mac ruminated soundlessly until he came to a decision. "There's no way I can make it on time, man."

"But?" Danny asked.

Mac consented, albeit grudgingly. "I'll do my best. With the exception of a ton of fucking essay exams, I guess there's really nothing I can't put on hold for a week or so."

"There is an airport near the site," Danny said. "If you can't drive there in time, I'll be glad to pick you up."

"I hate flying. It's inhumane. Packing human beings into fucking sardine cans. Besides, my knees can't take it anymore. If you change your mind, Danny, you call me, day or night. I do not want to do this, and I won't if you don't."

Mac hung up. He thought about the conversation, how strangely familiar it felt to talk to his former friend. He first met Danny and Anna in kindergarten. By the end of elementary school, they had become inseparable. After they graduated from high school in 1969, all three were accepted by and chose to attend the University of California at Berkeley.

He thought about their first year on campus, all the hours spent poring over journals in the library stacks, the afternoons hanging out in coffee houses on Telegraph Avenue, and the Friday nights at their neighborhood cinema watching movies by Bergman, Truffaut, and Cassavetes.

He remembered dropping a hit of windowpane acid and spending a summer day on the hillside behind campus; he'd laid on his back in the high grasses for hours, staring up at the sky, watching white cumulus clouds turn into stunning, shifting layers of color and form. He remembered the night he and a sweet brunette, whose name he'd forgotten long ago, put *Traffic* on the stereo, choked down some psilocybin, and rapturously lost their virginity to each other. He remembered thinking perhaps God did exist after all.

He had been living the hippie dream, until the dream became a nightmare.

He wondered why, more than four decades later, the three of them still held on to the sliver of remaining friendship. Or maybe it wasn't friendship that held them together for so long. Maybe it was fear.

He thought of the photo he kept in his wallet, the four of them in the photo booth, Anna's penetrating, defiant stare. *Are you still in there, girl? What are you doing conjuring ghosts? What kind of trouble are you in that Danny and I could possibly help you with, that the past would provide answers to? Damn it, woman, do not come back to haunt me.*

He took the letter with him into his study, turned on his computer, and typed the ten-digit number into a GPS app. The meeting would take place at N

36° 59.938, W 109° 02.710, the coordinates for Four Corners National Monument. Danny had been right on about the distance, about thirteen hundred miles traveling south and west on the interstates. It would take him at least two days to get there, if he stayed straight, which was highly unlikely. All that stood in his way were the forty-two blue books he had left to grade.

He decided he might be able to make it, if he really pushed. "And yes," he said out loud, "I will also need to take a lot of drugs and drive like a maniac. Twist my arm." In his best Doris Day voice, he began singing, *Que sera, sera*.

Danny went to bed after his conversation with Mac. He lay there awake, listening to the faint buzz of cars on the distant highway and the hooting of a nearby owl. *I have a good life*, he thought, *hard, honest labor; the sacredness of desert; the profanity of skimming electronically across the dark waters of the world; my old friend Jackson; Bolo to watch over, and to watch over me.*

He found himself thinking back to his early life in California, when his goals had been about forward movement, when he had best friends and high ideals and a future with unlimited potential. He had known fear then, but only as a rushing, free-floating anxiety running through him like a low-voltage current. He had known anger then, too, but only as the righteous outrage of a disenchanted adolescent who believed people could do better.

Now, his fears ran deep and dark, and his anger was no longer mitigated by faith in the human species. He didn't know if he was better or worse off now than he had been then; he only knew he was different.

Now everything will change again, he thought. Everything *is* changing. Everything will return, *is* returning. He imagined himself skating across the frozen surface of an alpine lake, and the ice breaking beneath his feet. He felt himself falling, all the way through and into the world again.

Chapter 8

After leaving the rest stop on Wednesday morning, Anna drove out of the narrow channel of the gorge. The storm that had plagued her for the past three days finally dumped the last of its moisture over the Cascades. The prevailing westerlies now carried nothing but hot air to the steppes and rolling hills of Eastern Oregon. *Oh my God, it's only May,* she thought as she drove past plowed fields and open grasslands already brittle and brown from the steady onslaught of high temperatures and extreme drought. In all directions, the smoky horizons confirmed what she already knew: the West was on fire.

She thought about turning around, going home. She ached to see Kate's face, to ask how her workday had gone, to hear about Gracie's adventures at daycare. She wanted to tell her daughter not to worry. She wanted to hold Gracie one more time. But by her own design, she could do none of that. The only road still open was the road ahead.

Kate went to work after dropping Gracie off at daycare, but she couldn't focus, couldn't stop worrying about her mother. She passed the morning in mindless industry: filing papers that had sat on her desk for weeks, cleaning her keyboard, deleting old emails. Just before noon, after canceling the lunch plans she'd made with a group of coworkers, she arranged for an Uber to take her home.

The answering machine on the living room end table blinked red. Kate sat down on the couch and pushed the 'play' button. The first caller, from the Sierra Club, wanted to remind Anna Sanders of an upcoming protest against the proposed Liquid Natural Gas terminal in Coos Bay.

The second message came from the neighbors down the street. "Anna, this is Ellie. The flight went well and we're on the ship, which is quite elegant, by the way. We want to thank you again for taking care of the plants in our absence. We'll give you a call before we board to come home. Bye, now."

Kate frowned. Her mother hadn't told her the Ryans were going out of town or that she had agreed to water their plants.

She listened to the third message. "What the hell?" She yanked open the end table drawer and dug around for a pen and paper. She hit the play button again, wrote down the number, and with trembling hand, made the long-distance call.

A man answered, "Bremerton Police Department."

"Hi, my name is Kate Sanders. I just got a message to call you. Actually, I'm not sure when the message came in but it said I should call as soon as possible."

"Detective Molinski is handling that case," the man said. "He's not in the office now but I should be able to connect your call. Please hold."

Elevator music played briefly in the background. A Beatles' tune, she thought, but so over-orchestrated she couldn't tell for certain. The music stopped. Another voice came on the line. "Detective Molinski here."

"Hi. I'm Kate Sanders. I believe you called me."

"Miss Sanders, yes. Thank you for getting back to us so quickly. Are you related to Anna Sanders?"

"She's my mother. Why?"

"Is your mother home?"

"No, she's not. I believe she's out of town." Kate actually had no idea where her mother had gone, but for some reason, she found herself on the defensive, and it was the first explanation that occurred to her.

"Is there a number where she can be reached?"

"What is this about?" Kate demanded. "What's going on?"

"Well, we're not quite sure what this is about. I'm calling because we found an abandoned car on the Olympic Peninsula yesterday. It's registered to your mother."

Kate's mouth dropped but she couldn't think of what to say. She sat on the couch, staring at a rough nick in the coffee table and gripping the phone so hard, her knuckles began to turn white.

She heard him say, "Miss Sanders?" His voice sounded too loud, as if he thought she'd set the phone down and walked away.

"Kate," she said at last.

"Kate, all right then." He repeated his request. "Do you know how we can reach your mother?"

Kate recited Anna's ten-digit cell number. "I tried to call her this morning but she didn't answer."

"That number won't help. We found her cell phone locked in the car's glove compartment, along with her wallet."

"Oh, my God," Kate whispered.

"Would it be possible to meet with you so we can put our heads together on this?"

She answered without hesitation. "I'm home today. Can you come now?"

"Well, right now I'm on the road, on my way down from Bremerton. I have to check in with the Portland Police Department when I get there, but I could be at your house by, say, 4 p.m. this afternoon. Would that work for you?"

"Yes," she said. "Yes, I'll be here."

She hung up and dialed her boss. She told him about the call from Molinski and he gave her permission to take as much time off as needed. He said he hoped everything would turn out for the best.

At a few minutes after 4 p.m., she opened the door to a fifty-something overweight man in a suit and tie, accompanied by a much younger man in a Portland Police Department uniform. Detective Molinski showed her his identification and introduced the other officer as Sergeant Devin. She showed them to the living room. The two men sat on the couch. She chose the recliner.

Molinski began the conversation. "I know you must be anxious to be brought up to date, so I'm going to get right to it."

"Please," she said.

"Wednesday morning, a scuba diver spotted your mother's car resting on the bottom of Puget Sound, roughly twenty feet below the surface."

Kate felt the blood drain from her face.

"The diver reported his discovery to my department in Bremerton and we contacted the state police. They arranged for a crane barge to go to the site. Last night, they brought the car up, a Fiji blue, 2005 Honda Civic."

Kate clamped her hand over her chin to stop it from quivering uncontrollably. "And my mother?"

"We haven't reached any definitive conclusions. In fact, we still have a team at the scene."

"But you *have* reached some conclusions," Kate said, reading between the lines.

"We don't want to assume anything, or mislead you before—"

"Listen, Detective," she said, sounding more hostile than she had intended. "I understand you don't want to give bad news unnecessarily, and you have to hold some things back during an investigation. But I do not want to be kept in the dark while you double-check everything six ways from Sunday. I want to know what you know, and what you suspect, every step of the way."

He raised his eyebrows and smiled, condescendingly, she thought. "Sure, Kate, we can do that, more or less. Let me tell you what we know so far. The car was driven off a bluff high above the Sound. To get to that spot, you have to drive up an old logging road, then up a rutted trail barely wide enough for a car. So this was no accident. Our theory at this point is that someone stole the vehicle and dumped it. Unfortunately, there's been a hell of a storm up there, so any evidence on the ground has washed away."

Kate saw him looking at her questioningly. She nodded for him to go on.

"However, we can't rule out suicide. Your mother's body wasn't found, but the driver's door was wide open and all the windows had been rolled down, so it's possible the currents…"

"There is no way she committed suicide," Kate said.

"The thing is," Molinski said, forging ahead, "the car itself doesn't have a scratch on it, at least not a recent one, and the undercarriage is intact. That poses something of a problem because according to the state forensic specialist, the only way a car could go off that cliff but not get banged up by the rock face on the way down would be if it went off at around sixty miles an hour."

"You're saying my mother drove her car off a cliff, full speed ahead?" Kate barely recognized her own voice it sounded so flat.

"We're not drawing any conclusions. We have a rope team there today looking for any evidence the car hit the rocks on the way down. But if we don't find any, well, we have to assume that the car was powered off the cliff by someone holding their foot on the gas pedal."

Kate heard herself ask, in a voice that sounded disembodied, "You think she's dead, don't you?"

Sergeant Devin, whose only role until then had been to take notes, got up and headed for the kitchen. He returned with a glass of tap water and handed it to Kate.

Molinksi resumed his summarization. "At this point, we simply do not know what happened. If you could help us pin down a timeline, maybe we can figure it out. When did you last see her?"

"Sunday night," Kate said. "I saw her Sunday night. I didn't see her Monday but I know she was home that day because she left me a note asking me not to disturb her. I figured she just wanted to avoid me."

Molinski raised an eyebrow. "Avoid you?"

"We had an argument on Sunday night. No big deal, just politics, but she holed up in her bedroom. She didn't even come out to say goodnight to Gracie." Kate glanced over to see Sergeant Devin scribbling furiously in his notebook.

"Gracie?" Molinski asked.

"I have a three-and-a-half-year-old daughter. On weekdays, if she and my mom don't have anything planned, I take her to daycare on my way to work and pick her up on my way home."

"So she's in daycare now?"

"Yes," Kate said irritably.

"You said your mother left you a note Monday night. May I see it?" Molinksi asked, sounding hopeful.

Kate shrugged. "Sorry, I tossed it, and the garbage has already been picked up. It didn't say much, just that she had a headache and had gone to bed early. She didn't come out of her bedroom Tuesday morning either. I was sure she'd be here when we got home that night but she wasn't. When I saw that her car was gone, I thought maybe she'd gone out of town."

"Has she ever done anything like this before?" He asked. "Just gone out of town without telling you?"

"No."

"Kate, has your mother ever been depressed? Has she ever hurt herself, or threatened to do so?"

"No, never. I mean, she does get depressed, but she's not a depressive, really, she's just…not an optimist. She describes herself as a realist. Look, she loves me and she is completely crazy about Gracie. And she's a fighter. I'm telling you, there is no way she would hurt herself."

"Are there any friends she might have talked to?" He asked. "Anyone else who might have information about her whereabouts? A husband, a boyfriend?"

She answered honestly. "My mother never married and she has never been particularly sociable. She used to have some friends at work but no one close."

"Used to?"

"She retired about three years ago."

"What kind of work did she do?"

"She has a Master of Science in applied chemistry. For the past thirty-some years, she worked for a firm that contracts with the state to carry out environmental impact studies."

"Do you think her past work could be related to her disappearance?"

She scoffed. "You mean like, did she make enemies or something? My mother worked as an analyst. She took the scientific data other people gathered through fieldwork and synthesized it into a report. She stayed in the background, a 'worker bee'—that's how she described herself."

Molinski rubbed his hands together, then pushed himself up off the couch. "Kate, would you mind if we took a look around the house? I'd like to see if anything jumps out at us."

She thought about it. "I guess that would be okay as long as I go with you. Mom would never consent to this, by the way, but she's not here, and I'm pretty freaked out, so if it would help…"

The walkthrough took less than ten minutes. "I didn't see anything to set off alarms," Molinski said when they returned to the living room. "Did she keep a calendar?"

"Yes, she does keep one," Kate said, pointedly emphasizing the present tense. "But it's on her computer."

"Do you have access to her computer?"

"I don't know her password," Kate said, "but I'm a programmer, so I may be able to figure it out."

"You should check it out, Kate, her computer, her personal correspondence, her emails if you can get into them." His suggestion sounded almost like an order. "If you can't get access, we could have one of our tech specialists take a look, but hopefully we won't need to go such lengths. Our plan is to put out a BOLO on your mother and distribute flyers with her picture to the local news stations in both Portland and Seattle."

"If she wasn't in the car at all, or had been but escaped before it went over the cliff, someone may have seen her. We'll start there and follow every lead. We'll do everything we can to find her, Kate. I'll get back in touch with you as soon as there are any new developments."

Handing her a business card, Molinski added, "If anything else occurs to you, or if you find anything relevant in her files or on her computer, please let me know right away."

Kate watched them drive away, then closed and locked the front door. In the bathroom, she splashed cold water on her face and practiced her smile in the mirror. She had to be able to hold it together when she picked Gracie up from daycare. Her daughter needed her, now more than ever.

That night, Kate cuddled with Gracie in the living room as they watched a Pixar movie. When Gracie fell asleep halfway through, she decided to leave her on the couch while she searched for answers. She hated invading her mother's privacy but she didn't see that she had any choice. She walked into Anna's bedroom and went straight to her desk. She moved the keyboard aside and lifted the blotter to retrieve the password list she knew her mother kept hidden there. But the list had vanished.

Frowning, she pressed the button to turn on the CPU. Nothing happened. She checked the power cord; it was plugged into the wall and firmly attached to the unit. She tipped the case onto its side and removed the cover.

The guilt she felt about violating her mother's personal space went out the window as soon as she realized the hard drive and memory chips had been removed. She began tearing the bedroom apart. She fanned the pages of every book in the pile by Anna's bed, dumped out the entire contents of her dresser and her under-bed boxes, and went through the pockets of every piece of clothing in her closet. "Damn you," she muttered under her breath.

Her last hope was the locked file drawer in the desk. She didn't have the key, so after retrieving a hammer and screwdriver from the garage, she got down on her hands and knees and pounded the lock until it broke apart. Glancing at the file names, she determined they held only the banal stuff of everyday life: financial records, appliance manuals, insurance policies, utilities and home repairs. None were labeled 'computer', or 'passwords', or 'My Vanishing Act'.

She was about to close the drawer when she decided the distinctive orange color of the first file made it worth a closer look. She sat down cross-legged on the floor, placed the file open in front of her, and began to examine the contents. The first document was her mother's will, the second provided contact information for an attorney, and the third detailed her mother's bank accounts and provided the passwords.

The fourth took Kate's breath away: a notarized form transferring the house, which had been paid for in full, and all of her mother's remaining financial assets, including over a hundred thousand dollars in a money market account, to Kate. It had been signed and dated by a notary the previous Friday earlier.

"Oh, my God," she cried out loud. "You planned this. You fucking planned this all along." Whatever 'this' turned out to be, she suddenly realized she was not to blame. Their Sunday night argument had not driven her mother out of the house, or over a cliff. Relieved of guilt, she began to cry. Alligator tears, her mother used to call them, and now they fell freely from her tired eyes.

She heard a sound in the living room and got up to check on Gracie but her little girl was sleeping peacefully on the couch. She returned to the bedroom and pulled the last item from the orange folder, a manila envelope stapled to the inside back cover.

She tore it open to find a single, four-by-five-inch color print. Clearly the work of a professional, the beautifully composed and developed photograph captured a young man and woman standing by a canoe on the bank of a slow-moving river. The setting was a desert canyon, with high limestone walls framing the sandbar on which the couple stood. The man, actually more of a boy at a close glance, was barefoot and shirtless. His thin, hairless chest was darkly tanned, and his faded blue jeans hung just below his narrow waist.

He had a red bandanna tied around his head, over long, brown hair that fell below his shoulders. His eyes were the same deep green as Gracie's eyes, and he was laughing. The girl also looked young. She had the slim build of someone in their late teens or early twenties, and she was wearing jean shorts, a t-shirt, and a big straw garden hat. Her thick, wavy auburn hair tumbled out and down. She, too, was laughing, laughing so hard her whole face scrunched into a grin.

Kate had never seen her mother look so joyful.

She turned the picture over and saw an inscription: *Great trip and great meeting you two. Ed and Marie, March 1973.*

The photo had been taken the year she had been conceived. Could this man-boy be her father? There was no studio stamp on the photo, no last names to help her figure out who Ed and Marie were, nothing to point her to an answer. Kate pressed the print against her chest. She held it there for a long time.

She went upstairs and slid the photograph into the corner of her dresser mirror, where she would see it when she woke up each day. If her mother didn't return, which seemed more and more likely, she would at least have this, a portal to a moment in time when her mother and possibly her father had been so amazingly happy and alive.

It occurred to her she should tell Molinski what she'd found, but she didn't like the man and didn't want him digging into her mother's secrets.

When she woke her daughter to put her to bed, Gracie asked, "Mommy, when is nana coming home?"

"Honey, she left me a message a little while ago. She's not coming home for a while, maybe for a long time."

"How come?" Gracie asked, tears pooling in her eyes.

"Well, you know nana used to have a very important job. Her boss asked her to come back to work and she just couldn't say no. They have a big project and need her help. But she did want me to tell you she misses you and thinks of you every single day. She wanted to make sure I told you how much she loves you."

"How much?" Gracie asked on cue, and held her arms wide like she did with her grandmother.

"Her love is even bigger than that," Kate said, "bigger than the whole wide world." She held out her own arms as far as she could stretch them.

Gracie looked relieved. "I love her that much too, Momma."

"I know you do, honey, I know you do. And so do I."

Chapter 9

Anna pulled off the freeway in Spanish Fork, Utah. Exhausted, and hungry for the first time since leaving Portland, she stopped at a local pizza parlor. She found an empty booth and ordered a slice of cheese pizza and a draft beer, polished those off, and ordered seconds. When she got up to leave, she felt almost human again.

On the outskirts of town, she turned in to park at the Big Oak Inn, a U-shaped throwback to 1970s motor courts. The neon vacancy sign was broken but she counted only three cars in the lot. No one appeared behind the desk when she entered the office, so she hit the call bell on the counter. After waiting a few minutes, she dinged it again.

A gaunt, sallow-skinned night clerk emerged from a side door posted with a 'private' sign. He was followed by a young woman with sunken cheeks, straggly hair and artlessly tattooed arms. His coworker, Anna thought, or girlfriend, or dealer.

"Yeah?" He said, as if throwing down a gauntlet.

"I'd like a room for one night, please."

"Thirty-two and tax."

She handed over two twenties.

He didn't ask her to fill out a guest registration form and didn't give her a receipt. He handed her the change and a key, then turned and followed his other half into the back room. When he slammed the door behind them, Anna caught a whiff of ammonia and sulfur, the unmistakable aroma of methamphetamines.

She parked the Volvo in front of a scuffed green door with the number eight painted on it in faded yellow. She lifted out the bag that held her bedding and clothes, retrieved her canvas satchel from the wheel well, and carried them inside. The room was about what she'd expected: a lumpy double bed and a fat television that looked so old, she thought it might still use a cathode ray tube. Other than a single wedge of soap, there were no amenities, not even shampoo.

Desperate for a shower, she stripped down and stood in the tub under a thin stream of warm water. She dried off with a threadbare, grayish towel hanging from a rack above the toilet.

Wearing nothing but a clean pair of socks, she grabbed the motel grade mustard-colored spread, the lightweight blanket, and the top sheet, and pulled them to the foot of the bed. She pushed the pillow aside to make room for her own, then wrapped her Pendleton blanket around her body like a cloak, and lay down.

She turned out the lamp and closed her eyes. She longed for sleep, but every time it began to approach, her excitement at its nearness chased it away again. She lay awake into the early hours of the morning, listening to the steady white noise made up of the distant rumble of trucks and the low hum of the wall fan.

She realized she was afraid to let go and sink into the darkness. She imagined Gracie in her arms, which provided some comfort, but didn't alleviate her fear. So she brought Kate, and Danny, and Mac into her fantasy. Like the survivors of a shipwreck, she imagined them huddling together and holding fast, floating on a cobbled raft of dreams above the turbulent waters of the world.

Mac knocked at the door of the third-floor apartment where his senior teaching assistant lived, then knocked again. Finally the young man, in a white t-shirt and sweatpants, opened the door.

"Steve, good morning to you," Mac said.

Steve rubbed his eyes and groaned, though it may have been a growl, Mac thought. He would have growled too if a manic professor had turned up on his doorstep at 3 a.m. on a Friday morning.

"Sorry for the early hour, Steve. I just need to drop these off to you and I'll be gone." Mac held out a grocery bag stuffed with blue books and Steve took it from him without a word. It would be Steve's job to log the essay scores, combine them with the mid-term scores, arrive at a cumulative grade for each student, and fill out all the attendant paperwork needed to turn in and post final grades.

"Due in the administration office by 5 p.m. on Monday," Mac said.

On the way back to his car, Mac felt a sudden celebratory urge to jump high in the air and kick his heels together. He stopped on the sidewalk and lifted one foot, putting his full weight on his bad knee. Grimacing, he decided that while he might be able to jump up, the coming down wouldn't be worth it. Instead, holding one hand behind his back, and the other up by his head, he did a little jig. It was enough.

When he got home, he opened a cold beer, polished off a few lines of coke, turned on the stereo and put on his wireless headphones. He spent the next few hours getting high and dancing to the music. He decided he moved with surprising grace for a man with a bad knee and a big gut. He finally collapsed on his bed as the sun was rising.

At 6:00 in the morning, Danny called the office from home.

"Good morning, Renata."

"*Hola*, Danny boy."

He cleared his throat. "Listen, I received a call late last night from a hospital in Minnesota. My sister was in a car accident and she's in bad shape."

"Oh, Danny, I'm so sorry. I didn't know you had a sister."

"We're not particularly close. She's always been a loner, kind of like me. Anyway, she doesn't have anyone else to take care of her, so I'm going to have to take a little time off."

"Of course you will, Danny. Don't worry about anything here. You know Eduardo. He thinks you can do no wrong."

"I do need to talk to him. Is he in the office yet?"

"He just walked in. I'm going to put you on hold for a minute."

While Danny waited, he realized he shouldn't have concocted such an elaborate story. He had accrued far more vacation time than he would ever use and Eduardo wouldn't have hesitated to give him a few weeks off if he'd asked. But he had screwed it up and now he was going to have to make up a lie about someone who didn't exist, injured in an accident that had never happened, living in a state he had never even visited.

Eduardo's voice came over the line. "Renata told me, Danny. I'm so sorry."

"Thanks, Eduardo. She's in bad shape but she's alive. I talked to the doctor a little while ago. He said she's medically stable and will be discharged to a nursing facility tomorrow. She should be able to go home a few days after that but only if someone is there to help her out. We're not close but she's the only family I have left."

Danny knew Eduardo was deeply involved in the daily lives of his and his wife's large, extended families, their community, and church. He expected an empathic response from his boss, and Eduardo didn't disappoint.

"I understand, Danny. Nothing is more important than family."

"Thanks, thanks a lot," Danny said. "I found a redeye that leaves tonight. I'm not sure how long I'll be gone, but probably a week, maybe two, depending on what I find when I get there."

"Take as much time as you need," Eduardo said.

"I'll coordinate with Renata to make sure she knows where I am on the different projects. Some can be re-assigned, and some can be put on hold until I get back."

"Okay, sure. Why don't you stop by before you leave this afternoon? Checks will be ready at 4:00, and I'd like to say goodbye."

"I will," Danny said. "I'll be there. And, Eduardo, thanks again. Really."

He was about to hang up when he realized Eduardo was still talking.

"You're a man of integrity, Danny, and I have great respect for your decision to help your sister."

Danny felt like weeping when he put the phone down but his body no longer seemed to know how.

In Spanish Fork, Anna woke in the rundown motel, in the bed alone, in the room alone. She looked around at the faded walls and stained carpets and windows grimy with neglect and found herself longing for home again. She wondered if Kate had found the photograph yet. She shouldn't have risked it but she had to leave her daughter something.

For the first time in years, she allowed herself to remember the seven-day canoe trip she had taken with Erin on the Green River, their last journey into the wilderness. She closed her eyes and pictured them floating lazily on the slow-moving river as it wound through slickrock sandstone canyons. Every bowed curve, every drop in elevation, took them further down through geological time.

They sought relief from the hundred-degree heat by paddling to rock overhangs that offered slivers of shade, or by repeatedly dousing their shirts in the river and putting them back on, dripping wet. At night, they camped on sandbars under starry skies and fell asleep to the sound of water gently lapping the shore.

She remembered one hot, still afternoon when a shimmery raven appeared above them. It flapped up and down to make a current to ride, and each beat of its wings echoed off the limestone walls. *Whoosh, whoosh, whoosh.*

One early morning, paddling in silence under a gray-green sky and a light rain, they heard a splashing sound, and looked up to see, from the tops of the canyon walls surrounding them, water falling down countless narrow chutes. It landed on rock ledges, then pooled, then tumbled again and pooled again, and kept falling until the streams thinned and disappeared, only to resurface in currents visible along the shoreline.

She was startled out of her reverie by the sound of footstelps outside. She opened her eyes and sat up, but whoever had walked by her room kept going. She looked at the clock: it was almost checkout time. She forced herself to get out of bed. After another skimpy shower, she stepped into a clean pair of jeans and pulled on a pale gray t-shirt decorated with silkscreened birch-bark canoes. She turned on the grainy television and watched the local news and weather while she stuffed her belongings back into the black bag. She loaded her car, closed the room door behind her and deposited the key in the drop box outside the office.

It's time, she said to herself. *Time to pull out of free fall, time to get wherever the hell I'm going.*

Around 2:00 Friday afternoon, Mac got out of bed, showered, dressed, and packed a small suitcase with clothes for the week ahead.

He pilfered his medicine cabinet, his kitchen cabinets, and his desk drawers in search of little stashes of Ritalin that his very easygoing physician had prescribed for 'attention deficit disorder'. He found around sixty pills altogether. He swallowed one dry and dumped the others into a plastic freezer bag that he zipped shut and stuffed into the pocket of his lightweight parka.

Last but not least, he dug around in the back of the hall closet and emerged with an Aqua plastic water bottle and a tall can labeled Fix-A-Flat, both purchased at a head shop in Chicago. He stuffed their roomy false bottoms with foil-wrapped pot. He worried that he didn't have enough to get him through the week to come but his dealer was out of town, so there was nothing to be done about it now.

He found it easier to lie when he didn't have to look his audience in the eye, so while Patricia was attending her weekly department meeting, he called her office to leave a message. "Hey, it's me. I just got an invite to stay with some old friends who have a house in Big Sur. Not an offer I can refuse. Sorry, I won't see you before you take off for Tennessee. When you get settled, let's find a way to meet up again. Take care of yourself, beautiful." He put the phone down. It didn't really matter if she believed him. She just needed to know that his absenteeism was planned.

He did a quick walkthrough, took a last hit off a joint, and locked the house. He placed the Aqua bottle in the front seat drink container, hid the Fix-A-Flat can in the wheel well, and put the rest of his baggage in the trunk. He hadn't been on a road trip in over a decade. In fact, for the past few years, he hadn't driven any farther than Chicago, and even then only when he had to catch a flight. It might be a kick, he thought, driving cross-country again.

The Prius motor purred to life and his iPod began blasting The Flying Burrito Brothers' *White Line Fever* through his amped-up stereo system. Mac sang along at the top of his lungs, and in key, as he drove through Madison's sprawling suburbs toward the Interstate.

At 4:00 Friday afternoon, Danny opened the door to the Pinyon office and froze. His crew, along with Renata and Eduardo, were all standing around his desk, hovering around a big box of mixed donuts. Above their heads, half a dozen colorful latex balloons broadcast florid messages: 'We wish you well', 'Get well soon', 'Hurry back'. Next to the food was a box decorated with a big

bow and wrapped in light brown paper with a dog-paw motif. The words 'Danny' and 'Thinking of you and your sister', were sprawled across it.

He just stood there, taking it all in, dumbstruck. His coworkers began to speak, one at a time, and he felt a deep blush spread up from his neck and inflame his cheeks.

"We'll be thinking of you, Danny," said Eduardo.

"Take care of yourself, man," said Tim, their newest employee, who had been in training with Danny all spring.

"Sorry to hear about your sister's accident, but if anyone can give her the support she'll need, you're the one," said Armando, his crew chief.

"Don't forget us, man," said Jorge, a small, sinewy man who was an unimpeachable expert on desert flora. "Just know you've got family here if you need us."

Tears welled up in Danny's eyes for the first time in as long as he could remember—years, maybe decades. He clenched his jaw and said, in a voice hoarse with emotion, "Thank you so much. You guys are the best."

His audience applauded and looked at him expectantly.

"I'm sorry to leave on such short notice, but these things happen, I guess. Really, thank you for this, for everything."

Renata lifted the present and handed it to him. "This is for you, from all of us."

His fingers shook as he pulled off the ribbon and tore open the paper. He pulled out a white fisherman-knit sweater from the box.

"That's for Minnesota," she said. "They're having a cold spell and we know you don't have many clothes to wear in that kind of weather."

Danny's voice almost got away from him. "It's beautiful. No one has given me a present in, well, a long time." He looked at Renata, silently pleading for help.

"The donut shop is now open for business," she announced, reaching for a glazed.

The staff stood around awkwardly, just long enough to eat, then began to disperse. On the way out, each person came up to Danny, as if he were the groom in a reception line. Some shook his hand, a few patted him on the back, and the others just paused to smile at him and nod.

Driving home afterward, he thought about blue-haired Renata, a vibrant single mother whose dry wit always made him laugh. And Eduardo, a devoted

Catholic with an Anglo wife and five beloved children, and a sense of decency that had earned him the loyalty of even his most intractable workers. And Tim, a recent graduate with a bachelor's degree in history, only twenty-two and already cynical about a world where the only job he could get was as a laborer. They were kind, hardworking, conscientious people.

He had kept his distance from them over the years, rarely socializing outside of the occasional large group gathering. But that morning, they refused to let him keep circling on the periphery of their lives. They reeled him in, and for a moment, held him fast.

A feeling of panic seized him. His perfectly trimmed boat of self-control was beginning to take on water.

As soon as he got home, he dialed Jackson's number.

"Hey, old man, it's me. Are you recovered from my last visit?"

"Danny," Jackson bellowed. "I'm good, good as new. I don't quite remember how Sunday evening ended, but I'm not really sure I want to."

"Don't worry, you didn't do anything I wouldn't do."

"I guess that's reassuring," Jackson said with a laugh.

"Listen, Jackson, I was wondering if I could stop by tonight, maybe bunk there. I've got a six-hour drive ahead of me tomorrow to meet some old friends and it would be easier if I split the trip into two legs."

"Hell yes, you can bunk here. I've got a fresh bottle with your name on it. But, Danny, stick to the speed limit when you get to Bernalillo County. Yesterday, the cops pulled me over again, this time in town. I was leaving the grocery store parking lot, for Christ's sake."

"Did they ticket you?" Danny asked.

"Nah, just the usual harassment. They asked if I was carrying, as if I'd carry a pistol to a supermarket. Idiots. They never have found one single thing to cite me on, and they never will."

"These were local cops?"

"They were, but I'm pretty sure they're being directed by FBI, or ATF, one or both of them. I don't really care that much, you know? I'm an old man. If they want to start a fight with me, they can have at it. I'll show them some fireworks." He laughed, apparently amused by his own bluster.

"Jackson, are you getting depressed?"

"Nah, I'm all right. I'm not going to do anything stupid. I'm just sick of being at odds with the world."

"I know that feeling," Danny said.

"I probably need to get out more, but the simple truth is, I don't have anywhere else to go."

Anna drove southeast from Spanish Fork on State Road 191, through Price Canyon recreation area and the La Sal National Forest, past Arches National Park, past Moab. She shuddered when she drove through Monticello, Utah, but she had no choice if she was going to pick up Highway 491. She knew the history of the town from her environmental consulting work: in the fifties, uranium and vanadium mining and processing had contaminated it with high levels of radiation.

After a fifteen-year Department of Energy cleanup project that ended in 2004, the area was supposedly safe again. Still, she was relieved to see the town recede in her rearview mirror.

She crossed into Colorado, continued south into New Mexico, and by late afternoon, reached the turnoff for the Broken Trail Lodge. She had chosen the location for the meet based on an account from a travel review on Google: *The lodge was built in the fifties in response to post-war prosperity and a renewed interest in travel at home. It consists of a two-story hotel with meeting rooms and a restaurant, and twenty-four extended-stay homes that are widely scattered across forty acres of largely undisturbed desert. No longer a prime destination for recreating celebrities and the nouveau riche, the resort is still admired for the mirage-like appearance of its low, sand colored adobe buildings, and for its conscientious preservation of place.*

She parked in the main lot. On the grassy median, she saw half a dozen skinny, black-tailed jackrabbits splayed out in the shade, looking as if they had been born to a life of luxury. Mourning doves called out from their perches on poplars and palms. Quails with topknots erect and families in tow darted to and from bushes like wind-up toys, no doubt provoking smiles, even from those who in another lodge might order them up for dinner.

At the front desk, she handed the clerk Ellie Ryan's driver's license and explained that she had already sent a cashier's check to cover a seven-day rental of one of their more remote guesthouses. The clerk found the reservation and acknowledged the payment had been received. Still, he asked her for a credit card to keep on file.

"I don't use plastic," Anna said, "but I would be glad to put down a cash deposit."

He looked skeptical, so she peeled off ten hundred-dollar bills from a roll in her pocket and set them on the counter.

"Thank you, Mrs. Ryan. This is rather unusual but we know where to find you," he said with a laugh, as if he didn't really mean the threat he had just made.

"And I don't want daily housekeeping," she said. "My family is dealing with the loss of a child, and we need peace and privacy." *My God*, she thought, *I lie so easily.*

"We could have someone come mid-week, say Tuesday around 10:00, to give you fresh sheets and towels?"

"That would be perfect," Anna said.

He handed her the key and the map, provided her with brochures on local attractions and recreational opportunities, and showed her the menu for the lodge restaurant. "The nearest full-service grocery store is forty minutes away, but we do carry some basic food items in our gift shop, like canned soup, bread and milk and cheese, if you don't want to go all the way into Farmington."

Following his instructions, she drove three miles east until she came to a dirt road marked by a wooden sign that read Cabin #23. She turned right and drove another half mile until she pulled up in front of a ranch-style adobe. The interior of the three-bedroom, one bath house had been built with typical Southwestern touches: red clay pavers on the floor, brushed white walls, colorful Mexican tiles on the kitchen counter, and open wood ceilings.

There was no television, no Wi-Fi, and no phone, but the clerk had assured her that cell phones could pick up signals from a nearby tower. The lodge-pole furnishings included a large living room couch upholstered in shades of tan and a black bear pattern. There was a similarly upholstered rocker, a coffee table, and a bookcase filled with diverse literary selections from a half-century of visitors.

The website had promised that every rental included a wall safe, an amenity offered by most hotels in proximity to native casinos. She located it in the hall closet. A foot-and-a-half deep and a foot-and-a-half high, it was easily large enough to hold the twenty-six, half-inch thick packets of hundred-dollar bills in her canvas bag.

At the back of the house, she slid open the sliding glass doors and stepped out onto a wide patio of unpolished pavers. She counted two outdoor recliners and four cushioned chairs around a glass topped wrought-iron table. Open, sparsely vegetated desert filled the expanse on all sides, though in every direction, she could also make out the distant outlines of mountain ranges.

She carried her luggage into the smallest of the bedrooms and locked her cash in the safe. She was hungry but she hadn't thought to buy food in town. She took one look at the deep claw-foot tub in the bathroom and decided she wouldn't starve to death. This was her last chance to rest and get her head straight before Mac arrived at the monument, if he arrived at all.

Chapter 10

Friday night, Danny loaded a forty-pound bag of dog food, a duffel bag with enough clothes to last him a week, a pair of hiking boots, two sleeping bags, a backpacking tent, and an armful of colorful Mexican blankets he'd picked up in Nogales, into the aluminum truck box bolted to the cab of his white 2010 Ford Ranger. He used nylon straps to secure a hard plastic, heavy-duty water container to bullrings on the side panel. He doubted he'd need everything he was bringing, but he believed in being prepared for any bump in the road.

"Bolo, let's go," he called. His dog came running from the back of the house. She jumped into the cab and took her seat on the passenger side, pressing her nose out of the partially open window.

After merging onto the freeway, Danny drove past a new housing development that had sprung up almost overnight. A gigantic billboard marked the entrance: fourteen feet high and forty-eight feet wide, it bore the picture of a smiling elderly couple standing in front of a cookie-cutter, one-story ranch house. The text read, *Welcome to Fair Acres, where you can find the home of your dreams.*

The home of your dreams, Danny thought. There's no vegetation within two miles of that damned suburb, not anymore anyway. But we humans want sterile. We want predictable. That's why developments like this crop up year after year, like poisonous mushrooms. Come home to Spring Meadows, to Saguaro Gardens, to Desert Vista. All a crock concocted by developers, who think their hyperbole will deceive the public into believing the crap they build has the very qualities they've destroyed to build it.

If billboards had to adhere to truth-in-advertising laws, the signs would say, *Come home to the meadows plowed under, to the riverbed drained dry, to the strip-mined mountain vista.*

He drove out of the city and past its populated environs, past cultivated fields and long stretches of dry land dotted with sage and creosote bushes and drought-tolerant weeds like black henbane and camelthorne. At last, his muscles began to relax, and his mind grew quiet. Bolo, too, settled down. She curled up next to him, and slept.

He pulled up in front of the hacienda, cut the engine, and rolled down his window to let in the cool night air. Stars twinkled in the deep black of the sky, and the silence was absolute…at least until Jackson's dogs came running out, barking dutifully to warn of an intruder on the premises. Danny called out the window to hush them but Bolo started barking fiercely and set them off again. The hounds circled the car. Bolo's ears and back went up and her bark became a deep-throated growl, but Danny knew she'd scream like a baby if one of the dogs actually went for her.

Jackson appeared on the patio, looking none the worse for wear since their Sunday liquid lunch and dinner. He whistled off his dogs. After a few final yaps, they turned and trotted away as if it was just another day in the hood.

Danny got out of the truck, walked up to Jackson and clapped his hand on one shoulder. "Hey, old man. You look like a goddamned teenager compared to how you were when I left you on Sunday."

"I have to admit I was a bit peaked by the end of that day," Jackson said with a groan.

Bolo jumped out of the truck and ran around the grounds, her nose hard at work, her tail wagging non-stop. She ran over to Jackson's dogs. After sniffing each other thoroughly, they joined ranks and started barking again en masse.

"I don't know about you," Jackson said with a wink, "but I'm ready to go another round."

"I'm sure you could," Danny laughed. "I, on the other hand, need to stick to beer tonight. Don't worry, though, I'll give you a chance to redeem your reputation another time."

"Well, let's go get you a cold one."

"Bolo," Danny called. She came running.

"Hey, girl," Jackson said, leaning over to pet her. "He's going to make you go inside with us, but I know you'd rather be with the big dogs."

"Too many rattlers out this time of year," Danny said.

Jackson winked at Bolo. "If that's how he wants to tend to you, that's how it is, girl. He is one stubborn son of a gun."

In the kitchen, Jackson opened two beers and handed one to Danny. They sat down at the table, and Bolo stretched out on the floor next to them, resting her head on one of Danny's boots.

"So, you're on your way north, huh? Who are these old friends of yours? I never heard you mention anyone in your life outside of work."

"Just some people I grew up with."

"And where exactly did you grow up, son?" He asked, as if it was a perfectly normal question for someone he'd known for two decades.

"Out west. You know I don't like to talk about it much."

"Much?" He creased his forehead and gave Danny a look. "You never talk about your life at all. Every now and then, you slip up and say something that lets me know you didn't just spring up out of the ground like a desert toad after a hard rain, but not often."

"Jackson," Danny entreated.

Jackson waved his hand in the air. "Ah, forget it. I don't need to know. I understand you have secrets. We all have secrets, and I don't mean to pry. But it does pain me sometimes, you not being willing to open up a little after all we've been through together."

"I'm sorry, man. There are a lot of times I've wanted to. But…" He shook his head.

"Just tell me this," Jackson said. "This meeting you're going to, it's a good thing, right? I'm asking because you look pretty miserable, son."

"I'm not sure I know the answer to that question."

"Well, I hope you're not in some kind of trouble," Jackson said, "but if you are, I'm here if you need me."

For the second time that day, Danny felt like crying.

Jackson was scrutinizing him. Fortunately, he didn't comment on the tears pooling in Danny's eyes; he just slapped the table with the palm of his hand. "Even if you're abstaining from the hard stuff, we could still do a little target practice out in the hinterlands tonight. There's a bit of a moon, the sky is clear, and there are about a million stars shining up there, so there may be enough light. You up for it?"

"Hell yes," Danny said. It had been a year or more since they'd spent that kind of time together, like brothers, or perhaps more like father and son.

"I've got a couple of new rifles I want to check out, see if they sight as well as they're supposed to, and whiskey with you is a fine nectar. Umm, if you change your mind about drinking, that is."

Danny grinned. "I'll tell you what. I'll be the designated driver."

After kenneling the dogs, Jackson loaded the truck with a fifteen gallon bag full of empty beer cans, a sleeping bag, and a high-quality self-inflating mat.

"Bringing a mattress with you now, old man?"

"I bought this a few months back," Jackson said. "I don't have enough meat left on me to cushion these old hips."

Danny watched him go into the house again. He returned with an unopened quart of Maker's Mark bourbon under one arm and a rifle in each hand. "These are brand new, mountable, twenty-seven-inch long, precision-guided firearms."

Danny took one of the weapons from him and examined it closely. "This is no hunting rifle, Jackson. If the cops find you with these, you're going to be in some deep shit."

"Yep," Jackson agreed, in a tone that put an end to the discussion.

Bolo jumped into the truck. Jackson let her sit on his lap so she could look out the window. He wrapped an arm around her chest so she wouldn't go flying when they went off-road.

With the windows rolled down to let in the cool night air, Danny drove past the hacienda and onto the open range. The compass on his rearview mirror kept him on course, more or less, but he still found it a challenge to navigate the roadless ranchland in the dark. Even when the stars were out and the moon was full, there were no signposts and no trees, boulders, or streams to give him a bearing. There was only flat scrub scratching noisily against the undercarriage, as if it wanted to get inside.

"About a quarter turn to the right," Jackson said. "We're almost there."

Danny smiled. He couldn't figure out how Jackson could orient himself by dead reckoning, but he did it every time.

Danny pulled up to the stand of skeletal cottonwoods that marked the spot. He cut the engine and turned off the lights. They sat listening to the metallic clicks and pings of the truck settling. When all they could hear was their own breathing, they sat a little longer. Danny found himself thinking back to a time when the cottonwoods grew tall and leafy and green, but that had been more than a decade ago, before the spring feeding the creek that watered the trees went dry.

Bolo whimpered slightly and strained for Jackson to let her out, but Jackson didn't respond, didn't seem to notice.

"Hey, are you all right?" Danny asked.

Pulling a metal compass from his shirt pocket, Jackson held the instrument in his open hand as if weighing it, but he was staring into the darkness. "I guess I don't really need this anymore," Jackson said, "but I like to keep it with me. You never know when a flash flood will change the face of everything familiar."

"Danny, I want you to come with me," he said. Slipping the compass back into his pocket, he got out of the car and started walking.

Danny hurried after him. About twenty paces from the truck, Jackson stomped the flat of his boot on the ground a few times, then held up one hand. "Stop right there," he said.

Danny stopped. He watched Jackson get down on his knees and begin running his hands over the sand. "What are you doing, old man?"

Using his hands like trowels, Jackson pushed the sand away from him, then crawled backward and did it again, and again. When he finally stood back up, Danny could make out a round plate on the ground. It looked like a manhole cover but with a larger circumference. He watched Jackson step to the edge of the circle, bend down and wrap his fingers around a handle of some sort. The old man straightened, raising the plate with him, then, with a shove, toppled it over backward. It hit the ground with a soft thud.

"Fiberglass," Jackson said, dusting off his hands. "It's on hinges. It used to be a steel plate, but that got to be too hard for me to lift."

Danny peered into the black hole. "What is this?"

Jackson pulled a small flashlight from his pocket. The beam illuminated a narrow ladder leading down into a hole in the ground. Danny felt Bolo rub against his legs. He grabbed her collar and yanked her back. "No, Bolo, that's a no," he ordered sternly. "I'll be back in a minute," he said to Jackson. He walked her back to the truck. She jumped inside and he rolled the windows up two-thirds of the way so she couldn't escape.

"Sorry," Jackson said when he returned. "I should have thought of her before I lifted the lid."

"No problem," Danny said.

Jackson returned his attention to the hole. "The ladder isn't angled. It goes straight down. Keep one hand on the railing until you feel the floor. Then you'll have to hunch down a little or you'll wallop your head."

Danny looked at him for more of an explanation but Jackson just pointed his flashlight at the hole. Danny shrugged and moved into position. He gripped the metal rail and lowered one foot until he found the first rung, then kept going as instructed.

"I'm on the floor," Danny called up.

Jackson turned off the flashlight, plunging them into darkness. "Stay there but step aside a little so there's room for me."

Danny heard Jackson's boots hitting the metal steps. All at once, bright, fluorescent light filled the room.

"The air in here is a little stale," Jackson said. "It's spacious, ten feet by twelve, but the ceiling is exactly six-feet-three inches high, a little design glitch. I have to bend at the waist to walk around in here, which kills my back, so I'm going to stay by the ladder. You should be all right, though."

Danny took a step forward and felt the ceiling brush the top of his head. "It would be perfect if I didn't have boots on, but it's close enough," he said, bending slightly and scanning the room. To his left, a small, square table, two folding chairs, and two collapsed cots had been shoved against the wall with a few sets of sheets and blankets piled on top. Above the furniture, the wall was lined with long metal shelves stocked with kitchen knives and silverware and dishes and pans, a two-burner propane stove, two electric hot plates, and other miscellaneous household goods.

On the wall directly opposite the stairs, he saw more shelves. These were filled with paper goods, dry rations, canned soups and meats, cases of bottled water, and jars of canned peaches, pears, tomatoes, and jam.

"How do you get power way out here?" Danny asked.

"The entry lights are battery powered. But look here." He bent down so he could step far enough away to reveal four large solar panels leaning against the wall behind the stairs. "Each one is rated at twelve volts and five amps, and I've set them up to run parallel, so the entire array is twelve volts and twenty amps. The outlets and solar charge controller are wired and ready to go. If I needed to run the system, all I'd have to do is carry the panels outside and connect the dots."

Danny was about to express his admiration for such ingenuity when Jackson reached for a chord and raised a bamboo curtain hanging in front of the wall to their right. He saw row after row of long iron pegs sticking out of the cement. Each was angled upward, and each held a firearm: assault rifles, sniper rifles, shotguns, or handguns. On the floor sat scores of ammo boxes.

"You can lift your jaw up off the ground now, Danny. Nothing on that wall is going to hurt you."

"It's not me I'm worried about. What the hell are you doing, man?"

Jackson frowned and ran his hand over his grizzled face. "I built this place in '62. You're probably too young to remember, but in the early sixties, when the Soviets and the Cubans seemed like such a threat, men all over the country were building bomb shelters in their backyards to protect their families."

"I remember," Danny said. "I was only eleven in 1962 but I'll never forget the duck-and-cover drills at school when we had to stuff ourselves under our wooden desks."

"Yep, those are the days I'm talking about. That's how paranoid we were as a nation. Anyway, when the Cuban missile crisis came to an end without bombs going off, I mostly forgot about this place. When I did happen to think of it, I always felt kind of foolish. Then in the eighties, when the S and Ls started to go bust, I decided to turn it into a vault, and for a lot of years I kept a goodly amount of cash down here."

"When did it become an armory?"

The bright florescent glare accentuated the deep wrinkles lining Jackson's forehead and cheeks, and lit up every clump of his thinning, sweat-soaked hair. Danny had never seen his friend look so old.

"I don't know how I got so far off course," Jackson said with a sigh.

Danny wanted to ask him if he was making a living by selling arms to drug dealers, or right-wing paramilitary training camps, or gangs of thugs. But he worried that such a question, or the answer, could cause a lasting rift.

"When I first stocked it," Jackson said, "I stored some guns down here, just a few. After all, the thinking back then was if we had to use these shelters, and if we survived, we'd be climbing out someday to a world in ashes. Who knew if it would be friends or enemies there to greet us? Anyway, I added a gun now and then over the years, just as a hobby. Then, after Estrella got sick, I guess my hobby took on a life of its own."

Danny wished Jackson had never showed him the shelter. "So why am I here?"

"Like I said before, Danny. We all have secrets. You may not want to know mine, but I think it's time you did. Just in case anything happens to me," he said, his voice trailing off.

Danny decided he had to know the truth. "If you want to tell me, then give me the whole story. What kind of people do you sell these weapons to?"

"Collectors."

"Meaning what?"

"Meaning collectors."

"Like what, *posse comitatus* collectors? Like drug cartel collectors?"

"Don't you know me any better than that, son?"

"You're saying you don't want to tell me?"

"I'm saying you shouldn't need to ask."

Danny stared at the floor for a long time but Jackson didn't speak.

"Once again, Jackson. Why are you showing this to me?"

"I guess I just want you to know it's here," Jackson said, sounding irritable. "These weapons are worth a hell of a lot of money. If anything happens to me, I'd like you to have them. They'd fetch a good price and boost your retirement fund. I'll leave the ranch to my boys but they'll sell it before I'm cold in the ground. Then somebody else will find this place. Or maybe nobody will ever find it; that would be all right too, I guess."

"Why do you keep saying, 'if anything happens to me'?"

"I don't rightly know, Danny. I've just got a bad feeling. The cops are hassling me all the time. And now you're involved in something that's got you all knotted up inside and won't tell me where you're going. All the news I read is bad. The weather is heating up. My dogs are restless. Hell, I don't know."

Danny nodded, as if Jackson was making sense, as if anything made sense.

"So now you've seen it. Let's get out of here before you get stuck all bent over," Jackson said.

Danny put his hand on Jackson's shoulder and held it there for a moment. "Okay, old man, okay. Let's do that."

Chapter 11

Mac woke to a buzzing sound. He had a vague sense it had been going on for some time, but it took him a few seconds to remember where he was: Kearney, Nebraska, in a Budget 8 motel. Despite his intention to drive all night, he had only lasted nine hours before the need for sleep and the craving for alcohol overtook him.

Groaning, he pushed the pillow off his head, reached for the clock, and shut off the alarm. The drive had taken a toll on his body. The simple act of sitting made every muscle from his waist up scream in pain. He located his ever-present bottle of ibuprofen and, with a glass of tap water from the bathroom, swallowed eight hundred milligrams. Moving slowly, he showered, got dressed, rolled a joint, downed a Ritalin and loaded the car.

At a McDonald's on the edge of town, he ordered two egg McMuffins, two hash browns, and a coffee too bitter to choke down. Merging onto the westbound lanes of Interstate 80, he drummed his hands on the steering wheel and sang along to Tom Petty's, *Free Falling*.

Fewer than a hundred miles from Kearney, he pulled off the freeway into a deserted rest stop. He got out, rubbed his eyes, and stretched like a cat waking from a long nap. He breathed in the dry air of the plains, shuddered with pleasure at the warm sun, and found a comfortable bench near the dog-walking area where he sat with his legs outstretched. With not another soul in sight, he lit a joint.

He looked out at the flat, dry vista. In the far distance, he saw a combine sitting idle, and even farther out, a white farmhouse. He remembered passing through Nebraska in the early seventies, past vast areas of untouched prairies and abundant wildflowers. Now, ninety-two percent of the land was being used to graze cattle or grow crops, mainly corn, soy, and wheat. Thanks to agricultural runoff and industrial toxins, the state's once pristine waterways were among the most polluted in the nation. It is so damned sad, he thought.

Only six hundred miles from home, with another seven hundred to go, he found himself sorely tempted to turn around and drive back to Madison. He missed his routine, his neighborhood bar, even his girlfriend. Yet for some reason he didn't fully understand, here he was, speeding away from the life he had built out of the ashes. *Ah, Anna,* he thought, *all I want is to be left alone so I can slip-slide away someday, drop like a stone from a barstool in some dingy dive. But you won't let me go in peace, will you? You would have made Dylan Thomas proud, my dear, but you scare the bejesus out of me.*

When he again became aware of his surroundings, more than an hour had passed, and a gargantuan Bluebird RV was pulling into the lot. Time to go. Past time. It would be physically impossible for him to make it to the monument before it closed. He wondered if Danny had arrived yet, and if Anna had shown up after all. Would they check back for him on Sunday? He decided they would. He stopped by the men's bathroom one more time, ate another Ritalin, then continued his drive west.

Anna turned into the Four Corners National Monument a little after 10:00 in the morning. She paid the five-dollar admission fee at the entrance booth and parked in the rough dirt lot behind the closest of the four rectangular, open-air buildings that framed the massive cement square. So far, there were only a few cars inside the gate.

The cement square was divided into four quadrants converging on a granite circle. At its center, she saw the round brass plaque, about the size of a dinner plate, marking the single geographic point where the borders of Colorado, Utah, New Mexico and Arizona meet. She had read that tourists traveled to the monument from across the country and around the world, all for the novelty of being able to straddle all four states by placing one foot on the marker.

She chose a bench in the New Mexico quadrant with a view of the parking lot and the square. Looking at the big X splitting the cement pad, she thought it looked like a helicopter landing pad, or a bombing target. The sun, a yellow ball rising in a clear blue sky, appeared to be taking aim. The day promised to be a scorcher.

She watched as tourists began to arrive. Most wore sun hats. Many of the older ones carried binoculars or had cameras slung around their necks. The younger ones typed into their cell phones, or used the devices to photograph the Four Corners plaque, the vista, and each other.

By 10:00, she started to think no one would come after all. As the sun leached her energy with its heat, she began to question herself: *Why am I even here? For the slim chance they'll show? For the slimmer chance they'll care?* Yes, and for the whisper of a possibility that love, not fear, still binds us.

She noticed a tall, sinewy man standing by the visitor's center, scanning the crowd. She stared at him, trying to make out the face behind the dark sunglasses. He started to move in her direction.

"Danny," she whispered.

"Anna, hey," he said when he reached her.

"Hey," she said in kind.

Their greeting felt awkward, but also practiced, as if they were acting out a familiar script, unearthed from the attic and dusted off for the occasion.

He stood a head taller than her. His body, clad in blue jeans, a blue work shirt, and cowboy boots, was lean but muscular. She felt small-boned and thin next to him. He looked like an aging dancer. She imagined she looked unkempt in some vague way, like a migratory bird at the end of its journey.

She embraced him, tentatively at first. He wrapped his arms around her. They held each other for a minute, two minutes. She breathed in his scent and lightly pressed her hands against his back, assuring herself he was not an apparition but flesh and bone.

"Thank you," she said at last, stepping back. "I feel like I can breathe again."

"On the phone, when you told me to disregard your letter, I thought you might not show. But here you are."

"As are you," she said.

He smiled. "Walked right into that one, didn't I? I came just in case you changed your mind."

"When I told you not to come, I wasn't being petulant. I meant it."

"But you're here, waiting for me."

"No," she said, shaking her head slowly. "I was waiting in case Mac showed up."

He stepped back from her, out of reach.

"Please don't be hurt," she said. "It's not that I didn't want to see you. I did, or I never would have called."

"Doesn't sound that way," he said.

She could hear the chill in his voice. He turned to look toward the parking lot and she wondered if he intended to bolt.

"Danny Shepard, don't you dare go all tight-lipped macho on me. I told you not to come. I would have told Mac exactly the same thing if I'd been able to. I will tell him exactly the same thing if he shows."

Danny squeezed the muscles at the back of his neck. "Jesus, Anna, I've been here less than ten minutes and I've already got a headache. Let me get this right. You want me to turn around, and go home? And when Mac finally completes the thirteen hundred mile cross-country drive he undertook at your behest, you're just going to look at him and say, 'Ah gee, sorry, Mac, my mistake, never mind'."

"Maybe he won't show," she said, covering her face with her hands. "Damn it, I can't seem to get anything right anymore."

Danny took a step closer, put one hand on her shoulder and lifted her chin with the other. She thought of the half circles under her eyes, dark as bruises, and turned her head away.

"What's going on?" He asked.

"It's a long, long story."

"I don't need every detail," he said with a shrug. "But you've gone to a lot of trouble to get Mac and me here. I'd like to know why."

"On the phone you said you didn't want to see me again."

"No, I didn't say that. I said I didn't want to stir up the past."

Then what the fuck is the point of you being here? Anna thought, but she didn't say the words out loud, didn't hurl them at him like she wanted to do. With all the self-control she could muster, she said evenly, "When I reached out, I didn't expect either you or Mac to welcome me with open arms. But I thought maybe we would still be able to connect…some kind of connection, you know? But there isn't any, is there?" She asked, looking up into his blue eyes.

"We will always have a connection, for better or worse," he said. "Why don't I wait here with you until Mac arrives? If I change my mind about staying, or Mac does, or you kick us to the curb, maybe we can still get together for dinner and drinks. No harm, no foul."

"No," she said, glancing around the square, planning her escape. "This whole thing is a bad idea. Even if Mac does show and you two agree to stay, even for a night, it would just be a drunken reunion like all the others, where all we do is bullshit each other."

"Anna, it's been a lot of years since we all tied one on together. I've changed since then, changed a lot, and I'm sure you and Mac has too. So I don't think that's how this will roll. Well, maybe the drunken part," he said, laughing.

She bit her lower lip and stared down at the ground, thinking.

Danny tapped her on the shoulder. "I need to go to my truck for a minute. Don't go anywhere."

Looking up, she gave the slightest of nods.

"I mean it, hon," he said. "Don't you run out on me when my back is turned. I know the desert like the back of my hand and I will find you."

Anna felt her chin begin to quiver. She bit her lip harder.

"Hey, I'm just teasing," he said. "You know that, right?"

Swiping at her eyes with the back of one hand, she nodded again.

Danny walked away. She watched him cross the cement pad and the parking lot, where he disappeared behind a Class A Motorhome with New Hampshire plates. Moments later, he reappeared. She couldn't believe her eyes. He had a dog at the end of a leash. When he reached her, he lifted the dog in his arms, high enough for her to look into its brown doe eyes.

"A dog," Anna marveled. "What do you know? You've got someone after all."

"Anna, this is Bolo."

"Oh, you are so beautiful," she cooed, in the same voice she heard other people use when talking to babies, in the same way she had talked to Kate when she was a little girl, and to Gracie just days ago. The thought caused her eyes to tear.

"What is it?" Danny asked.

Forcing a smile, she dismissed his question with a wave of her hand.

He lowered his dog to the ground.

Anna sat down cross-legged on the hard cement. Bolo came up close to her and leaned in with her whole body.

"Well, hello you," she said, stroking the dog's silky muzzle and scratching behind her ears. "She has such a sweet face, Danny. She looks so aware."

He crouched down beside her. "Yeah, those deep brown eyes get me every time."

"Are dogs allowed in here?" She asked, glancing around.

"I doubt it, but hopefully it's not closely enforced. I can't lock her in the car, not in this heat, so if someone hassles us, I may have to wait outside the monument. I did see a trail sign on the far side of the parking lot. Why don't we take her for a walk?"

From the circle where their lives now intersected, she looked out and around the plaza. More people were milling about or waiting in line to have their pictures taken while standing on the plaque.

She followed Danny through the crowd and out of the monument, to the start of the Dancin' Horse Trail. They started hiking, only to discover the trail ended a few hundred yards from where it began. Fifteen minutes later, they were back in the parking lot.

"I'm hungry," Danny said, pointing to a food truck near the entrance. The word 'Frybread' was painted on a sandwich board propped against the front bumper. They walked over and placed their orders with the cook, a gray-haired Navajo woman wearing a red t-shirt with a design that looked like the fragment of an ancient weaving. They watched her stretch the dough by hand, fry it in boiling hot oil, and lightly dust it with sugar. They carried their plates to a bench on the edge of the parking lot. Bolo crawled underneath, lay down in the shade and pressed her back against Anna's legs.

"This is better than any donut I've ever tasted," Anna said.

"I agree," Danny said.

Anna looked toward the entrance. "Do you think he'll come?"

Danny shrugged.

"It's strange," she said, "but I really don't know him anymore, or you, for that matter. I mean, he could be working for some Washington think tank, or retired, or dead. And you, you could be married with a slew of kids for all I know."

"No wife, no kids," Danny said, holding out his empty palms as if to illustrate how free he was of commitments. "As for Mac, he's still teaching at UW Madison."

"You know that for a fact?"

"I called him Wednesday night after you called me."

"You talked to him?" She asked, crossing her arms across her chest. "What did you tell him?"

"Nothing for you to be upset about. I wanted to see if he got the letter, which he did. I also wanted him to know you changed your mind."

"And?"

"He said if I came, he probably would too."

"What the fuck is that about? Strength in numbers?" She realized she sounded like an interrogator trying to corner a suspect, but she couldn't bear the thought of them forming an alliance against her.

"Mac made up his own mind, but I did tell him I intended to be here in case you showed."

She buried her head in her hands. "I don't get it, Danny. Why did you even come?"

He stared at her for a long moment before answering. "I thought you needed me," he said at last. "I came because I thought you needed me."

They spent the rest of the afternoon in the shade of an empty vendor stall, waiting for Mac.

Danny again asked Anna why she had set up the meeting, but again, she declined to answer. "Anything we say will just have to be said again when Mac arrives. If Mac arrives." So they talked about nothing of substance, not the past, not the future. In time, she grew comfortable with their silence, and Danny seemed to relax as well.

At 4:45 pm, a uniformed park ranger started his rounds, letting stragglers know the monument was closing and the gates would be locked in fifteen minutes.

"I assume Mac's just running late, since that's what he does," Anna said without rancor. "But the monument is closed tomorrow and he has no way to reach us, unless he has your cell phone number?"

"I don't own a cell phone."

"You're kidding, right?"

"I do own a laptop," he said, "but I didn't bring it with me."

"I guess I'm not entirely surprised. You never were much of a techie."

"Are you?" He asked.

"I have a computer at home. I used to own a smartphone but I dropped it in the drink a few days ago."

"Think we can survive without one?"

"Maybe." She laughed. "Though it feels strange to be untethered from the world. Danny, let's go home."

"Where is home?" He asked, raising one eyebrow. "I brought my sleeping bag, and brought one for you too, just in case."

"I brought my arthritic joints. I really prefer beds these days."

"Then you win, hands down," he said.

"There's a resort about forty minutes outside of Farmington called the Broken Trail Lodge. They rent vacation homes for extended stays. They call them cabins but they're all adobe, ranch-style houses. I reserved a three-bedroom."

"Some things never change," he said as they moved toward the parking lot. "Anna Sanders, always prepared, but definitely no Girl Scout."

"Yeah, here I am, sixty-five years old and I haven't earned a single goddamned merit badge," she joked.

"Does the place allow dogs?"

"I have no idea. I didn't know to ask when I made the reservations but I wouldn't worry about it. We're a couple of miles from any of the other units, at the end of a dirt road nobody will wander down by accident."

They drove out of the lot and onto the highway, Anna in the lead, Danny and Bolo following her taillights through the dusky night.

"Nice place," he said when they entered the house.

"It's spacious and private."

"It feels a little like my place, just a much larger, much more upscale version, and with real furniture."

"Oh good," she said, squeezing his arm. "Are you hungry or do you want to unpack first?"

"I'm starving."

In the kitchen, she showed him her meager purchases from her early morning visit to the Broken Trail Lodge gift shop/mini-mart: two bottles of wine, a case of beer, milk, bread, cheese, crackers, a few apples, and two frozen pizzas.

"Wow, what a selection. At least I won't have to worry about dying of thirst while I'm here, or getting fat."

Anna giggled. "I know it's not much. I didn't think. Well, I guess I did think, but I thought I'd be eating alone."

"I have some stuff in my truck," he said, walking away.

He returned moments later with a bag of dry dog food cradled in one arm, a case of beer in the other, and a plastic grocery bag dangling from his fingers.

"Great minds," Anna said with a nod to the beer. She took the bag from him and emptied it onto the counter: a loaf of bread, a jar of peanut butter, and a container of spun honey. "Our freshman year subsistence diet." She laughed. "Do you still eat this stuff?"

"Absolutely not. But I thought, in honor of the occasion."

He found a stainless-steel mixing bowl in a cupboard and filled it with water for Bolo. She arranged cheese and apple slices around a plate and unceremoniously dumped crackers into the middle. He grabbed a cold beer and she poured herself a glass of wine. She switched on the patio light and opened the sliding glass door and they carried their meal outside to the table. She sat down, but he remained standing, looking up at the night sky.

"I've got to do one more thing," he said, "but I'll be right back. Don't get up, and keep your eyes closed until I say."

"Why?"

"Don't be so suspicious. Just close them and wait."

She frowned, but complied, at least for a moment. When she heard him go inside, she stole a quick look, just long enough to see what he was up to. He was going through the house, turning off lights.

She closed her eyes again and waited.

"Much better," he said, coming up behind her. She felt his strong, gentle hands on her shoulders.

"Now, look up," he said.

As soon as her eyes adjusted to the darkness, she understood. "Oh my, billions and billions," she whispered. The stars were so clear and appeared so close she couldn't resist the urge to reach out to touch them.

Danny sat down next to her. Bolo sidled up between them and Danny rubbed the little lab's head and muzzle. In a somber voice, he said, "Bolo, Anna is with us now, so you have to keep watch over her."

Bolo wagged her tail, and Anna smiled. "I'm so glad you're here, Danny, both of you."

"Me too, hon, me too."

They sat there for a long time, listening to the silence, looking up at the stars, and breathing in the hot, dry desert air, redolent with the waxy scent of creosote.

Chapter 12

Mac, his head swimming after eleven hours on the road, sat down at a table in a dark corner of Farmington's Steel Rail bar and dance hall. He ordered nachos and a single pitcher of beer. The band in the main room was playing hardcore country, which wasn't to his liking. He tried to tune out the noise by concentrating on a captioned Fox News program being broadcast from a television over the bar, but that wasn't to his liking either. After finishing his food and draining the pitcher, he left to go in search of a cheap hotel.

Sunday morning, he woke to the piercing sound of a ringing telephone. He tumbled out of bed, and like a hound chasing a scent, tracked the noxious noise to a pile of clothes on the floor. "What?" He shouted at his cell phone after he unearthed it. He looked at the screen and tapped a button to silence the alarm he had set for 10:45 a.m.

After a hot shower, he wiped the steam off the bathroom mirror. He hated to admit it, even to himself, but he worried about how he would look to his old friends after a nineteen-year hiatus. Not pretty, he concluded, noticing, not for the first time, how much his gut had grown since his knee injury. Being forced to give up basketball had been bad enough, but no other form of exercise appealed, and it showed. He was sixty-five years old, going on seventy, his hair thinning, his chin doubling, his body an homage to self-neglect.

People change, he told himself. *People compromise. People give up*, he added, thinking his poor physical condition connoted a larger failure.

He dressed in a short-sleeved plaid shirt, blue Docker pants and an ancient pair of hiking boots he had unearthed from a box at the back of his closet. He spread a New Mexico map out on his bed and did the calculations. Sixty miles from the monument, at eighty miles an hour, the speed everyone seemed to drive in this part of the country, meant he could be there by one. He loaded his car, set his iPod to play Blind Faith, and drove out of town singing along to Steve Winwood's *Can't Find My Way Home.*

Fifty-two minutes later, he pulled up to the monument's gated entrance and parked next to an empty white truck with New Mexico plates. The truck's hood felt hot to the touch, but so did its roof. The outside temperature was probably nearing a hundred degrees, Mac thought. He could feel sweat trickle down his neck. The locked gate had a sign bolted to the crossbars: *Closed Sundays until further notice.*

"You've got to be kidding," he said under his breath. He scanned the distant open-air buildings and the cement pad but saw no signs of life. He checked his cell phone. Almost 1:00 p.m.

"Mac?"

Startled, he turned around. Danny. He was deeply tanned, more muscular than Mac had ever seen him, and his blond hair was graying, but it was him all right, tall and lanky, with the same shy grin and the same deep blue eyes.

"Danny, my man, where the hell did you come from?"

"I waited in the shade," Danny said, pointing across the road to the ruins of a metal outbuilding. "It took me a few minutes."

"I thought I'd missed you."

Danny smiled. "Nah, I knew you'd get here eventually."

"Who's this?" Mac asked, pointing to Bolo.

"My dog, Bolo."

"I'm not much of a dog guy."

"No matter. I'm glad you came, buddy."

"I am too, I think. I didn't really have much a choice, did I?" Mac took a second look at the building across the road, wondering if Anna too, might suddenly appear. Keeping his voice low, he asked, "Where is she?"

"Relax, man. She can't hear us," Danny said, grinning. "She went to town to buy groceries this morning. We'll meet at the house."

"What house?"

"You know Anna, she always plans ahead."

"You look good, man," Mac said, studying Danny's face. "Downright handsome, in fact. Hard labor suits you."

Danny looked at Mac, appraising him, and started to speak.

Mac interrupted to avert any comments about how *he* had changed. "So, how is she?"

"It's actually been good to see her, at least so far. She's not as intense as she used to be."

"Yeah, and how long will that last?"

Danny winced. "Mac, I know you're nervous about seeing her, but so far it's really been okay. She's…different somehow."

"Caving already, huh? But you always did have a soft spot for her."

"Anyway," Danny said with a shrug, "she wanted to wait for you before we 'really' talked, so I don't know much. We should get going though. It will take us about an hour to get there."

"Okay, man, okay. Lead on."

Anna wasn't at the house when they arrived but Mac heard her car pull up soon after. She found him in the kitchen, ran up to him and gave him a big hug and a kiss on his cheek. He hugged her back and began humming, *Here comes the sun*. For the length of a chorus, they swayed in place.

She stepped back, took a long, head-to-toe look at him, then reached out and patted his belly. "Tsk Tsk. Shame on you, old man, you've let yourself go. You need to get some exercise while you're here. I'll be glad to cook low-fat food for you if you'd like."

Mac laughed so hard, he had to reach into his pocket for a handkerchief to dry the corners of his eyes. After he finally composed himself, he said, "First of all, Anna, you do not cook. Never have, never will. Second, you have little room to criticize my appearance when you, my dear, appear to be the prodigy of a careless tryst between *Backpacker* magazine and *High Times*."

She made a pouty face, and he relented. "Actually, you look lovely, my dear. I don't see any birds flocking around your hair in search of a nest, so hey, it's all good."

He thought she looked pleased. They seemed to have slipped back in time without a hitch.

"Oh, thank you for bringing the groceries in," Anna said, when Danny appeared in the doorway.

Danny set the groceries on the counter and handed a second bag to Anna. "You went clothes shopping?"

"I only brought two changes of clothing with me," Anna said, "and nothing for hot weather. I stopped by a thrift store in town and bought some t-shirts and a couple of pairs of khaki pants. Their jean selection sucked big time."

"Mac, you have Danny to thank for today's culinary selection."

Mac helped Danny prepare the afternoon meal: peanut butter and honey sandwiches, potato chips, and beer. "Ah, LeRoy Street all over again," Mac said. "I didn't think I'd ever be able to choke down another PB&H after that year, but it does seem right and proper for this occasion, whatever this occasion turns out to be."

Anna set the table and they gathered in the dining room. Mac pulled a joint out of his shirt pocket, lit it, then passed it to Danny, who took a hit then passed it to Anna, who waved it away. "I haven't smoked one in years," she said.

"You're never too old to start again," Mac said, handing it back to her, but she waved it away a second time.

After lunch, when Anna and Mac went to their separate rooms to nap, Danny made a beeline for the laptop Mac had left on the dining room table next to a piece of paper with the Internet password. He turned on the power. "Yes," he said, thrilled to see that he had access to the Internet. *I am such a junkie*, he thought. *Like all addictions, reading the news satiates my immediate need, but the hangover is horrific, and the craving never satisfied.* He opened the browser.

Hundreds of large-scale, uncontrolled fires were once again burning across the west, from California to Alaska to the interior of British Columbia. In northwest Canada, fifty-two thousand acres of melting permafrost were releasing massive amounts of methane into the atmosphere. New studies published on @RogueNASA, the Twitter site created to foil Trump's efforts to mute climate science, confirmed a rapid acceleration in the rate of sea level rise. Southern California, despite rains brought by a powerful El Nino, would soon be in extreme drought again, and widespread water rationing was inevitable.

For political news, he signed in to the online editions of the *New York Times*, the *Washington Post*, and the *Guardian*. The left was fighting Trump's right-wing agenda on every issue of import, but the ultra-conservative Congress was notching up wins. Fundamentalism was on the rise around the globe, and the very notion of a tolerant, inclusive, peaceful civilization was under attack on almost every front.

"What are you doing?" Anna asked.

Danny jumped. "What's it to you? Christ, you scared the shit out of me. I thought you were taking a nap."

"Sorry," she said. "I didn't mean to sneak up on you. I couldn't sleep, so I came to find you." She pulled out a chair and sat down across from him. "I didn't know you had your laptop with you or I would have said something sooner. I'd rather you didn't use the Internet while we're here."

"It's not my laptop, it's Mac's. I was just reading the news. Why shouldn't I use the Internet?"

"I don't want to take any chance it could leave a trail to us, to this place."

"You think someone is tracking us?"

"You never know. Can you just shut it off, please?"

He stared at the open browser window, thinking her fears were silly, and itching for more news. Reluctantly, he agreed. "Okay. But before I do, did you read the news about Farmington?"

"No, I haven't seen the news in days. But please turn that off before you tell me."

Danny felt like a kid under the thumb of an irrational mother, but he didn't want to fight. He closed the browser and shut off the power.

"Thank you," Anna said. "So, tell me. What's the latest about Farmington?"

He leaned back in his chair and put his hands together behind his head. "Did you know methane gas is roughly twenty-five times more powerful than CO2 when it comes to warming the atmosphere?"

Anna smiled. "Danny, I am still a chemist. I know what methane is and what it does, and I know the Four Corners region emits more of it than anywhere else in the country. So much, in fact, that the gassy, invisible bloom surrounding us extends outward for about twenty-five hundred square miles."

"Oh," he said. "You already know about that?"

"Yes. You're surprised?"

"I am a little. I don't know many people outside of work, and none who really track what's going on with the environment."

"So, there's what, a new study out?"

"Yes," he said, getting excited. "It confirms the emissions are not a natural phenomenon, but—"

"A result of leaks from the forty thousand gas and oil wells in the San Juan basin."

He made no effort to hide his disappointment. "You're no fun at all. Do you always guess the ending before a person gets a chance to finish the story?"

Anna laughed. "Not always. Hey, what do you say we go for a walk while Mac is sleeping?"

"Sounds great," Danny said, though not as enthusiastically as he would have if she hadn't just crushed him. He called Bolo, who was lying on the cool pavers in the hallway. "Come on, girl."

They walked east over the flat, packed desert sand, looking for the subtle signs of life in the arid land. A Palo Verde beetle dove in their direction, its wings buzzing loudly, but it veered off at the last minute. They saw a lizard darting into a hole in the ground. They crossed a deep, dry wash, formed by runoff from the seasonal monsoons. Anna said she preferred the high desert to the plains, and he agreed.

He told her about the giant saguaros he'd seen on his hikes in Arizona, and explained how their skeletal, fiber-filled frames could soak up several tons of rain in a single day, which gave them enough water for them to survive another year and still provide sustenance for other desert creatures. He told her how swallows darted expertly between their long spiny needles to dig nests in the fleshy trunks.

"Do you have any idea how far back in geological time the saguaro appeared?" She asked.

"I haven't worked as a desert landscaper all these years for nothing," he said. "I do know my plants. The saguaro, at least the early iterations of it, can be traced back about seventy million years."

"Amazing," she said. "I knew desert flora and fauna were perfectly adapted to life in a land with so little water and such high temperatures, but I didn't realize it had taken them so long to evolve. Think there's any chance humans will fare as well?"

Sunday evening, the three old friends gravitated to the living room. Anna sat on one end of the couch, Danny on the other. Mac chose the lodge-pole rocker and immediately started it in motion.

"You look like Grandpa Amos from The Real McCoys," Danny joked.

"You look like a wise-cracking young whipper-snapper," Mac retorted with a spot-on impression of Walter Brennan. "Be kind to your elders or I'll take out my cane," he said, shaking a crooked finger at Danny while enthusiastically rocking the big chair. They all broke into laughter.

Mac turned his attention to Anna. "And you, missy," he said, still in the quavering voice of an old man, "you have some explaining to do."

"Yes, pappy, I s'pose I do," she said, laughing.

He and Danny both looked at her expectantly.

"Right now?" She half whispered.

Serious and tight-lipped, they continued to stare at her.

Anna dropped her head into her hands and roughly massaged her scalp. Mumbling, she said, "I thought maybe we could just hang out for a day or two before getting serious. This is complicated."

"I'm a patient man," Mac said, "but I don't want to sit around for two days wondering when the hammer is going to fall." He pulled a fresh joint out of his pocket and lit up.

After two minutes of dead silence, he spoke again. "Was I unclear when I just explained I'm not feeling patient? Help me out a little, Anna. Why are we here?"

"Why the Broken Trail Lodge, you mean?" She asked, stalling.

"Come on, woman, give me a break. You know exactly what I mean." He tapped the arm of the chair to communicate his impatience and he stopped rocking.

"Yes, of course, I understand what you're asking," she said with a loud sigh. "I just can't figure out where to begin. The thing is, since 1973, we've only seen each other maybe a dozen times, and not at all since 1998. Even when we did manage to get together, it was only for a day or a night, in an airport bar or a pub, any place where we could drink ourselves into oblivion."

"Exactly what's wrong with oblivion?" Mac asked.

"What's wrong with it is we never deal with anything, ever. What's wrong is I know who you once were but I don't know who you are now. I know of some of the events that make up each of your lives but I don't know how you feel about any of them, or about your lives as a whole. I don't know your passions, your politics, your relationships, what matters to you, what keeps you going."

"Yowza," Mac said, coining his favorite expression from the Big Band era. "That's quite a tall order, my dear. My shrink doesn't even know me that well."

"Once upon a time I knew you both that well," she said. "I knew you, and you knew me, inside and out."

"So?" Mac asked.

"So, I want to get reacquainted."

Danny finally joined the conversation. "Sorry, Anna, but there has to be more to this deal. Your letter implied you were in some kind of trouble. You want something more from us than a heart-to-heart."

"All I want from you is your support, and your advice, but first I have to know who I'm dealing with here."

"You don't trust us anymore?" Danny asked.

"Please don't get mad at me. I wouldn't have asked you to come if I didn't trust you deep down. I'm just saying—"

Mac finished her sentence. "You're saying you did trust us, but you're not so sure anymore."

"Fine!" She shouted, jumping to her feet. "You win. We haven't seen each other in nineteen years, and we haven't spoken an honest word to each other in forty-four, so no, I don't trust you. Happy now? I'm sure you don't trust me either, by the way, though apparently, neither of you is willing to admit it. And yes, I did ask you to come here because I am in a crisis of sorts."

"So, we're supposed to get you out of some mess you've gotten yourself into?" Mac asked.

Anna shook her head vehemently. "No, no, no. You don't have to fix anything, Mac. All I'm asking is that we finally deal with our collective shit. That's all I need. Afterward, I'll get on with my life. But I can't move ahead without finding some way to make peace with my goddamned past. If that doesn't work for you, then get out. Just fucking go."

She stormed out of the room. When she returned twenty minutes later, Mac was rocking and humming to himself and Danny was thumbing through an old copy of *Sunset*. Neither said a word as she set a bag of potato chips, a container of onion dip, and three beers on the coffee table before resuming her position on the couch.

Mac picked up one of the icy bottles and twisted off the cap. "Before I commit to anything, Anna, I need to know exactly what you mean by 'dealing with our shit'."

"There are things we've never talked about."

"Like what?" Danny asked.

"Like what happened that night and the day after."

"We've talked about nothing else," Danny said, sounding exasperated. "I went on a road trip, Mac finished Summa Cum Laude, and you moved to Portland. What else is there to say?"

"We've never once talked about what it meant to us," Anna countered. "We've never once talked about guilt, or anger, or any other human emotion for that matter."

"Whoa, girl," Mac said, holding up his right hand like a stop sign. He pulled a joint and a Bic lighter out of his shirt pocket, lit up, and took a long drag. He exhaled slowly, then looked directly at Anna and made a last-ditch appeal to her better judgment. "You don't really want to go there, do you?"

She pointed to Mac's joint. "May I have a hit?" He handed it over.

She inhaled but lost it to a cough. She tried again and held it this time. "Mac," she said, "I did not pull our friendship out of mothballs for one more stupid reunion. I brought us together because I need to talk about Berkeley and its aftermath."

"Again, Anna, why?" Mac asked.

"I can't explain why, not yet, maybe never."

"You don't trust us but you want us to trust you?" Danny said.

"Something like that," she said, taking another hit off the joint. She passed it back to Mac, batted her eyelids, grinned seductively, and crooned, "Ah, come on, guys. We can do this. It won't be so bad. Besides, what have we got to lose?"

Anna watched Mac get up out of the rocking chair. "I'll think about it," he said. "But it's already been a long day for me and all I've had to eat was a peanut butter and honey sandwich. I don't mean to diss this gourmet offering you've placed before us, Anna, but I'd like to have something more substantial than chips and dip on my stomach before we go down the rabbit hole."

"I agree," Danny said. "I could use some decent food and a break from talking. I saw cards around here somewhere."

The men dispersed, and Anna, left alone on the couch, had little choice but to follow. She went to the kitchen and turned on the oven. While it heated, she doctored a large frozen pizza by adding extra layers of cheese.

She found Mac sitting at the dining room table with his laptop open. As soon as he saw her, he rushed to his own defense. "Don't worry, Danny told me you didn't want us to use the Internet. I've turned off the WiFi connection. I'm just attaching my iPod to the speakers."

Danny walked in, holding two rubber-banded sets of cards. "We can turn these into a pinochle deck."

When the oven buzzer went off, they sat down at the table and ate pizza and drank beer. They found their stride in small talk and kept the conversation light. After dinner, they played three-handed pinochle until almost midnight.

Danny was washing the dishes and Mac putting them away when Anna came up behind them. She put her hands around Danny's waist, rested her face against his back, and asked, "Are you here or are you going, or do you know yet?"

He dried his hands and turned around to look at her, breaking her hold. "Let me make sure I understand what you have in mind. You want everything up for discussion, all the way in or all the way out, no middle ground. That about right?"

"That's my preference," she said, not wanting to risk an ultimatum.

"It's strange," Danny said, looking into her eyes. "When I arrived at the monument, I didn't know what to expect, who to expect. Your letter made me wonder if you were losing it, going off the deep end. But as soon as I saw you, I knew better. It was like I'd known you all my life."

"You have," she said, and she knuckle-punched his shoulder just as she had in grammar school when he teased her unmercifully.

"Ouch," he said with a grin. "Anyway, I'm not going to run out of here this minute. I guess I am willing to go where you need to go, for now, but, Anna, I can't promise I'll stay to the bitter end."

She put her arms around him and hugged him, hard. "Thank you, Danny, thank you. And maybe the end won't be so bitter." She turned toward Mac and extended one arm.

He waved her away. "I'm not going to go all mushy like you guys, but I will stick around for a while, and I'll do my best to really, really, really talk."

Anna clapped her hands together and bounced up and down on her toes.

"Don't get too excited," Mac said. "Before you get your hopes up, I want you to think about something, Anna, and think hard."

"Yes, Professor Caffrey?"

"Archaeological digs can be dangerous."

"I know, I know."

Mac transformed into a decrepit Walter Brennan again. "No, you don't know, and don't you sass me now," he croaked, shaking a suddenly palsied finger at her. "I don't think you have any idea of what can happen if you look back, little missy. Consider Lot's wife. You too could turn into a pillar of salt." He snapped his fingers. "Just like that."

She went over to him, took his face in her hands and kissed his cheek. "Oh, Mac, you are a love, crotchety or not."

Chapter 13

They woke early and scrounged their own breakfast: toast and coffee for Mac, cereal and coffee for Anna, eggs, toast and coffee for Danny. Lethargic from staying up so late the night before, they ate slowly, then leisurely washed and put away their dishes. Anna stepped onto the patio, and with a spark in her heart that had come to feel all too rare, heard herself cheerfully announce that the weather was absolutely perfect: sunny and not too warm.

Danny made a second pot of coffee and they moved outside, arranging themselves around the wrought-iron table. Mac rolled a joint, but when the others looked at him dissaprovingly, he set it aside.

"Okay, Anna, where do you want to start?" Danny asked.

"God, Danny, you sound like you're asking me which limb I'm going to amputate first. This doesn't have to be a horrible experience. I don't know where I want to start, not exactly. " She turned toward Mac, as if he might have an idea of how to begin.

"Don't look at me," he said with a shrug.

She squeezed the bridge of her nose between her fingers and closed her eyes for a few moments. "When we were kids?"

"You're kidding," Danny said. "That far back?"

Mac rolled his eyes. "Kindergarten should be safe enough territory. Oops, how childish of me," he quipped.

Danny gave him a dirty look, but that didn't stop Mac from forging ahead. "Middle school? No? Okay, okay, I've got it. How about our junior year at Lincoln High, when we sneaked out of our houses in the wee hours and met up at the elementary school playground?"

Danny smiled. "I supplied the Pall Malls. I cadged three a week from my mom. More when she was distracted during her fights with my dad. I don't think she ever suspected, but I've never been sure. She may have just been indulging me."

"It's hard to imagine ever liking cigarettes," Mac said, "but I did then."

"I have such a clear memory of those nights," Anna said. "Lying on our backs on the grass, staring up at the sky, talking about how dull our lives were, and how great they were going to be."

"Remember graduation night?" Mac asked. "We climbed down the bluffs to that isolated little cove in Santa Cruz. It was our first time tripping. We dropped windowpane acid and chased it down with rot-gut Red Mountain wine."

"It was pitch dark," Danny said.

"Until you started a driftwood fire," Anna said. "I remember how the flames illuminated flakes of mica in the soil. When I ran my fingers through the sand, I felt like I was dipping my hands into a galaxy and scattering stars."

Mac nodded. "And when Danny took off running down the beach, it looked like his heels were shooting fire."

They grew quiet, each, she supposed, thinking of those long-ago nights when their hearts were open and the world was still a place of magic and mystery.

"That summer went by so fast," Anna said with a heavy sigh. "And then there was Berkeley," she said.

"That's it?" Mac said. "That's all the bonding you want to do before we cut to the chase? No more reminiscences? No more nostalgia about the good-old days?"

"We have to go there sooner or later," Anna said.

"I vote for the latter," Mac said. "I drove two and a half days to arrive in the middle of fucking nowhere—oh, I mean to arrive at this lovely desert oasis—and now you're telling me I did all that for a quickie?"

"Sorry, Mac. Not enough foreplay?" Anna shot back.

Mac lit his joint, took a hit, and took charge of the conversation. "Okay, Berkeley. I don't know about you but I loved that city. Telegraph Avenue was *la creme de la creme* in those days, before it was turned into the equivalent of a strip mall. All we had to do was stroll down the sidewalk and in no time at all, some longhaired druggie would whisper 'acid, hash, grass' under his breath, like a siren calling so sweetly. We were nerds who stumbled into the magical, mystical land of hippies. Easy to score, easy to be a part of, easy to live."

Anna didn't match Mac's excitement but she went along with him. "I did love that big three-story monstrosity we moved into on LeRoy. Seven private one-room apartments, two shared bathrooms, and a brilliant, bizarre, and stoned cast of characters. We spent a lot of hours in that kitchen, talking and drinking coffee with each other and anyone else who might wander by."

She heard Danny push his chair back and she glanced over at him as he stood. He looked tense, like a runner at the starting block.

"Unlike you two," he said, "I can't take those three and a half years and just pluck out the good memories. For me, that Thursday night in Berkeley was the departure point for our journey into darkness, and the next morning, that was the last light burning out. So a trip down that particular memory lane is not one I want to take. It is, in fact, one I've spent most of my adult life trying to avoid."

"It's not one any of us wants to take," Mac barked.

"You seem to be enjoying it," Danny said. "But you always did know how to have a good time while the world around you burned."

"Fuck you, man."

"Face it, Mac," Danny said. "After our world fell apart, you went on as if nothing happened. You went to class, finished your coursework, and graduated right on time. You never missed a beat, man. But hey, the party must go on, right?"

Mac gripped the seat of his chair, as if to hold himself down. "It was your choice to drop out of school, Danny, your choice to take off on some retrograde on-the-road adventure, on the road to nowhere."

Danny balled his fists and took a step closer to Mac. "I didn't have a choice, man, not then. What I've never understood was how you went on with your career as if nothing had fucking even happened, you cold son of a bitch." With that, he turned and walked into the house.

Anna heard the front door slam. Bolo emerged from under the table and went to the patio door, where she waited with her tail wagging and her nose pressed against the glass.

"He left her behind," Anna said. "That worries me."

With Bolo at their heels, she and Mac walked through the house to the front yard, where they scanned the horizon for Danny. Bolo, staring into the distance with her ears cocked, whined. He had vanished from sight.

Mac gave Anna a puzzled look.

"We should put this conversation on hold until he gets back," she said, a statement with a question inside.

"Yeah," Mac said, "I guess that's right."

Less than a mile from the house, Danny stepped down into the dry wash that he and Anna had crossed the day before. He laid down flat on his back, closed his eyes and focused on breathing, on letting his muscles relax and his thoughts just float by, like passing clouds. He listened to small desert sounds, the clicking of beetle wings, a lizard skittering into dry brush. He caught the faint scent of sage.

His memory of their beginnings was less colorful than Anna's or Mac's, just a simple black-and-white thirty-five millimeter film playing in his head. He saw the suburban neighborhood twenty miles south of San Francisco where they'd grown up together. He saw them riding tricycles around the cul-de-sac, chalking squares on the sidewalk for hopscotch, playing King of the Mountain on a massive pile of gravel that would be used in the construction of a new housing development.

He remembered carrying neatly wrapped gifts with carefully tied bows, courtesy of their mothers, to friends' birthday parties, he and Mac dressed in checkered shirts and pressed trousers and Anna in starched dresses and saddle shoes. Later, there were school dances, football games, first joints, first dates, and high school graduation. Then there was Berkeley.

Danny sat up and grasped his head. He shut his eyes and pressed hard on his temples. He wanted the memories to stop. He willed them to stop, but it was already too late.

He saw the three of them on the roof of Birge Hall, looking out over the campus. The day was surreal from the start: the weather so fucking gorgeous, the bay so blue, the sun so bright, their hearts so wrecked. That was the morning they decided to wall off their collective history so they could move on with their lives. Move on they did, though every few years they showed up like clockwork at a preordained time and place; in noisy restaurants and dark bars, they met over pitchers of Guinness, or boilermakers, or straight whiskey.

On the surface, there was easy familiarity, friendly harassment, and drunken laughter between friends who had once known each other almost as well as they knew themselves. But no matter how well they mimicked intimacy, they were always on guard, always vigilant, always terrified a wrong word would wake the sleeping dragon of their memories.

He knew Anna had called them together to give the walls a push, but to what end? He still couldn't imagine anything good coming of this. A shudder coursed through him. It felt like excitement, or maybe fear; he wasn't sure if he could tell the difference, or if there was a difference. He knew if he let her in, he would risk becoming vulnerable to pain in a way he hadn't been for many years. He wondered, for the briefest moment, if that meant he would also become vulnerable to joy.

Anna was on the patio when Danny returned. She noticed his weathered face looked drawn, as if the hot, dry air had sucked something essential out of him.

"You were out there a long time," she said when he pulled up a chair next to her. "I don't know how you do it—walk for hours across the same empty, repetitive landscape of sand and scrub. Like I said yesterday, I do love the desert…but the high desert, with its saguaros, pencil cholla, teddy bear cactus, and piñon pines. Not this tumbleweed-filled flatland."

"It suits me," Danny said with a shrug. "Where's Mac?"

"He went to his room. Probably sleeping."

"I guess I came down pretty hard on him."

"Yes, you did."

"Yeah, not cool, I know. It's just, all the old interpersonal stuff keeps surfacing. I mean, here we are, almost fifty years later, and I still feel like the odd man out, and Mac is still the joker, and you, hon, you can still wrap us both around your little finger. And that's just a tiny sample of all the ways we bump up against each other."

"You're right. We have issues, have always had issues."

"That's an understatement," Danny said.

"Look, I know Mac was goading you, but I have to admit, I've never really understood why you left so quickly. You were this close to finishing your degree," she said, holding up her thumb and forefinger so they were almost touching.

"That's easy," he said. "I was devastated by what had happened. Terrified we'd be arrested. And Christ, Anna, the three of us had just renounced our friendship. Splitting seemed like the only option."

"Going home wasn't an option?"

"You've got to be kidding. You remember my father, how uptight he was. When I was in high school, he tried to force me to attend Annapolis. He was furious when I accepted a partial scholarship to Berkeley instead. To him, the university was anathema, the place where aspiring commies went to learn how to overthrow the government. He didn't warm up to me again until I got the job at Vanguard and cut my hair. He was downright chummy after that, but it wouldn't have lasted. Let's just say there was no unconditional love awaiting me."

"What about your mother?"

"She never could stand up to him. She was so intimidated by his bullying, so self-conscious and constrained, that I never really knew her at all."

"That was true of many women of that generation."

"That may be, but my point is, there was no one to go home to. So I grew my hair long again, bought an old bus, did a lot of drugs, and drifted from place to place, doing odd jobs here and there. At a music festival in Oregon, I met a woman who lived in a commune in the hills north of San Francisco, and I moved back to California to join her there. It was cool for the first few years—a decent enough relationship, a solid community."

"But eventually, the scene changed and things got pretty messed up. There were too many bad drugs going around—heroin, Quaaludes, amphetamines. There were too many people running from, instead of to, something. Too many people like me, trying to find refuge in an idealized counter-culture that no longer existed, maybe never had."

"So I ran again, but this time, I ran *from* people rather than *toward* them. I spent the next few years on foot, hitchhiking, hiking and backpacking most of the coastal mountain ranges out west, including the Pacific Crest Trail. Slowly, very slowly, things started to change. I found that if I physically wore myself down to a husk, empty of wants and needs, I could experience something resembling peace."

"I'll be back in a minute," Anna mumbled, getting up from her chair. She hurried to the bathroom, closing the door behind her just as her tears started to fall. She put her elbows on the sink and her head in her hands and tried, unsuccessfully, to push her emotions back down. When she finally stopped crying, she splashed cold water on her cheeks and headed back to the patio, putting on what she hoped was a brave face.

"Are you okay?" Danny asked.

"No," she said, shaking her head. "It's hard, hearing what you went through, and hearing you describe emptiness as synonymous with peace."

"Emptiness isn't so bad, Anna. It's not the same as nothingness. It's just a radical letting go, and it saved my life. Anyway, to go on with my story, at forty-five years of age, I finally wound up in southern New Mexico and put down roots. That was also the year the three of us decided to stop seeing each other."

"You settling down in Las Cruces was why we stopped meeting," Anna said. "I'd bought the house in Portland, and Mac got tenured at the university, so there was no longer any need for us to schedule meets two or three years into the future. For the first time since leaving Berkeley, we all knew exactly where to find each other."

"But we didn't find each other, did we?" Danny said. "I never saw my folks again after I left Berkeley. Dad died when he was about the age I am now, and my mom passed four years later. I didn't know about either of them until I found their obituaries online. I wasn't even listed as next of kin."

Anna reached across the table to take his hand. "I'm so sorry, Danny. I didn't know."

"Yeah, well. I have a good life now. I like my job and the people I work with. I have one close friend, an old man, a lot older than me anyway, who owns a defunct cattle ranch near Albuquerque. And I have Bolo, who I found abandoned on a desert highway when she just a pup."

Bolo perked up at the sound of her name and came over to Danny to check things out. He put his hand on her head and rubbed her ears. She wagged her tail and pressed her side against his legs.

The sliding glass door opened and Mac, his eyes puffy with sleep, stepped onto the patio. "Ah, the prodigal son has returned," he said, nodding to Danny. "I'm glad you came back."

"Sorry about before," Danny said, sounding contrite.

"I've been called worse than a cold SOB," Mac said. "So, what's up, guys?"

Chapter 14

After lunch, while Anna and Danny napped in their bedrooms, Mac put in his ear buds and took his iPod to the couch. He stretched out, closed his eyes, and lay there unmoving, but he didn't turn the iPod on, and he wasn't sleeping. He was replaying history.

In 1970, at the start of their sophomore year, his younger brother, Erin, moved to Oakland to attend Grove Street College, often considered the 'home' of Huey Newton and Bobby Seal because it was there they adopted the radical politics that gave birth to the Black Panther Party. In 1971, the district decided to relocate the school from the heart of the black community to the posh Oakland foothills. Many students dropped out in protest, including Erin, who found a job at a food co-op. When a room opened up at the LeRoy Street house in Berkeley, Mac talked him into moving.

And then they were four.

In the fall of that year, Anna and Erin fell in love.

And then they were two, and one, and one.

In the winter of 1972, Danny, still a month away from finishing his Bachelor of Science degree, accepted a highly-paid position at Vanguard Chemical.

And then they were none, until all hell broke loose during campus protests against the war in Vietnam.

In the spring of 1973, on a Thursday night, all four of them crowded into Anna's room. Danny carefully taped together eight sticks of dynamite. Anna checked and rechecked the accuracy of the travel alarm that would serve as a timer, then attached it to an electric blasting cap. Erin carefully placed the device in the backpack he'd bought at an army surplus store. He insisted that since the bomb was his idea, he should be the one to deliver it.

Anna explained that once he set the backpack down on the second floor of the Vanguard Chemical building and lifted the small knob to start the alarm ticking down, he would have a full ten minutes to make it outside to safety.

Mac was in the front seat, riding shotgun as Danny drove through West Oakland. Anna and Erin were sitting in the back, holding hands. They never had been able to stop touching each other. Danny pulled over to the curb and parked but he left the engine running. Erin, wearing patched jeans and a dark shirt, and his trademark red bandanna to hold his long hair back, stepped out of the car. He must have been nervous because the underarms of his shirt were wet with sweat.

He paused to kiss Anna goodbye, then hoisted the pack with the grim determination of a warrior marching into battle. Without looking back, he walked quickly across the dark street to a door off the alley, a door Danny had disarmed before he left work that evening. Erin opened it with Danny's key.

Three minutes later, the two-story Vanguard building exploded with a deafening roar.

Windows in adjacent buildings shattered and the car they were sitting in shook like jelly. Anna screamed, and Mac heard a guttural cry erupt from his own throat. Tears began to stream down all their faces. They didn't talk on the drive home, just moaned and whimpered, 'Oh, no', 'Oh, God', 'Oh, God, no'. When they pulled up at the house on LeRoy, they spoke only long enough to set a time and place to meet the next morning.

As soon as Mac walked into his room, he saw a letter-sized piece of paper folded on his pillow, with his name written on it in Erin's tiny, precise print. He opened the page with a trembling hand. Typical of his brother, it began with the 'back to the garden' song lyrics from Joni Mitchell's 1970 ode to Woodstock, and it ended with the Neil Young lamentation about Mother Nature being on the run. Following the lyrics were Erin's own words. *No matter what happens, keep fighting for the earth. Love each other. Take care of each other.*

The next morning, they left LeRoy Street separately. Each took a different route, and each in turn, after arriving at Birge Hall, took the elevator as high as it would go, then climbed stairs to yet another floor and opened yet another door to get access to the roof. When everyone had arrived, Mac brought up the letter, only to find out Erin had left exactly the same message for both Danny and Anna. Thinking back now, he still felt a bit pissed off about each note being identical, as if Erin had thought he belonged equally to all of them.

Mac remembered watching Erin's face in the rearview mirror that night. He didn't see a warrior, not then. He saw his little brother—the wild child ignoring his mother's call to dinner until Mac tracked him down outside, hoisted him over his shoulder, and carried him inside to the table. He saw him forging through sucking mudflats in the East Bay so he could get a little closer to seals and seabirds, and coming home so encrusted Mac had to hose him down in the front yard.

He saw him carefully placing sprigs of sage and seed pods from pine trees on a shelf in his bedroom, as if they were sacred. And they were, Mac thought, they were.

Now, lying on the couch in this place where old friendships were being painfully rekindled, Mac thought again about Erin's words: 'Keep fighting. Love each other. Take care of each other.' *Okay, Erin, okay. I hear you now, and I will do better. I promise you, little brother, I will do my best.*

That evening, the household came together on the patio once again.

"Is anyone hungry yet?" Anna asked.

"I think I'll drink my dinner tonight," Mac said.

"Sounds like a plan," Danny said, standing. "I'll get the beer. What about you, Anna?"

"I'll have wine, thanks. But I'll need to make a sandwich or something later."

"Then let's do this," Mac said.

"Do what?" Anna asked.

"I think it's time for me to tell you two a story," Mac said.

Anna groaned. "I don't think I can take another one today."

Mac leaned back in his chair and began speaking in the deep, sonorous voice of a parent reading a child to sleep. "Sure you can. Both of you just sit back, let your bodies relax, close your eyes and listen, and I will tell you a tale of love and betrayal in the city by the bay."

They did as they were told. Mac, lost in thought, finally realized they had opened their eyes and were staring at him expectantly. "Sorry, I was going to tell this in my fairy tale voice but I don't think it will work. Usually, it works, but this time I think I need to use my own voice, if I can still remember it."

"You don't have to do this, Mac," Anna said. "We don't have to give a blow-by-blow recounting of everything that happened and has happened since."

"Oh yes, we do, Anna," he said. "You called and we came and by God, we are going to do this once and for all—finish it so we can fucking let go of it and move on."

"A friendly warning, Mac," Danny said. "Talking about it this morning did make me feel a little better, but it didn't make the past go away. In some ways, it brought it closer."

"Great, just what I want to hear before I spill my guts," Mac said.

"All right, close your eyes again. It makes it easier for me to focus." They obliged, and he began.

"There's nothing I want to say about the night of the bombing, so let's move on to the next day when we met on the roof of Birge Hall. What a brilliant backup plan: if anything goes wrong, let's all show up at our usual hangout."

"I don't think we ever really considered the possibility anything would go wrong," Anna said. "We were so naive."

"That we were," Mac said. "Anyway, as you might remember, on the way to Birge Hall that morning, I lifted a newspaper from someone's doorstep. All it said was a gas line blew in the middle of the night and turned the Vanguard building into a burning heap of rubble. They didn't know yet what had triggered the explosion. They didn't know yet if anyone had been inside the building. I mean, it had been less than six hours since we'd left the scene."

"We were so freaked out," Anna said.

"By the time we met that morning, 'we' no longer existed," Danny said.

Mac nodded. "You're right, but we couldn't face that reality, not then. We hugged, and we did that hokey little thing with your penknife, Danny, smeared our cut thumbs together, swore never to betray each other, swore blood brothers and sister for life. And we set up a date and place to come together again: two years to the day, San Francisco, Pier 29. We figured by then, we'd either be in the clear or in prison."

"But by the time I got back to LeRoy Street, I had become certain of two things. First, I never wanted to see either of you again, ever. Second, I wanted to finish what I'd come to Berkeley for—namely, my degree. So I closed the door to my room. I opened my books and started working, and didn't stop until the semester ended and I graduated on time and with honors."

Anna opened her eyes and glared at him. "You sound so smug."

He shot back. "You're the one who set the rules for this reunion, Anna, all in or all out, no bullshit."

"Back off, Mac," Danny said, leaning forward as if about to pounce.

"Ah, the hero arrives to rescue the maiden. But the hero tied her to the railroad tracks in the first place, didn't he?"

Danny turned beet red, visible even under his dark tan.

Anna pushed her chair back and stood up as if preparing to leave. "Hold up, Anna," Mac said with urgency. "Please." She waited.

"I'm sorry, that was a slip, and way out of line. I won't do it again. But I'm not done here. *We* aren't done here." His hostility had evaporated and his words were a plea.

She gave him a cold stare but she took her seat again, and Mac resumed talking.

"You know, I have wasted many good benders trying to unravel the pathology that drove us like lemmings to those miserable reunions. Every few years, we showed up like clockwork at some preordained time in some dark bar in some strange town to share pointless details of our daily lives, or fabricate tall tales, or reveal half-truths. Anything to get us to the end of the night relatively unscathed."

"But, Anna, you are right about one thing. We never 'really talked'. We should have. I realize now that we should have." Anna's eyes brimmed with tears.

"The hardest moment for me, other than the night itself, was when the next edition of the paper reported they had found a body in the rubble, burned beyond recognition." He rubbed his eyes, trying to wipe out the image. "And you know what was really weird? No one at the house even noticed he'd gone missing. I mean, not Ted, or Arnie downstairs or the ballerina woman on the third floor. What was her name? Cynthia?"

"Even weeks later, none of them had mentioned his absence, or Danny's, for that matter. Maybe I was giving off a danger signal and they were afraid to approach me. Or maybe they were just preoccupied with their own lives."

"My parents, they of course noticed Erin had stopped calling them every weekend, but I managed to stall them until I went home at the end of the semester. The cops hadn't been able to identify Erin's body yet, and I doubted they ever would, but I couldn't look my folks in the face and keep telling them bullshit stories. They had a right to know. So I told them what had happened, more or less."

"You told them?" Anna asked.

"Yes," Mac said.

"You really mean that?" Danny asked.

"How could I not tell them? They were our heroes in those days, remember?"

"I do remember," Anna said. "Your dad and mom were both hardcore lefties. But still…"

"No buts," Mac said. "Can you imagine what it took for my mom to get a doctorate and become a researcher for the Academy of Natural Sciences at a time when most middle-class married women didn't even have careers? Or what a huge risk she and my dad took when they marched with Women Strike for Peace, the national antinuke group? Who do you think taught Erin about the natural world? Who do you think taught him to fight for what was right?"

"They were great parents, and I owed them the truth. Most of the truth, anyway. I told them Erin had been killed in an explosion of his own making, and that he was alone."

"He was, in the end," Anna said, her voice breaking.

"Still, I wish I hadn't lied to them, but I didn't see any other way. I mean, they put their hearts and souls into advancing progressive issues, but they never condoned violence. I was afraid they would turn us in if they knew we'd been complicit in Erin's death. So I didn't tell them, though I'm sure they suspected."

"Anyway, we argued all summer, never over Erin overtly, but over my attitude, which I admit was piss poor, and my out-of-control drinking and drugging. In September, I left home for UCLA. I managed to clean up my act, and after I finished my doctorate in physics with a sub-specialty in climate studies, I moved to Madison for my first faculty appointment. I've been there ever since."

"Did you ever reconcile with your folks?" Danny asked.

"I went back to visit in the summer for a few years, but my relationship with them never felt right again. I wrote them, they wrote me, and we called each other once in a while, but over time they became more and more distant.

Eventually, the calls stopped, and we all let go. No big blow-up, just a relentless deterioration of affection. My father died of a heart attack when he was seventy-two, and within the year, my mother also passed. I found out because their lawyer contacted me through the university to inform me he had settled their estate. They left everything to charity.”

“Anyway, I’ve lived in Madison ever since I left California. I’ve had a number of serially monogamous relationships, some longer than others, none very deep. No pets, no kids, and since I tore up my knee playing basketball, no hobbies except microbrews. Actually, I do understand that drinking is an addiction, not a hobby, but most of the time, I don’t give a shit. I teach and continue to do some research in the field of climate studies. I try to inspire students, but the more despairing I feel, the harder it becomes, and the more despairing I feel. That’s what scientists call a positive feedback loop.”

He slumped down in his chair and rubbed his eyes. “That’s it, kids. Story over, start to finish. True confessions spoken, duty done. Can I go home now?”

Anna came around behind him. She leaned down and wrapped her arms around him. He accepted her embrace, held her hands against his chest and leaned his cheek against her arm, resting there. Danny, too, came over and put a hand firmly on Mac’s shoulder. “Here we are,” Anna said. “Here we are again, and at last.”

That night, Anna looked out of her bedroom window to see a starless a starless sky lit only by low thunderheads rolling in and over the desert plateau. She turned out the bedside light. The speck of a house that was number twenty-three went dark, and the rain came down hard, the dusty earth embracing every drop.

The once-upon-a-time friends and once-upon-a-time enemies fell into fitful slumber.

Chapter 15

Anna was pouring her second cup of coffee when Mac wandered into the kitchen in his boxers and a t-shirt.

"Hey, sleepyhead," she said, giving him a brief, full-bodied hug he didn't resist. "You slept late. Hungry yet?"

He looked down at his belly. "When am I not?"

Danny and Bolo came in through the patio doors.

"Ah, there you are," Anna said. "You've already been out for a walk?"

Danny nodded. "It's muggy out thre, and heating up fast."

Anna looked at him closely. "You look more worn out than you did when you went to bed. Bad night?"

"You could say that."

"So, what's on our agenda for today?" Mac asked.

Anna pulled a carton of eggs and a pound of bacon out of the refrigerator. "How about breakfast? Even I can cook bacon and eggs, or bacon and French toast if you'd rather?"

Mac and Danny placed their orders and carried their steaming cups of coffee into the dining room, where she could still see and hear them.

"Another meal, another day," Mac said.

Anna smiled seeing Bolo bump up against Mac's legs and start exploring his bare feet with her nose. Mac reached down to pet her.

"Danny," Mac said, "I keep petting your dog and telling her 'good girl', but I know I sound like I'm reading out of an instruction manual."

Danny laughed. "She doesn't care what you sound like. Just keep it up."

"Okay, I'm cool with that. Man, it seems like I've been here for a month, but this is only Tuesday. Hard to believe," Mac said.

Anna shouted, "Fuck," from the kitchen, followed by, "The maid, the maid." She rushed over to them. "It's Tuesday," she said emphatically. "The maid will be here in fifteen minutes."

They stared at her, uncomprehending. "The maid," she said, waving her arms around like she was flagging cars. "Fifteen minutes. No dogs on this property, no marijuana in this state. Get it?"

They jumped up and joined her in a frenetic search of the house. Mac wiped down all the surfaces where he'd rolled or smoked joints and the pot and paraphernalia into a large freezer bag with a zip lock. She tried to get rid of any lingering orders by opening all the windows and furiously fanning the air with a magazine.

Danny washed out Bolo's dog food bowl and tossed empty wine and beer bottles into a trash bag.

"Where are you going?" Anna asked when he headed for the front door with his load.

"To put these in my truck," he said and kept walking.

"We are grown-ups here," she muttered to herself. "We do have the right to drink."

Danny returned to the kitchen, grabbed a piece of bread, folded it over two pieces of bacon, and stuck it in his shirt pocket. He picked up his keys and the bag of dog food and Mac's zip-locked stash of pot and paraphernalia, called Bolo, and walked out of the house. Anna ran to the front door and yelled after him as he climbed into the truck, "She'll be gone in two hours."

He shouted back, "Later," then drove off with his dog and the contraband.

It was 9:57 a.m.

The bacon and eggs were cold by the time Anna dished them onto two plates. She and Mac carried them to the table and took their seats. They sat up straight and folded their hands in their laps, as if waiting for someone to say grace, but Anna doubted they could pass for reverent. Mac, at least, had the conspiratorial look of a disobedient child.

"Whew," he said.

"Whew," Anna said and giggled.

The doorbell didn't ring until almost 10:30. Anna opened it with a yawn and an *Arizona Highways* magazine in hand, as if she'd been having a lazy morning and enjoying a light read. The housekeeper, a young Navajo woman barely out of her teens, stood on the step with a bucket of cleaning supplies. Anna smiled and invited her inside.

At 1:00, Danny returned with two more cases of beer, a fifth of Maker's Mark, a gallon of milk, and a tub of fried chicken and French fries he'd bought from a fast food place in Farmington.

"Oh yeah," joked Mac, as they took their places around the patio table for lunch. "We are some hardcore old hippie pot-smoking saboteurs. We are so, so bad."

They all laughed hard and long at the sudden rush of paranoia that had swept them into frenzied action.

Anna woke from a nap around 3:00 in the afternoon, and saw Mac standing in her doorway, tapping his fingers on the wall. "What's up?" She asked, yawning.

"Tag, you're it," he said, and was gone.

She emerged from her bedroom wearing cotton pajama bottoms and a ratty t-shirt, her hair disheveled, her eyes barely open. She found the men in the living room in their usual positions.

"You look like the waif in a Keane painting," Mac said. "Your bad luck to be last," he added, with a wicked grin.

She scowled at him, then turned her attention to Danny. "I think I need a break. Is there anywhere near here where we could go for a long, but not terribly difficult, hike? And why are you sitting inside with all the curtains closed?"

"We're inside because it's ninety degrees outside," Danny said, "and humidity is at about eighty percent, I'd guess. Unless you want to spend the day in a sauna, a hike is out."

Anna made a low moaning sound and headed back to her bedroom.

Mac caught up with her in the hallway. "Anna, I don't have time for a recreational outing. I have to leave here on Friday so I can be on campus Monday. That's when grades will be posted and the wailing will begin."

"I know, Mac, I know. I'll be back in a minute, I promise, but I really have to take a quick shower."

Forty minutes later, her hair still dripping wet, she returned to find Danny sitting in Mac's rocker with his hands locked behind his head and a satisfied smile. Mac had taken over her usual seat on the couch.

"It's all cool," Mac said, smiling at her. "We're shaking it up today."

"Welcome back," Danny said. "I thought maybe you'd slipped through a cosmic wormhole, you've been gone so long."

Flummoxed by the new seating arrangement, she said, "I'll be right back. I just have to grab a snack."

She returned, carrying an almost empty bottle of beer and a plate of crackers, thinly sliced apples and pieces of cheese, all neatly arranged around a small bowl of hummus.

"For a woman who thinks food presentation means dumping the potato chips and Cheetos into two different bowls," Mac said, "this is quite the accomplishment."

Anna, unperturbed, set the food down on the coffee table. "Oh, damn, I forgot beers for you guys. I'll be right back."

Danny jumped up off the couch. "Sit down for Christ's sake," he said. "I'll get them." She obediently sat. Danny returned in less than a minute, bottles in hand.

As soon as he took his seat again, she stood up. "Oops, I forgot the napkins."

"What the fuck are you doing, woman?" Mac barked.

"I'm stalling, Mac. What do you think I'm doing?" She barked back. Then she sat back down and chugged the last of her beer.

Danny took the empty from her hand and replaced it with a cold one.

She fixed her gaze on Mac. "Okay, I'm going to be good now. No more pleading, hiding, or acting out, I promise. But, Mac, I need to warn you, the story I tell will not make you happy. Or maybe it will. I don't know. Maybe happy and sad." As an afterthought, she added, "And probably mad."

He raised an eyebrow and shrugged. "You set this thing in motion, hon. It's your show."

Anna pulled her knees to her chest and took a slow deep breath. "What I remember, after our delightful meeting on the roof of Birge Hall, was somehow ending up on the steps of Sproul Plaza. I sat there for hours watching people go by. They looked so normal, as normal as anyone looked in Berkeley in those days, and they were going about their lives, walking to and from classes, carrying books, laughing with friends."

"When I finally got back to my room, I hung a sheet over the dresser mirror so I wouldn't have to look at myself, then I took off my clothes and got into bed. The pillows smelled just like Erin, like salt and pine and a hint of patchouli. You know?" She paused to keep herself from breaking into tears.

They both gave solemn nods.

"I stayed in bed for a long, long time. When my eyes got tired, I closed them. When I couldn't stand being inside my head, I opened them and stared at the wall. I heard you come and go a few times, Mac, but I never heard Danny; I didn't realize he had already left. I didn't want to see either of you, though, didn't want to see anyone. For over a week, I drifted in and out of sleep, only getting up to sneak a glass of water from the kitchen, or to use the bathroom."

"Then one night, I accidentally caught a glimpse of myself in the bathroom mirror. It wasn't a pretty picture. My hair was matted; there were dark circles under my eyes; my lips were peeling. And I was emaciated, having eaten nothing but a box of crackers I had in my room. It was the middle of the night but I immediately went to the phone and called my parents. I don't remember what I said to them, but I must have sounded pretty bad, because my dad caught a redeye from Portland and showed up at my door late the next morning."

"He packed three boxes with my clothes and books and a few other things from my desk and put them in the trunk of a rental car. Then he wrapped his arms around me and helped me walk out of there. I think he would have just picked me up and carried me if he hadn't had a bad back. So, home again, home again, not to our house in the old neighborhood but to the house in Portland they moved to after I left for college."

"I'm so cold," she said. The air in the room must have been in the high seventies, but she was shivering, chilled to the bone. Danny got up and felt her forehead.

"You're not feverish. This isn't helping," he said, taking the beer from her hand. He disappeared into the kitchen and came back a few minutes later with a cup of hot tea.

"We can stop, you know," he said, handing her the cup.

She took a sip of the tea. "Mmm, the honey is good. Buddy, if I stop talking now, I don't think I'll ever start again," she said and resumed her story.

"My parents knew I'd begun dating Erin at the start of my junior year but they didn't know we were basically living together. To them, he was still the scrawny kid who had climbed every tree in the old neighborhood. When we visited them that summer, on our way to Mt. Adams, they teased him about hearing his disembodied voice calling down to them from the big fir in our front yard, 'Hi, Mr. and Mrs. Sanders.'"

"They were nice to him, and I know they liked him, but they respected Mac, and they just couldn't fathom why I had chosen to be with 'the wild Caffrey boy', or why losing him the following spring was so devastating. I never told them the circumstances, of course. I just told them we had broken up."

"I'll never forget that trip with Erin," she said. "We hiked Mt. Adams, drove to Zion, canoed the Green River. He opened my eyes to the natural world, and I've never closed them again."

"Wasn't there a massive wildfire on Mt. Adams a few years ago?" Mac asked.

"Yes," she said. "The smoke reached all the way to Portland. I remember thinking I was breathing in the ashes of Bird Creek Meadows, which was where we camped that summer. I was heartbroken."

The tea had grown cold but Anna emptied the cup and ran her finger around the bottom to get every last drop of honey. "This was good, Danny, much better than beer. Thank you."

"You're welcome," he said.

"Sorry, I got a little sidetracked. Anyway, after Dad drove me to Portland and Mom fed me home-cooked meals for a few weeks, I did start to feel better physically, though I was still fucking depressed. Then the nausea hit. Day after day of getting sick to my stomach, day after day of throwing up." She paused, pulled her legs up onto the couch, wrapped her arms tightly around them. She glanced at Mac, then away. "My mom took me to see her doctor. He ran tests. He asked me if I knew I was three months pregnant. I didn't, but I was."

There is a moment, an infinitesimal gap between the time a bullet leaves its chamber and the time it enters the body. In just such a moment, Mac did the calculations. "You mean you had another child before you had Kate? That's not possible," he said.

Anna looked down and bit her bottom lip.

"But, how…"

There is a second moment, between the time the bullet enters the body and the time the brain understands it's been shot. In just such a moment, Mac answered his own question. "Erin?"

Anna nodded.

Mac, moving as if his body hurt all over, slowly got to his feet. The room was perfectly still, perfectly quiet, except for the sound of his labored breathing and the tick-tock of the kitchen clock in the next room. A mourning dove called in the distance. "You miscarried?" She shook her head no.

"Did you abort it?"

Anna looked him in the eyes for the first time since she'd begun speaking. "No, Mac, though I did consider that option. We did a lot of drugs for a lot of years, including LSD, and there were all the warnings about birth defects, which turned out to be hype, but they scared me. Even so, I couldn't do it, not to Erin's child. Thank God, she was a healthy baby."

"Erin had a daughter," Mac said, almost under his breath. "What happened to her? Did you give her up for adoption?"

"No, Mac."

He stared past her with a puzzled expression, as if trying to make out something moving in the far distance.

"Look at me, Mac, please," she said.

He turned his gaze to her but his expression was unreadable.

"I named her Kate."

"No, that can't be," Mac said. "I remember clearly when you first told us about Kate because of course I wondered. It was during our first reunion, in March of 1975, in San Francisco. That's right, isn't it?" He asked, turning to Danny.

Danny nodded.

"It was the two-year anniversary of Erin's death," Mac said. "I distinctly remember you telling us about your daughter. She was six months old, and you said your parents were watching her. I remember feeling like it was a betrayal of Erin, you starting another relationship so soon after…"

Danny leaned forward in the rocker, concentrating, trying to put together fragments from that long-ago night. "Mac, I thought she said it wasn't a relationship, just a one-nighter with some guy she met in Portland."

"That's irrelevant," Mac said with a dismissive wave of his hand. "There's no way Kate can be Erin's child."

Anna turned to face him. Looking directly into his eyes, she kept her voice firm but tender.

"Mac, there was no other relationship. There wasn't even a one night stand. When we met in San Francisco, I lied about Kate's age. She was a year-and-a-half old then, not six months."

A look of pain and confusion contorted Mac's features. He stood there, unmoving, his body rigid, his eyes glazed. Then he blinked and took a few steps back. He held up his hands and stared at them, as if just realizing they had become fists. Finally, in a strangled voice, he asked, "You had his child? And you lied to me? Why in God's name would you lie to me, Anna?"

"Mac, I couldn't have told you when we were in Berkeley because I didn't know I was pregnant then. And after…"

"Just what the fuck is your excuse for *after*, Anna?" He asked. He wasn't yelling. His voice was flat, his body motionless.

Roughly massaging her temples, Anna said, "I didn't know what you'd do."

"What the hell did you think I'd do?"

"I don't know…I don't know. But I thought you blamed me for what happened to Erin. I thought you hated me."

Mac's dissociative calm shattered like a plate glass window in the path of a wrecking ball. He started pacing the living room in long strides, clenching and unclenching his hands. He stopped, bent over double and clutched his stomach. An anguished moan escaped him. Then he straightened up and took two steps closer to Anna.

"I did hate you, and Danny," he said through clenched teeth, "but I stopped hating a long time ago. The only person I blame now is myself, just to get the facts straight. But for this bullshit, this subterfuge, this lifetime of lies, only you are responsible, Anna Sanders. Only you," he said, in a dark rumble of sound.

"Mac, please," she said softly. "I'm almost done talking, if you can just hear me out."

"Fuck you, Anna. Forty-three years since we last met and you've never said a word to me about her? You fuck. You selfish bitch. You cunt. You whore." The expletives seethed out of him like poisonous black smoke.

"Mac, I'm so sorry," she said and began to cry.

"You sure as hell are," he said in a strained whisper. He moved closer, looming over her. She found herself cowering.

Mac had never hit another human being in his life but she knew he wanted to hit her now. She got up from the couch and backed away from him, kept backing away until she bumped into the wall. Mac moved in close and she instinctively raised her arms in front of her to shield her face from blows.

"You weren't the only one who lost him," she said, her voice breaking. "He was the only boy, the only man I slept with until I was in my forties. And he is the only man I have ever loved. I loved him just as much as you did."

Mac seethed. "Who the fuck are you?"

Anna stopped cringing. She lowered her arms, clenched her own fists and stepped forward, facing off against him.

With only an arm's length between them, Danny jumped up and inserted himself in the middle. He held his fisted hands at his side, like pistols in a holster.

Mac had to take a step back to keep his balance.

"What is it with you, Mac?" Danny said. "This whole scene needs to cool down."

Mac tried to elbow past him but Danny blocked him. "You're scaring me, man, and my dog, for Christ's sake." Bolo, who had been sleeping at Danny's feet, had squeezed under the coffee table and was whining pitifully. "Take a walk, man. Now."

Mac started to protest but Danny said again, "Now, Mac. You need to go. Now."

In a menacing voice that was entirely his own, Mac said, "I'll be back." He turned abruptly and stormed through the house and out the front door, slamming it behind him.

Anna heard his car start and his tires spinning out on the gravel as he fled.

Chapter 16

Mac, reeking of sweat and alcohol, returned late the next morning. He found Anna on the floor in Danny's bedroom, sleeping, curled up with her head on a pillow. Bolo, lying next to her, looked up when she saw Mac enter, but she didn't move, didn't wag her tail. Danny, sitting in a lotus position at the top of the bed, looked ragged, like he hadn't slept for days, but he was wide awake. His eyes, like Bolo's, followed Mac's every move.

Mac stopped just inside the door.

"You look like shit," Danny said to him.

"I feel like shit," Mac said.

Anna woke but didn't rise. She covered her head with her hands and arms and pulled her knees closer to her chest, as if she could disappear if she just made herself small enough.

Mac turned around abruptly and walked down the hall to the shower, where he stood under a steady stream of hot water with his eyes closed. He didn't get out until the water turned tepid. He smelled better, but one glance at the bathroom mirror told him he still looked like hell, with large, puffy bags under his eyes. In the kitchen, he poured a glass of orange juice, swallowed a handful of ibuprofen, then refilled the glass with tap water and drank that down too. The leftover coffee in the pot had grown cold but he poured a cup and dosed it with two heaping spoonfuls of sugar.

He returned to Danny's bedroom with the mug in hand. Anna, still on the floor, had moved into a sitting position. Bolo lay next to her, watching. Danny didn't appear to have moved an inch. He eyed Mac warily.

Mac took one step into the room and one step to the side so he could lean his back against the wall. "Anna," he said softly.

She raised her head. Her eyes were red and swollen, her face ashen.

"Anna, I am going to try very hard to stay on an even keel, but I need to say some things, and I need you to listen. Can you do that? Will you do that?"

She didn't answer but she didn't look away from him either.

"I am all over the map emotionally, which is pretty obvious, I guess. But I'm doing the best I can, given the circumstances. I'm sorry I freaked out on you last night. It's just, after all this time, finding out Kate is Erin's daughter…I feel so sad, just so damned sad about losing all those years of knowing her," he said, his voice breaking. "She's my niece, and for all I know she may even look like Erin, but I've never met her, never even seen a picture of her. Or Gracie. In truth, I don't know if I can ever forgive you."

"I know, Mac," Anna said, tears starting to stream down her cheeks. "I know what I did is unforgivable."

Mac nodded, took a deep breath. "What I need to tell you, though, is I remembered something last night when I was driving through the desert in an alcohol-induced stupor. I'm sober now, in case you're wondering. Anyway, what I remembered is that you, Anna, are the woman Erin loved. And his was no small love, hon, no small love. That matters to me, you know? In all honesty, I don't know how I would have reacted if you'd told me about Kate when you first found out you were pregnant. I was so full of rage in those days."

Mac glanced over at Danny, who remained unmoving on the bed with his legs crossed and his hands folded, as if meditating with open eyes.

He pulled the remains of a joint out of his breast pocket. He lit it, took a hit, then drowned it in the cup of cold coffee. "You know, I only came to those reunions because I was paranoid. We all had the goods on each other, so keeping the enemy close seemed like a sensible idea. I did blame you, both of you, but most of all you, Anna. Not because I thought you screwed up the timer or anything like that. I blamed you for the same reason my parents blamed me: you loved him as much as I did, yet you let him carry a live bomb into a building, just as I did."

Mac slid down onto the floor and pulled his knees to his chest. "You know, I don't condemn the action we took, not anymore. Vanguard Chemicals was a nightmare factory, and we took them down. We stopped them from manufacturing that particular poison at that particular moment in time, which is something, I guess. Though given the volume of deadly chemicals we still broadcast in order to bend the earth to our will, it was a pretty small victory."

"But my guilt, my relentless fucking guilt, is this: I didn't protect my little brother. It's just that simple, and that terrible. I miss him every day, and some days, it feels like every minute." Mac began crying, then sobbing. He felt as if the knife that had pinned him down so many years ago was being ripped out again, tearing the old wounds open. "Anna, I wish you had felt safe enough to reach out to me. I wish I could have been there for you, and for Kate. But more than anything, I wish Erin could have known his daughter. My God, he would have been ecstatic."

"Oh God, Mac, I wish that too, more than you can know," she said.

She crawled over to him. He reached out his arms to embrace her and she wrapped hers around him and they held on tight, as if they could keep each other from careening into chaos. Then slowly, tenderly, Mac took Anna's hands in his and pressed her palms against his cheeks. He held them there for a long moment before placing them back on her lap. Then he pushed himself up to a standing position and staggered off to his bedroom.

Mac woke up late in the afternoon to find the rest of the household sleeping. He banged around in the kitchen, unloading the dishwasher, putting pans away, making enough noise to rouse the others. He was putting away the silverware when Anna walked into the room. He looked at her and gave her a tentative smile. She kissed him lightly on the cheek.

Danny came in a minute later and took a seat at the table. He rubbed his drawn, grizzled face with both hands, and groaned.

Anna sat down next to him. "You look so tired, Danny."

"I am tired, and burned out on talking."

She nodded. "Me too. It would feel good to move, walk, do something, anything. And I think it's cooling down a little outside."

"Is there somewhere we can go?" Mac asked. "Aren't there some rivers around here?"

"Yeah," Danny said, "there are, but none I'd want to step into right now. Do either of you remember the massive chemical spill into the Animas River a few years back?"

"I saw the pictures," Anna said. "The water turned bright orange. Very creepy."

"Creepy is an understatement," Danny said. "Toxic levels of heavy metals, including lead, selenium, arsenic, and cadmium, flowed down the Animas into the San Juan River near Farmington. It wasn't the first time either. There are thousands of abandoned hard-rock mines in southwestern Colorado, and for years many, if not all, have been leaching toxins into the Animas and San Juan watersheds."

"How about a hike on dry land?" Mac said, moving on.

Danny frowned and wrinkled his brow, as if considering the options. "We're surrounded by mountain ranges, but this late in the day, we couldn't get to any of them in time to hike in and out before dark. The only thing I can think of close by is the Shiprock formation on the Navajo reservation. It's maybe forty minutes from here."

"What is it?" Mac asked.

"I'll show you if you'll grab a pen and paper from the counter." Mac retrieved the items and handed them over.

Danny sketched a jagged tower with six lines emanating from its base. "Shiprock is the exposed lava core of a thirty-million-years-old volcano. It rises sixteen hundred feet above the desert floor. Six wall-like sheets of magma, shaped like inverted Vs, radiate outward, but only three are clearly visible above ground. A hike up the tallest one would give us a view of the whole valley."

"Looks pretty cool," Mac said.

"According to a glossy photo book I found on the bookshelf in the living room," Danny said, "the Navajo name for Shiprock is Tsé Bit'a'í, which translates as 'rock with wings' or 'winged rock'. In ancient times, when the Navajos were under siege from their enemies, their shamans prayed for deliverance. Their prayers were answered when the ground beneath them rose up like a winged bird and carried the entire tribe to safety here in the southwest."

Sounding wistful, Anna said, "Maybe if we stand on the same ground and pray for deliverance, it will carry us off as well."

"Where would you want it to drop us down if it did?" Mac asked.

Anna shrugged. "A decade ago, I might have said the wilds of British Columbia, but they're on fire now. Or maybe California, but it's on fire too, and in drought. A week ago, I would have said my home in Portland. Now, I just don't know anymore. I guess I'd trust the winged rock to decide."

"It should be an easy climb," Danny said. "We probably can get there in time to watch the sunset."

"Yes, please, let's go," Anna said. "We can pack sandwiches and fruit."

"And water, not beer," Mac suggested, followed by an anxious moment of regret. "Did I just say that?"

"You did," said Anna.

"Then water it is," Mac said.

They packed a picnic dinner and gathered up their coats. Dogs weren't allowed in the Navajo Tribal Park, so Danny fed Bolo early. They left her curled up on the couch to await their return.

They crowded together in the front seat of Danny's pickup. He drove while Mac and Anna took turns complaining about the paucity of anything to look at other than the same old boring desert and the same old empty sky. As soon as the road turned to the west, they could see Shiprock's solid tower of rock, rising higher than the Empire State Building. The complaints were replaced with 'wow', and just 'wow'.

Once inside the park, Danny drove to the nearest trailhead. He carried the food and water in his backpack, and Anna and Mac followed him up the sharply crested dike. It was a relatively short hike but the ascent grew steep in places. Danny clambered up the rocky slope with such ease, he might have been strolling down a sidewalk, and Anna, though breathing hard, kept up with him. Mac trailed behind, pausing often to swig water and gulp air. Two-thirds of the way to the top, he stopped at a small outcropping just big enough to allow the three of them to sit comfortably together.

"Hey, what about here?" He called to the others, who were fifteen paces ahead.

They turned around and came back down to sit on either side of him. Anna took off her coat and rolled it up so she could cushion her back from the jagged rock. Danny handed out cheese sandwiches and apples. They shared a bag of potato chips and a bottle of water.

Eating in silence, they looked out at the vast desert surrounding them. The sky to the south was pale and cloudless, empty and endless. But to the west, a dark, wide band of cumulus clouds slowly moved in their direction.

Mac passed the water bottle to Danny. "I've been thinking about the morning we split up, remembering what you said." Danny looked at him with a puzzled expression.

"You brought up Erin's letter. You said you didn't know if you could keep fighting like he asked us to do, but you thought you could honor the part about us taking care of each other. You said you loved us and would be there for us, any time we needed you, and Anna and I said the same."

"Yeah, I remember," Danny said. "I didn't exactly live up to my promise, did I?"

"No, but I sure as hell didn't either," Mac said.

"Me either," Anna said. "When we pulled away after hugging goodbye that morning, it was so painful, like tearing off skin. I knew then we would never be the same. Nothing would ever be the same. Then we all let go of the lifelines."

"Anna," Mac said, "this is hard for to admit, even to myself, but you were right about us never really talking. We didn't talk about how fucked up we felt, or how we could go on from there, or what life would be like without him, or without each other…not then, not ever. All we talked about was how to cover our tracks."

"We barely covered our tracks at all," Anna said. "It was just dumb luck we weren't found out. Luck, and the fact DNA testing wasn't in the picture in those days. I mean, nowdays, with cameras on every corner …"

Mac put a hand on her arm to interrupt her. "What you're doing now is exactly what we did then. We ran straight to facts and away from feelings."

Anna looked taken aback at first, but then she nodded. "You're right, Mac, you're absolutely right. The feelings are just too damned painful, even now. I still miss him so much, and still feel so responsible. I handed him the backpack. I told him it would be okay."

"Talk about guilt," Mac said. "He was my little brother and I failed him completely. I couldn't face that reality for years, still can't, not really, not at a gut level."

Danny joined the conversation. "I'm the one most at fault."

"Why you?" Anna asked, sounding incredulous.

"My greed is what set this whole thing in motion," Danny said. "When I got the job offer from Vanguard, saw how well it paid, and thought about all the doors it would open for me, I didn't hesitate."

"Of course you didn't," Anna said. "The job sounded like a fantastic opportunity. You had no idea what you were getting into, or how fucked up they were."

"I should have known, though. I mean, they told me straight out it was a weapons development project."

"But, Danny," Anna said emphatically, "they also told you the deforestation agent they were making would have none of the unintended side effects of Agent Orange, which was sickening American soldiers and burning the flesh off the Vietnamese."

"Yeah, that's what they told me, and I told myself I could take the job with a clear conscience because I would be on the side of a lesser evil, one that didn't contain dioxin."

"Dioxin," Anna said, as if spitting out venom. "It's still one of the most poisonous toxins ever invented. Remember the chemical explosion in Italy in 1976? A lot of people died, and over three hundred school children who were coated by clouds of dioxin broke out in lesions and boils."

Danny grimaced. "Even in 1973, I knew it was a horrifying chemical. In fact, that's exactly how they sold me, or bought me, to be precise. Their new liquid concoction was dioxin-free, hip, hip hooray. What they didn't tell me was it contained dozens of other herbicides that would accumulate in hundreds of species and poison water tables for decades. Some of the compounds they added to the mix had already been banned for use in the United States, but Vantage planned to get around that problem by manufacturing and distributing the final product through a foreign shell company."

"You were so devastated when you figured it all out," Anna said.

"Yeah, I was freaked. When I met with my boss about my concerns, he basically threatened to destroy my career if I opened my mouth. I thought about quitting but the problem wouldn't have gone away. I thought about calling the *San Francisco Chronicle* but I didn't think I had enough credibility for them to take me seriously. The term 'whistleblower' hadn't been coined then, and I was just a twenty-one-year-old kid who hadn't even graduated from college, not someone with the stature of a Berrigan or an Ellsworth."

"There's one thing I've never understood," Mac said. "Why didn't you ask for my help?"

Danny looked at him with a hint of pity. "Buddy, you were just as nerdy as we were. You didn't have any connections or influence either. Not in those days. In retrospect, I am sorry I didn't include you from the start, but the fact is, I was ashamed of what I had been suckered into, and I never intended to tell anyone. Then one evening when Anna and Erin and I were just hanging out in the kitchen getting high, Anna asked me how things were going at work. All of a sudden, I just blurted everything out. She was upset," he said, looking over at Anna, "but Erin—he was outraged."

"Of course he was," Mac said with deep affection. "He was such a tree-hugger."

"You should have seen him, Mac," Danny said. "He rose up like an angelic superhero whose soul burned with the fire of righteousness. He said we had to stop them, no matter what. We talked options, and I honestly can't remember which of us first brought up the idea of blowing the place up. I mean, we talked about all kinds of crazy shit in those days."

"Yeah," Anna said, "I used to dream of shooting flaming arrows onto the roof of the campus ROTC building."

"One of many absurd fantasies we indulged but never considered for a minute," Danny said. "They were just our way of venting, at least until that night in the kitchen."

Anna took Mac's hand in hers. "We did want to tell you about it but Erin said you would stop us cold if we did."

Mac smiled ruefully. "The little shit. The only reason he finally came to me at all was because he wanted to borrow my car so you guys could drive to Vanguard and back in the middle of the night. I told him absolutely not. I told him the three of you were insane and I'd turn you all in if you went through with it."

"So how did you end up agreeing to come with us?" Danny asked.

Mac sighed. "Erin was opinionated and obstinate and self-serving, like we all are at times, but those qualities didn't run deep, didn't propel him through the world. Religion didn't either. Though our parents had done their best to turn us into good Catholics, neither of us believed in a metaphysical god, or in any god for that matter. But ever since Erin was a little kid, the natural world captivated him. His connection to the earth was deeply spiritual, though how one can be spiritual without a god in the picture, I don't know."

"What I do know is he revered nature. So, when he found out Vanguard was manufacturing a poison that would denude the land and sicken every living thing it touched, all for the sake of money, well, that was a sacrilege in his mind. How could I not help him?"

"He understood what was at stake," Danny said with a rueful laugh. "He saw the monster in the box and he tried to slay it."

"Yeah," Mac said. "He was a flaming superhero and a bit of a flaming fanatic when it came to this place we used to call 'Mother Earth'. You may not know this, but when Erin was about fifteen, he saw *Gone With the Wind* on television. He fell in love with a line from Scarlett O'Hara's father." Mac stood up and opened his arms wide to encompass the view before them. In his ruddiest Irish accent, he said, "'Why, the land's the only thing worth having, worth fighting for, worth dying for! Cause it's the only thing that lasts!'"

Anna laughed. "I never heard Erin say that but I can hear him saying it now. I can hear him."

Mac sat back down. Anna reached over and squeezed his hand. "My God, it is such a blessing to be able to laugh and say his name in the same breath."

"We humans are messed up in so many ways," Danny said. "Racism, misogamy, poverty, fanaticism, greed, warfare, you name it. We've made some headway against those problems, and I suppose it's possible we could work through them someday, but not if we destroy the planet. Gerald O'Hara and Erin were right. The earth is the single object we cannot do without. It is the single condition on which all other conditions depend."

After a long silence, Mac took a swig from the water bottle. "It was such a mistake for us to let go of each other after. We've all had to deal with the loss on our own. All these years, there's been no one to share with, no one to know what we were grieving, who we were grieving, no one to give comfort, or forgiveness."

The bottom edge of the sun touched down on the western horizon. As the sky darkened, a band of burnt orange blazed above the sinking ball of fire.

Anna pulled her coat free and wrapped it around her shoulders. "It's getting chilly. Let's go home, boys."

They were quiet on the ride back and remained quiet when they entered the cabin and readied themselves to turn in.

Anna, before closing her bedroom door, called out, "Good night, Danny. Good night, Mac."

Danny, in his own room, said, "Good night, Mac. Good night, Anna."

"Goodnight, John Boy," Mac called out. He turned off his bedside lamp and the house went dark.

Chapter 17

In the kitchen, Anna, still in her pajamas, lifted the coffee cup with both hands and took a tentative sip. "Mmm, it's strong."

Mac, in boxers and a t-shirt, poured himself a cup. "It's hard to believe we've been here almost a week."

"You were a late arrival," she said, "but the time has gone by fast. Anyway, we were supposed to check out today, but I called the office as soon as I got up this morning."

Danny, fully dressed, came in through the patio and joined them. Bolo was with him, panting hard. She slurped up the cool water in her bowl then sprawled out in the kitchen on the cool paver floor.

"You've been out for a walk already?" Mac asked him, sounding incredulous.

"It's 9:00, dude," Danny said, grinning. He opened the refrigerator and poured a tall glass of orange juice.

"Morning," Anna said. "I was just telling Mac I extended our reservation by a few days, so we don't have to check out until Monday at noon. I don't know if either of you can or want to stay that long, but at least you have the option."

"Thanks, Anna," Mac said, "but I need to be back in my office, fully functional, by Monday. I can stay through today, but I have to get on the road tomorrow."

They spent the rest of that morning lounging and reading: Anna, the *Arizona Highways* magazine she'd been holding when the maid came to the door; Mac, the *Sunset* magazine Danny had discarded; and Danny, another bookshelf find, a 2001 paperback on the spiritual world of the Navajo.

In the early afternoon, they made a light lunch, and by 2:00 were back at their places on the patio, watching dark clouds amass in the western sky. Another storm was coming.

"It will be strange to go back home," Mac said. "It's felt weird to be so disconnected from normal life, to not even be able to check emails or read the news. I've missed not knowing what's going on in the world."

"I think it's a relief not to know," Danny said.

Mac looked at Anna. "I imagine Kate and Gracie will be happy to have you back."

"Just a minute," she said, getting up from her chair. She disappeared into the house. When she returned and took her seat again, she said, "I have something for you." She lay two photographs face down in front of her. She slid both to the middle of the table and turned the smallest one over.

It was one of the four photo booth shots taken the day of the bombing, in commemoration, in celebration, of their decision to battle Goliath. She could tell by the smile on his face that Mac recognized it immediately. "I have one of those in my wallet," he said.

"Then it's for you," she said to Danny.

He picked it up and examined it closely. She watched his expression shift from curiosity to amusement, to tenderness, to sorrow. "God, we were so young, and so hopeful," he said at last. "Thank you, Anna," he said, carefully tucking the photograph into his shirt pocket.

"Another picture?" Mac asked, nodding at the one she had yet to reveal.

"This is for you, Mac," she said, turning the photo over. Mac reached for it and Danny craned his neck to see.

"That's Kate, and Gracie," Anna said. "Last fall, we took a day trip through southern Oregon to see the foliage. We stopped at a roadside stand to buy hot apple cider."

In the photograph, maples and elms painted the landscape in burnished oranges, yellows and reds, in vivid relief to the canvas of tall evergreens ubiquitous throughout the Pacific Northwest. Kate, flushed from the cold air, her short hair sprouting from under a woolen cap, was crouched down with an arm around her daughter. Gracie was dressed in OshKosh B'gosh overalls and a red undershirt, and appeared to be huddling against her mom for warmth. Both were laughing hard for some reason Anna could no longer remember.

Mac examined the photo closely.

"I think Kate looks more like Erin than me," Anna said. "They both have his green eyes."

"Does Kate know about any of this?" Mac asked. "Does she know about me?"

"No, she doesn't. She doesn't even know about Erin really. She thinks her father died in a car accident before she was born. I did tell her we loved each other, and I told her he was brave and funny, and passionate about the wilderness, and social justice, and life. But that's all I had the courage to tell her. She doesn't know he went to Berkeley, or that I did for that matter. I raised her in Portland, and she thinks I went through the undergraduate program there, since that's where I finally completed my Bachelor's and Master's degrees."

"Will I ever get to see them?" Mac asked, sounding doubtful.

"I'm not quite ready to have that discussion yet. It's a complicated question."

Danny groaned, and Mac's shoulders drooped as if he'd been deflated.

"Another bombshell waiting in the wings?" Danny asked.

"Just not today, okay?" Anna said. "I promise, Mac, we can talk tomorrow before you leave."

"That bad, huh?" Danny said.

"Yes and no," she said.

"It's always 'yes' and 'no' with you," Mac said, sounding irritated. "But since I do not want this day to go south, which I suspect it will if we continue this conversation, I'll let it go for now."

Danny offered to cook dinner that night. He fried pinto beans, rice, and chicken together with saffron and Mexican spices, and the pungent aromas wafted through the house. He spooned the mixture, along with salsa and onions, into large flour tortillas topped off with guacamole and sour cream. Anna made a fruit salad and uncorked a bottle of wine, and Mac sang the chorus to *A Little Help From My Friends* while he set the table.

"You sound so good, Mac," Anna said. "I still can't carry a tune."

He adopted his W. C. Fields' voice and with a pained, exaggerated grimace, quipped, "I do remember, and no need for you to try, my dear."

"Very funny," she replied.

When Danny served them, Mac mumbled, "The hostess with the mostest. All you need is an apron."

Danny laughed. "Just count your blessings someone in this house still knows how to cook actual food."

"Thank you, Danny," Anna said. "This does look like real food, and it smells wonderful."

They cleaned their plates, with many compliments to the cook. Bolo eyed Danny eagerly as he scraped remnants from the frying pan onto her kibble. She practically inhaled her dinner that night.

Mac plugged his iPod into the computer.

Nina Simone sang *O-O-H Child* and they all kicked off their shoes and joined in, not quite dancing but moving around the room with the music, touching each other lightly, singing, on key and off, about the brighter world to come.

Richie Havens, recorded at Woodstock, cried out *Freedom* again and again, and Mac accompanied the breakneck guitar riffs by drumming his hands on the table at manic speed. Neil Young came on, singing about Mother Nature in the 1970s, and they all stopped and looked at each other, thinking of Erin's letter. They talked about how different things would be if environmentalists and climate scientists had been taken seriously half a century earlier.

They were cheered by the music, the jokes, and the banter, but at last, they started to wind down, their stamina sapped by the long week behind them, the hot, humid weather, and their age. There was talk of bed but Mac was acting as DJ and wanted to play one last 'feel good' song, so he turned the lights down and turned up the volume. Van Morrison sang *And It Stoned Me*, and they danced once more, moving their heads in time with the music, hair flying, legs keeping time, hands raised skyward, feeling the music in their muscles, feeling it vibrate and skim across their bodies, feeling the high of coming home.

They called it a night, and Anna claimed first dibs on the bathroom. She washed her face and brushed her impossible hair, which seemed to be getting wilder as it got grayer. She looked at herself in the mirror, noticing the deep lines across her forehead, the deep circles under her eyes, and the paper-thin quality of her skin. "I am so fucking worn out," she sighed.

As she drifted toward sleep, she did not dream of Erin so much as conjure him. They were backpacking Bird Creek Meadows on Mt. Adams, their first trip into the wilderness. They were such innocents, Anna at twenty, Erin a year younger. She remembered them hiking uphill until the dense pine forest opened onto a vast sub-alpine meadow. She remembered stopping, feeling herself receding, getting smaller and smaller as the world grew large. A slender, meandering stream caught the pink light of dusk and reflected it back in every rill.

All around them and beyond, as far as she could see, there were wildflowers. He was teaching her the names: Indian paintbrush, lupine, bear grass, chocolate iris, avalanche lily. He was showing her the petals opening, colors deepening toward the center. He was holding her hand in his hand and guiding her to touch and feel the knobbiness of fern spores, the fragility of trillium petals, the waxiness of huckleberry leaves. He was pointing to the delicate blossom of a wild iris, its color like the thinnest white cloud against the palest blue sky.

When darkness started to descend, he put his hand on her arm to start her in motion, and she followed. They made a small fire and sipped Jim Beam from a pint bottle. Soon they were enveloped in utter silence and in the blackest darkness she had ever known. Cold descended, and big, dry snowflakes glowed brightly in the light of their campfire. The smell of sweat and whiskey and wood smoke followed them into the tent, where they crawled into her childhood sleeping bag and made love on a field of flannel while painted cowboys bucked ponies around them.

She thought, *It is memory, not a dream, waking the next morning with our faces inches from each other, breathing in the cold morning air, warming it inside us, breathing it out again. I was shape-shifting, morphing into someone still unknown to me.* She remembered the taste and smell and feel of his body: the flat belly, the boyish hips, the downy hairs on his forearms, as soft as fronts of maidenhair fern.

She spoke to him from the house in the desert, without speaking. "Such tenderness and such bravado. It is a wonder one boy was given both in full measure." She loved him as deeply as she ever had, but she ached to be free of all the years of longing and grief.

Outside her bedroom, beneath dark thunderheads, hundreds of lightning flashes appeared in the west. The storm was moving closer. That night, the rain came down hard and fast, and soaked the parched desert until the washes filled and the rivers ran.

Chapter 18

The thunderstorm came and went during the night, leaving a bright blue sky and a cool breeze in its wake. Desert plants that had been pale and anemic looking the day before were already sprouting new growth, transforming the landscape into a panorama of brown and green.

Mac banged on Anna's bedroom door at 8 a.m. "Hey, rise and shine, woman. It's a gorgeous day. Coffee's on."

She didn't answer, so he knocked again, harder. "Seriously, Anna, it's time to get up. I have to get on the road this morning."

He returned to the kitchen to find Danny serving up an egg, cheese and green chili omelet.

"The air smells wonderful," Mac said, carrying their plates out to the patio.

"Nothing better than the desert after a light rain," Danny agreed, coming up behind him with two mugs of coffee.

They had just finished eating when Anna appeared at the sliding glass doors in pajama pants and a t-shirt, her hair a frightful mess and her face looking drawn. Stopping at the threshold, she said in the voice of a pouty teenager, "You ate without me."

Danny laughed. "Sorry, kiddo, we wanted breakfast, not lunch."

"I can fry some eggs for you," Mac suggested, getting up from his chair.

"No, no," she said. "Sit. I need to wake up first."

She left them. When she returned a few minutes later, her hair was brushed and she had swapped out her pajama bottoms for blue jeans.

Mac looked her up and down. "I'm sorry I had to wake you so early. You don't exactly look rested."

"I was in bed for a long time," she said, "but sleep? Not so much."

They sat together on the porch, drinking coffee and looking out at the vista. Yesterday, the air had been lightly infused with a fine brown dust, but last night's rain washed it clean again. The Chukka mountains and the Sangre de

Cristo and the San Juan ranges were visible in the distance, their outlines so clear they might have been etched against the sky.

"A fine last morning," Danny said.

Mac looked into Anna's dark, troubled eyes. "Are you looking forward to going home? You must be missing Kate and Gracie."

"More than you can imagine." She attempted a smile but nothing else about her expression conveyed any semblance of cheerfulness. "So, Mac," she said, as if the thought had just occurred to her, "you said you might want to look them up someday, get to know them?"

Mac's eyes widened. "Are you kidding? But yesterday...I don't understand. You wouldn't even consider the idea. Now you're implying it would be okay with you?"

She reached for his hand and squeezed it hard. "Better than okay. I would be grateful."

Mac, thrilled by the sudden change of course, grinned and squeezed her hand in return. He noticed Danny, who had been staring out at the desert as if barely listening to their conversation, was now sitting up straight and paying attention.

"It will take some work on your part," Anna said. "As I explained yesterday, Kate is in the dark about my past, and knows nothing about you. You'll need to explain who you are, how you fit into her life. But I know she'll come to trust you, Mac, and love you. How could she not?"

"I'm a little confused," Mac said. "You want me to be the one to tell her about our past?"

Anna nodded. "How much you say is up to you."

"What are you talking about?" Mac asked. Hope began to slip through his fingers and he felt a sudden sensation of falling. "Where are you going to be when this meeting takes place? Hiding under the covers?"

Anna's expression hardened. "Look, I don't quite know how else to say this, but after you guys return to your respective lives, I don't think we'll ever see each other again. I know I won't see Kate or Gracie again. I won't be returning to Portland, not when we leave here, not ever."

"What the hell?" Danny asked.

"What the fuck?" Mac asked.

Anna shoved her hair back from her face with both hands and crossed her arms against her chest. Her eyes didn't look tired anymore: they looked clear and intensely focused. "I wasn't going to tell you because I didn't want to do anything to implicate you, at least not any more than I already have."

"Implicate us in what?" Mac asked.

"I did something recently that was, well, illegal. You don't need to know the specifics."

"That is an unacceptable answer," Danny said between clenched teeth. "After what we did to get here, and after all we've been through this week, you owe us more of an explanation."

"You are exasperating men," she said, pushing her chair back and getting to her feet. "Trust me, you don't want to know anymore, and I don't intend to tell you."

"But I *do* want to know," Danny said.

"So do I," Mac said.

"Fuck," she shouted. "I'm trying to protect you for Christ's sake."

Danny's voice turned hard with anger. "Anna, you've been doing this dancing around thing all week, where you drop little hints, then veer off in another direction and leave us hanging. You're pissing me off."

Anna brought her fist to her mouth and bit down on her index finger, as if to stifle a scream. "This is not what you think, Danny. I am not playing some fucking game."

"Then what the fuck are you doing?"

Anna, clutching her arms around her, began to cry. "Look, I was foundering before I came here, badly. I needed to see you both, to work things through in my head and heart. But that doesn't mean it was an easy or a right decision, to involve you. I've tried to be careful about what I say and what I don't say. That's why I 'dance around' as you put it."

Danny, his rage apparently diluted by her tears, said calmly, "Anna, stop trying to manage us. Just give us a straight answer."

After a long silence, she knew she had no more fight in her. She wiped away her tears and said softly, "All right, fine." She sat back down in her chair and fixed her gaze on the edge of table. When she began speaking, her voice sounded flat, disembodied. "The Volvo in the driveway isn't mine. I stole it from my neighbor the night I left Portland to come here."

"That is a really strange thing to have done," Mac said. "Like, really strange. However, I can't see how it would pose a threat to me or Danny. But why on earth would you steal a car? Don't you own one, or have the money to rent one?"

Danny didn't say anything, just watched and waited.

"I did own one once," she said. "The night before I stole the Volvo, I sent my car over a cliff. It's now sitting on the bottom of Puget Sound."

Mac's eyes widened. "An insurance scam?"

Danny chimed in at last. "That's not the story, is it, Anna? You're trying to go underground for some reason, aren't you?"

"Please," she said, raising her head to look at them. "I can't tell you anymore. I really can't. The cops will think you were part of it."

"Part of what?" Danny said. "That's the question I want answered."

"If I tell you," Anna said, "and if I'm ever arrested, and if the cops figure out our past, or our present connection, you and Mac will be interrogated. You could even end up being arrested."

Mac took a hit from his pipe as he silently grappled with the implications of Anna's hypothetical cautionary tale. He looked at Danny and saw the expression on his face shifting like dark clouds on a windy day. Even Bolo, who had been sleeping under the patio table, must have sensed the tension; her anxious little whine broke the moment.

"Mac?" Danny said.

Mac blinked hard, shrugged. "I guess I'm willing to chance it."

Danny nodded. "Why don't you start talking, Anna? If at any point either of us decides we don't to know more, we'll ask you to stop. At that point, I'll be out of here for good."

"Ditto," Mac said.

"It's a bad idea," Anna said, looking at them with a worried frown, "but if you insist, I don't see how I can refuse you, not after the week we've had. But I'll only give you the big picture, for my safety and yours. Even that is more than either of you should know, but it's probably not damning."

"What time is it?" She asked Mac, the only one of them who wore a watch.

"A little after noon," he said. "Why?"

"What time do you need to leave?"

"Whenever. I have plenty of time to hear this."

She sighed. "Okay then. Would you mind getting me a beer?"

Mac went into the house and returned with three cold ones. Anna took a long drink and began.

"I've hidden from my past, our past, for so long. I've had to tell so many lies, make up so many stories, cut off so many parts of myself. For decades, I felt like I was trapped in one of Escher's impossible paintings, with no entrance and no exit. But three and a half years ago, everything changed. The day I stepped into Kate's hospital room and saw her newborn daughter in her arms, and saw her own face shining like the first light, that was the moment I found myself again."

"I felt alive for the first time in years. I felt like an old she-bear waking from hibernation and lumbering into spring, nosing the air, catching the scent of fresh grass, rich earth, and wildflowers. Things began to matter to me, things that hadn't since Berkeley. My granddaughter and my daughter mattered to me. It's not that Kate hadn't mattered before, but my love for her had been so intertwined with grief. This time, the only thing I wanted out of life was to make her and Gracie happy, and to keep them safe."

"Safe from what?" Mac asked.

"Life, the world, whatever might come." Tears started to roll down Anna's cheeks again and she made a hiccuping sound as she pushed back a sob. "Kate often accuses me of being dark but I think she just means I am easily depressed by the problems of the world. Still, her criticism cuts me, because ever since that night in Oakland, I have been afraid I am, in fact, a dark person. Not evil exactly, but twisted somehow."

Mac moved his chair closer and took her hand. "You aren't a bad person, Anna. None of us are. As for what happened in Oakland…we were young, and idealistic, and impulsive, but we weren't evil, or twisted. Vanguard was the dark force, not us. We were good people trying to stop a terrible thing from happening."

Danny nodded. "He's absolutely right, Anna. Nothing about you is dark, though you've always seen the world unfiltered, and you've always taken your news black, no cream to cut the bitterness. You were fun and irreverent, curious and dogged, and ferocious at times. You were all alive-oh, like Gully Jimpson's Sara. That's why Erin loved you. That's why we all loved you."

She reached across the table for Danny's hand and squeezed it hard. "Thank you for that, Danny. You are such sweethearts, both of you."

"But what does any of this have to do with keeping your family safe in the present?" Danny asked.

"It has everything to do with it," she said. "I've known for a long time I needed to do more to protect them, but after Oakland, I couldn't entirely trust my moral compass." She pushed her chair back. "I have got to get some Kleenex. Maybe we can take a short bathroom break?"

They all went into the house. Ten minutes later, they were back on the patio, Anna looking pale and shaky. "I know I still haven't answered your questions but I'm getting there. Okay?"

They both nodded, and she began again. "For three and a half years, I hesitated, stalled, and rationalized, but didn't act."

Danny smiled. "You did what you do with us when you're uncertain about whether or not to talk to about something."

She shot him a grateful smile. "Thank you, and yes, just like that. Then one day, over lunch with a friend, I saw an opportunity. I realized if I didn't take it, I would never act at all."

In a tremulous voice, she said, "Here comes the hard part." She drew a ragged breath. "I sent my car into the drink because I wanted to fake my death. I don't know if the ruse worked, since the Internet is off limits and I have no access to a Portland newspaper from here, but if the police think I'm still alive, there's nothing I can do about that now anyway."

"But Kate?" Mac said. "She knows you're okay, right?"

"No, Mac, she doesn't. And please don't start lecturing me. I know it was a terrible thing to do to her and Gracie. But if I had just disappeared, she would have spent years worrying and wondering when I would return, and when I didn't, years imagining something terrible had happened to me. This way, she'll have a shot at getting closure and moving on with her life."

Danny, who had been staring at her fixedly, finally blinked. "No, she won't waste her life worrying about what happened to you. Instead, she'll spend years wondering why you committed suicide and what she might have done to cause it."

Anna nodded. "I know that's a possibility. But what I'm counting on is the fact Kate has never been inclined to interpret anything I do as her fault, so I don't see why she'd do so now."

"I don't get it," Mac said, incredulous. "None of this makes sense. How does abandoning them do anyone any good?"

"It doesn't, not directly. But I had to take a leap forward, and it had to be an irrevocable leap. If I had left myself any room at all to change my mind, to reverse course, I would never have made it out of Portland. I would have turned the car around before I even got to the freeway ramp. I would have turned it around a hundred times along the way here."

"She'll never forgive you," Mac said, so quietly he might have been talking to himself.

"You're probably right, but I'm less worried about the forgiveness of past sins than I am about committing future ones."

"Meaning what?" Danny asked.

"Meaning, humanity's addiction to fossil fuels is destroying the climate and imminently threatening the survival not only of my daughter and granddaughter, but every child and grandchild in the world. The poor are the most vulnerable, but we're all at risk, as are the eight million other species occupying this planet. Many good people are sounding the alarm, many are trying to protect the vulnerable, but few are listening."

"I know I'm just one person, but I have to do everything I can to help— and I mean everything. If I just sit on my hands and watch this unspeakable tragedy unfold, I will be committing a sin of omission so grave no god would forgive me."

She stood up suddenly, decisively. She walked over to Mac, leaned down and kissed him hard on the cheek, then did the same to Danny. "We're done here, guys. This is the perfect time for you both to pack your things and go."

"Are you serious?" Mac asked. "Is that what this is all about? Some kind of climate action?"

"Please," she said. "You should both go now."

Danny looked up at her as if she was a puzzle he was trying to solve but he didn't speak.

Suddenly, Mac saw the pieces fall into place. "You're planning to blow shit up again, aren't you?"

"Yes," she said. "Yes, I am."

Danny stood without a word and went inside the house.

"Hold on just a minute," Mac called out, rushing to catch up with him and leaving Anna alone on the patio. "Didn't you buy a bottle of whiskey? Beer just isn't going to cut it."

"Bottom cupboard on the left."

"You okay?" Danny asked, looking pointedly at Mac's hands, which were trembling as he set the bottle on the counter.

"No. Not okay. Totally flipped out. What about you?"

Danny laughed. "I don't know, man. But I'm with you. It's almost 1:00 and we're not drunk yet. Once we take care of that little problem, everything should become crystal clear."

They returned to the patio with the bottle and three glasses. Anna was still standing with her arms folded, biting her lip, thinking hard.

Danny poured a stiff drink and touched her shoulder lightly. "You're a little white around the gills, hon. Why don't you have a sip of this and sit back down? We probably don't need to hear any more details. You were right."

She accepted his offering absently and took her seat.

Mac poured himself a short drink, swallowed it in one gulp, and poured another. "Anna, I have one thing to say. Whatever you're planning to do, don't."

"Oh, come on, Mac. Are you telling me you don't think it's necessary? You're a climate scientist, for Christ's sake. You know how bad things are."

"Yes, things are bad. So bad I can't see any way a sixty-five-year-old, five-foot five-inch tall woman, weighing maybe hundred and twenty pounds, can make a difference even if she is armed with a bomb."

"So what, I should do nothing? Just watch the planet fry?"

"No, I'm not telling you that. What I *am* telling you is violence always creates a backlash, and from the perspective of someone who has been sounding the alarm for years, we can't afford to alienate people right now. There are a lot of other ways to have an impact, ways that will build the movement, not undermine it. Look at what thousands of Dakota Access Pipeline protesters accomplished at Standing Rock before the fucked-up election set us back decades."

"Hell, look at your own hometown of Portland where protesters created a human blockade by filling the river with their kayaks to keep Shell Oil's Fennica icebreaker from leaving for the Arctic. Media from all over the world covered their actions."

"True," Anna said, "but the reason the protesters got so much attention was because of the Greenpeace volunteers dangling from the bridge. The world loves a circus. And the ship plowed through them anyway."

Mac, indignant, corrected her. "No, it didn't plow through them. Portland Fire and Rescue cut down four of the repellers, which created a gap in the line. But, Anna, protesters are never going to physically overpower machinery. Their goal is to make the public aware and to put pressure on the policymakers."

"But, Mac," she said, "in the end, the ship did go to the Arctic, and it did sink its test well, and the oil would be flowing now if they had found enough of the stuff to make it worth their while. You know they'll try again. The oil companies are not going to stop digging until every ounce of poisonous black slime is sucked out of the earth."

"So, you're going to do what? Physically stop them? You must know, whatever you're planning to destroy—a terminal, a drilling rig, a tanker—they'll just rebuild."

"I know," Anna said. "I'm not naïve. But it will take them time to rebuild. If they can't get their products to market as scheduled, international buyers will lose confidence in the U.S. supply, and the profit margin for such ventures, which is pretty borderline anyway since the market is glutted, will go into the tank."

Danny shook his head. "It won't work, Anna. There's too much money at stake. Our corporate sponsored government will support the oil and coal companies to the bitter end with subsidies, and with the National Guard if they need to. If you think Big Brother is watching now, just wait."

"He's right," Mac said. "The only way we can put an end to the mining of fossil fuels will be by convincing more people of the danger, not by becoming outlaws and alienating the entire country. We're making progress. Look at all the universities and corporations divesting from oil. And over ninety percent of people polled in the United States agree climate change is an issue. That's huge."

"But Mac," Anna said, "half the people we've just elected are climate deniers, and even though more than seventy-percent of the population in the US say they believe protecting the environment is worth the risk of slowing economic growth, they scream like pigs when oil prices rise. Being aware of an impending disaster means nothing if people aren't willing to make real sacrifices."

"One point for Anna," Danny said.

"This isn't a game show, Danny, and you're not the fucking moderator," Mac snapped.

"Modern economies are built on perpetual consumption, so they are inherently unsustainable. Mac, modern economies are built on perpetual consumption, so they are inherently unsustainable. If we were to globally cut the use of fossil fuels, and globally make massive investments in green infrastructure, which Biden and some other countries are trying to do, we might have a shot at survival. But the fact is that neither our citizens nor our governments are willing to bear the burden of the economic hardship that would ensue."

Mac slapped his hands down on the table. "We are making progress, goddamn it. For thirty years, I've researched and written and taught, and every day I work to convey the urgency of what we're facing. We are making progress, Danny, not enough, but progress. And the use of violent tactics would just make things worse."

"Oh Mac," Anna said.

"Don't patronize me, Anna," he warned.

"I'm not, Mac, not at all. I know how much you've done, far more than I have, far more than most people, and I have nothing but respect and gratitude for your efforts. I think the same of all the people who march, who write letters, who spend time and every spare dollar to try to get the public and the politicians to pay attention. Their commitment, their resolve, is amazing. I mean, the protesters in North Dakota were absolutely heroic."

"I have great hope environmental activists will turn this thing around in the long run. But we have to buy them a little more time, buddy, because we're almost out of it."

Mac's words seethed out of him. "Then go buy a fucking kayak, march in a different protest every day, put your body in front of oncoming coal trains for all I care. Get a thousand other people to put their bodies out there with you. But don't bomb shit. We do not need an eco-terrorist in the headlines."

"It's not terrorism, Mac," Anna shouted. "I'm not doing this to intimidate or frighten anyone. I'm not even doing it to send a message. I'm doing it because it's the only way to actually, physically stop coal and oil from getting to market, even if just for a while. It's not as good as keeping it in the ground, which is what really needs to happen, but it's something."

Mac couldn't look at her. He pulled a pipe out of his pocket and focused intently on packing a marijuana bud into its bowl.

Danny picked up the open whiskey bottle and poured the amber liquid into his empty glass. "Anna, the problem I have with your plan is I am in fact less optimistic than you are. I don't think we're almost out of time. I think the bell has tolled. The horrors to come will make the Four Horsemen of the Apocalypse look like wannabe delinquents egging neighborhood houses."

"And you told me you were keeping depression at bay," Anna said.

"Yeah, well," he said. "I do still read the science news every day. This climate thing we've set in motion has taken on a life of its own. I just don't think there's anything you can do, Anna. No matter how many bombs you build, it won't make a damn bit of difference."

"But difference for whom, Danny?" She asked. "For our children? Our grandchildren? Our great-grandchildren? Every fucking molecule of CO_2 we keep out of the atmosphere means every child and every grandchild born in this century will have a little more of a chance to survive into adulthood. We have to try to give them at least that much."

"I need to go lie down, just for a few minutes," Anna said, pushing back her chair.

Mac watched her go, then turned to Danny. "You and I need to talk."

"I agree," Danny said. "Let's go for a walk." He turned to Bolo. "You be a good girl and stay here so Anna will know we haven't abandoned her altogether."

Through her bedroom window, Anna watched them walk across the desert. It worried her, the two of them going off together. What were they up to?

She was back on the patio when they reappeared in the distance an hour later, two little stick figures rippling in the heat.

"Have a good walk?" She asked.

"Hot," Mac said, pointing to the sweat pouring down his face and neck.

"A little hot," Danny said, looking unscathed.

"Need to cool down," Mac said. "Inside."

"Inside it is," she said, following them into the kitchen.

Mac downed two large glasses of water, then made a beeline for the bathroom.

"He'll be glad to get back to Wisconsin," she said to Danny. "He's not built for this climate."

"No, he's not, but he isn't leaving just yet."

"I didn't mean right this minute, but…" She heard something in Danny's voice, a catch, a verbal wink of sorts that made her do a double-take. "What are you saying?"

"Mac's not leaving quite yet. Neither am I."

"When are you leaving?"

"Hold onto your horses, Anna." He looked down the hall. "Ah, here he is now. Let's go to the living room and have a little talk."

Anna took her usual seat on the couch. "All right, what's going on?"

"Nothing bad," Danny said, sitting down next to her.

Mac sat in his rocker and started it in motion. He began speaking in his old man voice. "Keep your britches on, missy. It's time for you to listen to your elders. Well, elder, anyway. That would be me."

"Oh God, not an intervention," she said.

"Not exactly," Mac said. "Though I do think you need to lay off the moonshine."

"Me? Me! What about you?"

He pretended to threaten her with an imaginary cane. "Don't you sass me, now."

Anna couldn't help but laugh. "Seriously, what's going on?"

He stopped rocking, leaned forward in the chair, and dropped the voice. "At the end of every semester, I feel like I'm hanging on by my fingernails. I want so much to encourage the kids I teach, to convince them they can make a difference. But I have to take on other personas to help me because I don't believe it myself anymore. Anyway, there is a part of me that thinks, given the situation we're facing, maybe, just maybe, it's the right thing to do."

"What's the right thing?" Anna asked.

"Stopping fossil fuels in their tracks, by whatever means necessary."

Anna moved to the edge of the couch and leaned forward, elbows on knees. "Wow, you've come a long way from telling me if I blow anything up, under any circumstances, I'll be undermining decades of progress."

Mac frowned. "You have to understand I've spent many years entrenched in a fight against my own despair. Such battles tend to feed black-and-white thinking. I still think blowing shit up is a risky way to go, on many levels. But I have to admit, I'm becoming more reconciled to the possibility we're doing so much damage to the earth, if we don't take drastic action, and soon, humans will be extinguished altogether. Some days I think maybe it wouldn't be such a big loss."

"I thought you were the optimist in the bunch," Anna said.

"Even optimists can have moments of doubt," he replied.

"Anna, I'm on the same page as Mac," Danny said. "We've decided we're going to join up with you."

"Join up with me? Danny, I'm not a bandit looking to form a gang. I don't need a crew."

"We think you do," he said.

"We could be 'the bifocal bombers'," Mac suggested, "or 'the caned crusaders'."

"This is not a joke," she said, getting to her feet. "And this is not why I asked you here. I do not, under any circumstances, want either of you involved."

"I know," Danny said.

"I know," Mac said.

She relaxed just a little. "I do hear your support, though, and I appreciate the sentiment."

"Don't be so condescending," Mac said.

"Then don't be so cavalier," Anna said. "You have no idea what you're talking about, either of you. You have no idea of the costs."

"That's bull," Mac said. "My last, my only, radical act cost me my brother, the love and respect of my mother and father, and for way too many years, the friendship of the only other people on the planet I really care about. I know the costs, Anna. But I've spent my life teaching kids about how we're destroying the climate, and for the last decade, I've been telling them it's time to put it all on the line, now or never. Telling, not doing, mind you. The fact is, I'm just another privileged old white man sending the young to fight while I give advice from the comfort of my easy chair, or bar stool, depending on the day."

"And I'm just useless," Danny said. "I don't teach, don't protest, don't write letters. I don't even sign petitions anymore, since most are just thinly disguised requests for money. I do donate to some environmental groups but I don't do anything else to change the future except to keep my footprint on this earth a small one, and that's clearly not enough."

"I'm sixty-five years old and I figure I have maybe ten or twenty more left. I would like to do something useful before I die. After a lifetime of running away, I think it's time for me to step up." His voice broke with emotion, which made both Anna and Mac look at him with alarm.

"I'm fine," he said, waiving away their concern. "Look, I have nothing to lose, and no one I love who is not in this room, except Jackson, and he's as old as God."

Anna stood abruptly and stepped away from the couch so she could see both of them at once. "This is crazy. Mac, you need to get on the road if you're going to make it to Madison by Monday. And, Danny, you should go too. I'm going to pack you both a lunch and send you off."

"We're staying," Mac said. "That's the deal."

She started pacing, fiery in her determination to make them understand.

"The choice I've made means I will never again see my daughter or my granddaughter, though as long as I live I'll feel that loss, and the weight of the pain I've inflicted on them. I will never again sleep in my home, which was safe and warm and paid for in full. And if the cops figure out I'm not dead, it's entirely possible I'll end up in prison for car theft even before I have time to make a bomb, much less set it off."

Mac interrupted. "But, Anna—"

"Hold on, I'm not done. I'll lost access to my health insurance, my Medicare, my pension. If I don't end up in a federal prison, I will definitely end up living in poverty—if I live at all. A future spent in homeless shelters or sleeping in doorways is not out of the question, because unless I get arrested or blow myself up, I'll be in hiding until I drop dead. I will never be safe. The more people who know what I'm doing, the greater the risk, to them and me."

She had listed the consequences of her intended action like a furious actuary, whipping them at Danny and Mac, wanting them to sting. "Is that the life you want?"

They looked at her, shamefaced. She had put their fantasy under a microscope, and so diminished it.

"Anna," Danny said, but she held up her hand to stop him.

The air felt as still as stone and as heavy. Even the desert seemed to be holding its breath.

"I've put you at enough risk by asking you to come here. It's time to cut your losses and go home."

With that, she turned her back to them and walked away and into the house.

Mac felt the floor drop out from under him like an elevator going into free fall. "Well, well. She painted quite a different picture of the future than the one I was imagining. Pretty damned scary. I have to admit, I'm having second thoughts."

"Yeah, she is something," Danny said, with a bemused look and a crooked smile. "She doesn't scare me but she does impress me. It's good to see her back in form, the Anna we once knew and loved. You know, she believes she can pull this off alone, and she does have a goddamned steel rod running through her. But if anything goes wrong, I'll never forgive myself. I don't want to lose her again, Mac. I don't think I could bear it."

Mac leaned forward and looked Danny straight in the eyes. "Is that why you want to join her, for love of Anna? Not for love of the world?"

Danny stared down at his folded hands for a long time, thinking. "Maybe," he said finally. "I guess I could say I'd be doing it for the world, or for humanity, but the truth is I've never loved either in the abstract. Nature as a concept doesn't make me catch my breath, but a coyote's howl, a forest of aspens, a Golden Eagle in flight? I am touched by the particulars, the manifestations. I don't love humanity per se, but I do love you, Mac, and Jackson, and yes, Anna. Do you think that is somehow invalidating?"

Mac considered the question. "No," he replied. "No, I don't. No more than Anna's love for Kate and Gracie invalidates her decision."

Danny, looking relieved, said, "Thank you, Mac. And I understand why you might not want to get involved."

"I'm still thinking about it."

"We can't jerk her around. We have to make a decision and stand by it. It's okay if we don't end up making the same one."

"I know, you're right. But I need a little time to think this through."

"Meet up again in a couple of hours?"

"Sure. I think I'm going to hole up in my bedroom for a while."

Danny watched him leave, then got up and went to find Anna. He found her lying on her bed, staring at the same old *Sunset* magazine that had passed from hand to hand all week. "Anything new in there?" He asked her, grinning.

Anna laughed. "Not yet, but all that's left for me to read is the small print, so who knows what I'll find."

"Listen, Mac and I are both going to take a little time to process all of this."

"You're not coming with me, so process all you want."

As he turned to go, she called out, "Danny?"

He paused, and she got up off the bed and walked up to him. "Will you hold me for a minute?"

He wrapped his arms around her and she wrapped hers around him, resting her cheek against his chest. When she spoke, he felt the warmth of her breath through his shirt.

"You have fought so hard to heal, buddy, to become whole again. You are such a good soul, you know. And you have Bolo to consider. You can't do this to your life, Danny, not again."

Though he knew he wouldn't change his mind, and he doubted Mac would either, he didn't argue, he just held on for a little longer, pressing his open hands against her back, feeling her fragility and her strength.

Part III
A Fighting Chance

Chapter 19

Danny drove away from the desert house before the sun rose. The *Daily Times* predicted Saturday's temperature would reach hundred and ten degrees, an all-time high for Farmington in the month of May. His truck was air-conditioned, at least in theory, but in reality, only a thin stream of cool air blew through the vents. He told himself he should have fixed the leaky compressor years ago.

He pulled up at the hacienda a little after 9:00. He hadn't called to inform Jackson he was coming, so he parked the truck, rolled down the windows, turned off the engine, and waited for the barking hounds to rouse the old man. Finally, he heard him shouting at the dogs, ordering them to be silent.

Danny watched him walk out onto the patio, place one hand over his eyes like a salute, and stare into the distance to see what was causing such a ruckus. He was quite a sight, standing there with tufts of white hair sticking out from his head at every angle, shirt buttoned lopsided, jeans not buttoned at all. Danny felt such a surge of love for the old man, he wasn't sure he could go through with the plan. Still, he rolled down his window and shouted, "It's me. Danny."

Jackson squinted at the truck. With nothing on his feet but sagging white socks, he walked across the dirt to the driver's side window and clamped his gnarled hands on the sill. "Danny? Are you trying to scare me to death?" He asked irritably. "Why didn't you call first? I was dead asleep."

"Sorry, man," Danny said. "I should have called. The thing is, I've decided to quit my job, and I'm feeling responsibility poor and cash rich, so I was thinking about heading to that big old Sandia casino everybody talks about. But then I thought of you."

"You're quitting Pinyon? Well, that's something I never thought I'd hear."

Danny had expected the news of his sudden retirement to worry Jackson, but he hadn't anticipated the pained look on his face, or the suspicion in his voice.

"Yeah, it's a long story. I'll tell you all about it on the way."

"On the way where?" Jackson asked, scrutinizing Danny's face as if he still wasn't any too sure about him.

"To the casino, for a little retirement celebration."

"Danny, it's not even 10:00 in the morning. Even if it was midnight, I don't like casinos. I didn't think you did either. How about you just take me to town, to the grocery store? I need a few supplies. Then you drop me back here and go celebrate all you want."

"Okay, sure, that's fine. It was just a wild hair."

Jackson walked around the truck to the passenger door.

"Before we go, you might want to put some shoes on and button up your pants." Jackson looked down at himself and grinned. "See there, I'm all discombobulated. There's a reason I want you to call first. It's so I can check my 'how to get dressed' instructions before I make a fool of myself."

He retreated into the house for maybe ten minutes. When he reappeared, he was wearing a blue-checkered cowboy shirt with pearl snaps. His hair was combed, his pants secured, and his feet clad in well-worn, intricately tooled cowboy boots.

After Jackson got in the truck and Danny started driving in the direction of town. "Son, are you really going to quit your job?"

"Yes, on Monday. I didn't want to call Eduardo at home on the weekend."

"You know, Danny, over the years, I've learned not to ask about your comings and goings. I figure your life is your business and you'll tell me what you want me to know. But now I'm asking. What the hell is going on and how much trouble are you in?"

"There's no reason to worry. As for the details, trust me, you're better off not knowing."

Jackson stared out the window as if sightseeing but the veins on his forehead were distended and his jaw tight. "That's one 'trust me' too many, especially when you've already told me two lies this morning. First, there is a reason to worry. Second, your secrecy has nothing to do with what is or is not better for me."

Danny, shamed by Jackson's rebuke, felt blood rushing to his face.

"These friends of yours, the ones you were going to see when you passed through here last week, are they part of this?"

"Yes," Danny said.

"You trust them?"

"With my life," Danny said. "As much as I do you," he added, his voice choking.

They were getting closer to town. Danny turned west onto another deserted single lane road, one of many crisscrossing the county. He couldn't think of anything to say in his defense, so he drove in silence, past a seed company's fields and warehouses, past a couple of Angus cattle ranches, past the skeletal remains of old homesteads abandoned long ago.

"What do you need, boy?" Jackson asked, in a voice so heavy with resignation, Danny felt the weight of it on his own chest.

"I need to go underground, disappear. So do my two friends. I thought you might know something about how to go about that, or someone who could help us. I hate asking you. I hate it. But I don't know where else to turn."

Danny glanced over at Jackson, saw tears in his eyes, and suddenly wanted nothing more than to take it all back. "I'm so sorry, man, this was a bad idea. I don't mean to take advantage of you, ever, or to do anything that would come between us. I'll figure out some other way."

"If you find another way, then what? You'll just disappear on me? Never stop by again, never call, never tell me what's become of you?"

Danny pulled the truck over to the side of the country road and turned off the engine. He looked at Jackson, but couldn't hold his gaze when he saw the disappointment in his friend's eyes. "Of course, I'll keep in touch with you," he said, but he didn't sound convincing, even to himself.

"I'd like to believe you, Danny."

"I'll probably have to be out of touch for a little while, but only for a while. I will never abandon you." This time, he thought he sounded like he meant it, and he did. He looked at Jackson again. Emotions he could only guess at were sweeping across his friend's face like rough waves.

When Jackson finally spoke, his voice was flat, matter-of-fact. "I'll help you, and the others because they matter to you. To establish a new identity, you'll need new driver's license. Ideally, you'd also get passports, but they're a lot harder to come by since 2007 when the U.S. State Department began issuing high-tech e-passports. They're embedded with computer chips that carry biometric data, which makes them hard to forge. I don't know anyone who does that kind of work. But if you're willing to pay for a birth certificate to match the license, you can apply for a new passport."

"Wow, who knew you had such a wealth of knowledge?" Danny said, as if taking a lighter tone would somehow smooth out the tension between them.

"You don't know the half of it and I don't want you to. If you need any munitions, let me know."

"I could use a decent rifle, a sniper rifle, if you've got one handy."

"Are you planning to shoot someone with it?"

"No, no. I may need it to set off a charge, though." Jackson looked at him askance.

"No one will get hurt," Danny said. "I promise."

"And how are you going to get your hands on a charge to set off?"

Danny hesitated. "One of my friends is a chemist."

"Holy shit, you're going to mess with homemade bombs? You'll blow each other up."

Danny felt his jaw drop. He had never heard Jackson swear before.

"We could always break into a road construction site." The words seemed fine in his head, but coming out of his mouth, he knew they sounded like a bad script in the hands of a lousy actor.

"No reason to," Jackson said with seeming indifference. "I can get you pretty much anything you need."

"Jackson," Danny said, pleading.

"Take me home, Danny. This is about all the excitement an old man can take for one day."

When they pulled up at the ranch, Jackson opened the door and started to get out of the car. Though it tortured him to say it, Danny had to ask. "How much cash do you need upfront?"

Jackson answered without turning back to look at him. "There is no upfront. There is only full cash payment. The going rate is five hundred dollars for a license, and another four hundred dollars to counterfeit a birth certificate. How many of you did you say there are?"

"Three, including me."

"So that's twenty-seven hundred dollars. You'll also need photos for the passports and the licenses. You can them made at any big drugstore. Drop the pictures off Monday around 4:00. I won't be here. Put them in the pot by the front door."

Danny reached into the back seat and grabbed the small paper bag Anna had stuffed money into after showing him and Mac the contents of the hallway safe. He pulled out a banded roll of hundred-dollar bills and handed it to Jackson. "This will cover the cost and leave you a little extra, for the risk you're taking."

Jackson carefully peeled off twenty-seven bills and handed the rest back to Danny. Avoiding eye contact, he got out of the truck, closed the door behind him, and disappeared into the hacienda, not once looking back.

Late Sunday morning, the three friends drove into Farmington. They cruised around until they saw a sign for Vi's Beauty Salon hanging on a house in a mixed-use neighborhood about a mile from downtown. They parked the truck a few blocks away, across from a small playground equipped with one swing set, one teeter-totter, and one picnic bench.

"If they can fit me in at Vi's this morning," Anna said, "I'll take the truck and go to the sporting goods store. The mall we passed is only about six blocks from here, and it should have a salon or two, maybe a barbershop. I'll park back here to wait for you."

"What if they're booked?" Mac asked.

"We can always drive to another part of town. You have the list, Mac? Most malls have a Radio Shack or some kind of electronics store. Even a toy store might carry walkie-talkies."

"Got it," Mac said.

"This should be interesting," Danny said, handing her the truck keys. "I haven't been in a mall in probably fifteen years."

"Brace yourself," Anna said.

Mac and Danny split up. They took slightly different paths to the mall and staggered the timing of their entrances. They had no reason to think anyone was watching them, not yet anyway, but they didn't want to chance being filmed together on a CCTV parking lot camera. Danny found the Sassy Salon and Spa on the second floor. He counted two customers and two staff inside, all women.

He felt conspicuous, not because he was a male, but because he was an old male with a gray-blond ponytail halfway down his back, dressed in blue jeans, a t-shirt, and hiking boots. He took a seat in the waiting area. One of the stylists, who looked to be his age despite her pitch-black hair, pulled the drape off her client and walked her to the front desk. After processing the woman's credit card payment, the stylist turned to Danny. "Can I help you?"

"I was hoping to get a haircut," he said, trying to be deferential.

"We're booked this morning," she said dismissively, as if she wanted him out of there in a hurry.

He walked up to the counter and held out a hundred-dollar bill. "I washed it this morning, so I just need a cut," he said.

She took the payment. "I guess I can squeeze you in." She led him over to one of the red vinyl chairs, draped him, and fastened the cloth tightly around his neck.

"How do you want it styled?" She asked.

"No idea," Danny said. "I'm starting a new job. I need to look like a businessman."

She wet his hair with a spray bottle, then took her scissors and began cutting. From the corner of his eye, he watched his beautiful, long locks tumble to the floor.

"This is a classic side cut," she said when she finished. "Keep it parted on the left and loosely combed."

On his way out of the mall, he saw Mac through the window of the barbershop, waiting for his turn, looking glum. Mac looked up at him but gave no acknowledgment. Danny kept walking. When he reached the playground, he saw Anna sitting at the picnic table, trying to stay cool under the shade of an elm tree.

"Danny," she said, "I barely recognize you. Your hair is so short, and so gray."

He groaned. "Yeah, it's bad, isn't it? I look like a retired accountant."

"Hon, accountants don't dress like construction workers. You look like a stud."

"You look pretty hot, yourself," he said, feeling the blush spread up his neck and into his cheeks.

"I don't know about that. But I do think I could pass for a desperate housewife," she said, pushing the back of her hair up with the palm of her hand. "It's the Boho Chica look, layered and styled to give me a 'bohemian flair', or so I'm told. But now every gray hair is visible and there are a lot more of them than I realized." With a wicked smile she added, "But thank God, I have nowhere near as many as you."

They were still sitting at the picnic table when Mac arrived. "Are you two from Hollywood?" He asked, in his best country bumpkin voice.

"Oh, Mac," Anna cried. "Where's your mustache?"

"I told the barber I wanted to clean up my act. He recommended a 'wavy comb-back', with enough length on top to minimize my receding hairline. He also shaved off my mustache and suggested I grow a close-cut beard. He said I would look sexy, and thinner. Who would have known?"

"You are almost good looking now," Danny said. "But thin?"

"That was a grueling experience," Mac said.

"I kind of enjoyed having my hair washed by someone else," Anna said. "It was so relaxing, I almost fell asleep in the chair. But I agree, under normal circumstances, not worth the time or money."

"Normal circumstances being we are all fine with looking like disheveled throwbacks from the sixties," Mac said.

"Did you find everything on the list?" Anna asked.

"Got it. You?"

She nodded. "It's getting late. We should head back."

They paused to look at their reflections in the truck windows. "Oh, my God," Anna said.

"I know we're supposed to be going underground," Danny said, "but I never imagined the underground looking so corporate."

They made it home by 2:30 p.m. Anna dumped out her purchases from Office Max: an expensive digital camera, a small printer designed for easy photo processing, and a thirty-sheet box of four-inch by six-inch photo paper, the smallest the store carried. She read the camera's instruction manual while Danny took a white sheet from the linen closet and hung it on the living room wall with duct tape.

"You're up first, Mac," she said. Once he got tired of making silly faces for the camera, she took half a dozen headshots and sent them to the printer. They watched the pages drop into the tray, each with a one-inch square image of Mac in the center.

"I look psychotic in these," he said, sounding completely demoralized.

"Yikes," Danny said, leaning over his shoulder. "Yes, you do. It could work for you, though, Mac. Driver's license photos often make people look like serial killers."

"True," Anna said, "but it's not really the image we're going for here. We'll do another set, Mac. This time, don't smile."

They cheered when the printer spit out new images of Mac looking somber, but not insane.

Each took a turn in front of the camera.

Before they went to bed that night, Anna turned to Danny. "Do you know of a cheap motel in Albuquerque? Or is this going be a hunt and peck operation?"

"I don't spend much time in the city but I do know where to find a strip of cheap motels, the kind of places where no one asks for ID or credit cards. The kind of places the Health Department routinely condemns and every junkie in town seeks out. For a little extra cash, I'm sure they'd give Bolo a pass."

"Wouldn't we stick out? Now that we have these frou-frou hairdos, I think we'd look more like middle-class gawkers than the down and out."

He arched his eyebrow, looked her up and down. "Anna, I think you could easily pass for a homeless drifter even with your new cut."

"Just a minute," she said, and she hurried off to the bathroom to check herself out in the mirror. Her jeans were threadbare, her t-shirt faded, her face unadorned, no jewelry, no makeup. And once she washed the styling gel out, her hair would return to its natural state of dishevelment.

"I guess I could pass," she said when she returned.

"I know you could," Danny said. "And I don't think we'd attract too much attention if you and I got a room together, since I look like an old farmhand, which I more or less am. But, Mac, you present a problem."

"Yeah, this makeover did nothing for my laid-back hippie image," Mac said, running his fingers over the stubble where his mustache should have been.

"And you dress so straight," Anna said, looking pointedly at his beige, permanent press Dockers. "Without your hair and beard…I don't know. You look like you could be handing out religious pamphlets."

"Ha ha," he said.

"That's your comeback?" She said, smiling. "That's the best you can do?"

He ran his hands over his receding hairline and his bald face.

"I'm too depressed to bother with you."

"Even if Mac dresses down," Danny said, "we'd have to split up. Three people checking into one of those dives would raise all kinds of alarms. If the cops are paying attention, they'd probably think we were up to something illegal—drugs or prostitution. I don't think it's worth the risk if we have an alternative."

"Such as?" Mac asked.

"How do you feel about campgrounds?" Danny said.

"Old bones. Arthritis. Remember?" Anna said, referring to the first day at the monument when Danny had arrived, prepared with his sleeping bags. "But if we could get some good padding, like a piece of foam rubber, I'm willing, under the circumstances."

"Mac?" He asked.

"I'm game, I guess," Mac said.

"KOAs allow dogs, and there's one in Albuquerque on the east side of town, right off the freeway. They have campsites, yurts, and cabins. If we luck out, we could rent a cabin, which would be more comfortable, more spacious, and more private. If not, we could camp there for the first night, which would give us time to look around."

"Sounds like a plan," Anna said. "What do you say to one last game of pinochle before we blow this popsicle stand?"

Chapter 20

Early Monday morning, they went through the house and gathered up their belongings. "This is it," Anna said.

"I still need to make my call," Mac said.

"Me too," Danny said.

Anna handed out the burn phones and the twenty-eight dollar walkie-talkies Mac had purchased at the mall's Radio Shack the day before.

Mac went to the patio for privacy. Danny walked outside to the front of the house.

"How did it go?" Anna asked when Mac found her in the kitchen a little later.

"Fine. I talked to Steve, my TA. He said he turned the grades in on time and he agreed to cover my office hours next week."

"What about your girlfriend? Won't she wonder where you are?"

"I had to let my dean know I would be delayed getting back, so I called him too. He said she's already left for Nashville."

They found Danny back in the living room, staring out the window as if watching something off in the distance.

"How did your calls go?" Mac asked, but Danny didn't appear to hear him.

"Danny," Mac said emphatically.

Danny turned slowly to face them. "I built my house in Las Cruces pretty much single-handedly, over a long, hot summer, from nothing but dirt and straw and a few wooden poles. I've lived there for twenty years now and I'm having kind of a hard time envisioning the place sitting empty. I console myself with the thought that eventually the door will open to winds or wayfarers, what little food there is will be scavenged, coyotes will find shelter, spiders will spin webs, and life will go on. But it's the only real home I've ever known, and I'm going to miss it."

"Danny, you don't have to..." Anna said.

Danny shook his head. "Let it go, Anna. My phone service is canceled, the electricity turned off. And I called Eduardo. I told him I had to stay in Minnesota long-term and he asked if there was anything he could do for me. He also asked if I'd stop to say goodbye when I came back to town to clean out my place, and I said of course I would. You know, I'm sick of deceiving people I care about. At least in the future, I'll only have to lie to strangers."

When the cars were packed, they checked the house again to make sure they hadn't left anything behind but the keys. In the driveway, they stood facing the house with arms linked, Mac in the middle, Danny and Anna on either side, and Bolo at their feet. They took one last, long look at #23.

Anna wondered if it was as hard for them to leave as it was for her. The desert house had been both a sanctuary and a crucible. They had been transfigured there, as they navigated their way from isolation to community, broken to whole, despairing to hopeful. They had mourned and celebrated. Now they would move forward into an impossible battle.

"It was a good decision, to come here," Danny said.

"Maybe we'll come back someday, for another reunion," Mac said.

"I hope so," Anna said. She realized there hadn't been a single morning she hadn't woken up aching for Kate and Gracie, feeling desperate to see them, wondering how they were, what they were doing. It was almost as if they had been with her the whole time, which made leaving that much more painful.

They broke apart, got into their separate cars, and drove away from the house, first Danny in his truck, then Mac in his Prius. Anna slowly pulled away in Ellie's Volvo. It was getting late and they had a schedule to keep.

They caravanned into Farmington, then turned onto US-550 going south and east. Mac quickly fell in love with his two-way radio and began broadcasting in a gruff southern drawl, "This here is Six Pac calling Hissy Missy," followed by, "This is Pub Crawler, checking in with the Desert Rat." Danny, who was the farthest back, didn't play.

Anna, like Mac, had read the instructions that came with the walkie-talkies and she tried to stump Mac with a '10-9', which meant he was supposed to repeat what he'd just said, and a 'skateboard coming your way', meaning she had just passed a flatbed heading his direction.

Forty-five minutes later, they exited the freeway at Nageezi, New Mexico, population two hundred and sixty. Anna drove through the tiny town, past a few houses, a general store, and a post office, past any sign of human encroachment other than the road itself. Finally, she slowed and stopped, using the binoculars to scan the horizon. She saw no sign of any cars coming her direction, so pushed the talk button on the radio. "Over and out, boys."

She eased the Volvo down into a ditch on the side of the road and cut the motor. Before they left the cabin, they had thoroughly wiped down the interior of the car, and since then, she'd worn a thin pair of glove liners to ensure no fingerprints were left behind. She shoved the radio into her back pocket, hung the binoculars over her shoulder, grabbed a hammer and nail from the passenger seat, and got out of the car. She drove a single hole through the tread on the front tire. The air whistled out and the carriage tipped to one side.

"Need a ride, good looking?" Danny called out of the window when he pulled up next to her.

Anna grinned and climbed into the front seat. She was greeted by Bolo with whimpers and a hard lick to her face. "Good girl," Anna said, rubbing the dog's back and sides. "Good girl. I told you I'd be right back."

"I feel bad about the tire," she said.

"You feel bad about a tire?" He scoffed.

She shrugged. "Silly, I know, but it is Ellie's car."

"The highway patrol will be a lot less curious about it than they would be if it was abandoned for no reason."

"I know, I know, but it still doesn't seem right. Where's Mac?"

"He pulled over just off the exit. He'll fall in behind us when we pass by."

They pulled onto the freeway and Mac soon trailed behind. Danny drove to the Albuquerque airport, where Mac left his car in the long-term parking lot. Danny and Anna picked him up and they drove another ten miles north and east to reach the KOA. As soon as they pulled in, Anna, grinning, pointed out the swimming pool and hot tub in the center of the campground. "Oh, baby, we will be sitting in the lap of luxury."

Mac patted her knee. "Anna, one of the things I love about you is you mean that."

The two-room camping cabin was occupied, but they were able to rent the one-room deluxe for a full week. It had a shower, a refrigerator, a microwave, and a kitchen table with four chairs. Sleeping accommodations included a two-tier bunk bed, a double bed, and a pullout sofa. Since they paid in cash, Danny didn't have to show his driver's identification, but he did have to give them his truck's license plate number.

They carried everything they had with them inside: Anna's canvas bag of cash, Danny's backpack, and the entire contents of the truck box. They made a rule that someone had to be in the cabin at all times. Anna laid claim to the bunk beds, which were partially closed off behind a partition. She said she liked the snugness of them, said it reminded her of being a kid in her parent's house, made her feel safe. The sofa bed in the living room was too short for Danny's long legs, so Mac offered to take it and let him have the bedroom.

"Danny, did you call Jackson this morning before we left the cabin?" Anna asked.

"No, I decided not to take the risk. I'm just going to drive over there later and drop off the photos."

"Are you sure you'll be safe?" She said.

"Nothing is safe now."

"I don't know, Danny. I'm having second thoughts. I know we don't have a lot of choices, but is working with a weapons dealer consistent with what we're trying to do here?"

"Ah, so that's what's been bugging you. You too?" He asked, directing his question at Mac, who had been watching their interaction with interest.

"I don't know, man. I mean, I'm a doper, but otherwise, I'm normally a law-abiding citizen. I don't even cross the street until the walk sign flashes."

Danny ran his hand through his short hair and frowned. "Look, I understand why you two might object. I'm not wild about the idea myself but I don't see an alternative. I'm sorry you haven't met Jackson, and I doubt you will, but I think it would be easier to swallow if you knew him. He's more of a gun collector than a gun runner, though he has admitted to selling them on occasion. But he's not some paramilitary guy arming a militia. His paranoia is about the omnipotence of the military industrial complex, and his hero is Eisenhower, not the *posse comitatus*."

"These days," Mac said, "I don't think such fears would be considered paranoid. I think they'd be considered insightful."

"I don't know," Anna said, shaking her head. "It's a weird partnership. The action we're planning to carry out will be widely condemned, but I really believe it's the ethical choice, all things considered."

"And you think what? Jackson's questionable ethics will taint us?" Anna frowned.

"Is Exxon Mobil ethical?" Danny asked. "I've bought gas from them many times, like most Americans have at some point or another. But as far back as 1981, they fucking knew their product would raise CO2 levels high enough to cause global warming. Still, they spent the next twenty-seven years spending tens of millions of dollars on a media campaign to convince the public burning fossil fuels was harmless."

"Is Pepsi ethical? They sell soft drinks in India with thirty-six times the level of pesticides permitted by the European Union, yet they still capture twenty-five percent of the U.S. soft drink market and continue to expand overseas. And look at Wal-Mart. The *New York Times* reported their Mexico subsidiary paid twenty-four million dollars bribing local officials to sidestep safety regulations so they could obtain construction permits for new stores. If we buy a gun from Wal-Mart, is that somehow cleaner than getting one from Jackson?"

Mac said, "I'm impressed, Danny. You are quite the newshound."

Danny shrugged. "At least Jackson is just an individual, not a corporation, so his criminal activity is less far-reaching."

"Okay, okay," Anna said. "You win. You're right. We need his help. And I certainly wouldn't pass any kind of ethical litmus test. For one thing, I invested my savings in mutual funds with a high rate of return, and never asked which corporations benefited. I could have been funding Exxon Mobil myself, for all I know."

"You wouldn't be the only one," Danny said. "God knows how many people unknowingly invest in companies that pollute the earth or exploit the poor or build weapons of war. Most people have no idea how complicit they are."

"You do trust him, though, Danny?" She asked, not because she didn't know the answer, but because she just wanted to be reassured one more time.

"Funny, he asked me the same thing about you. The answer is yes, I trust him absolutely."

"Well, then, he must be trustworthy. Just be careful, please."

Danny pulled up at the hacienda at the appointed time. He was surprised to see Jackson's pickup parked by the barn, and even more surprised when Jackson stepped out to the courtyard carrying two cold beers. Danny got out of the truck and walked up to him, envelope in hand.

"I didn't think you were going to be here."

"I changed my mind," Jackson said, staring at Danny's short hair. "Well bless my soul, looks like some woman worked you over good. You look just like a fed, boy."

"Just a haircut," Danny said with a laugh.

"Well, you look mighty pretty with your new do, but I see a lot of gray coming through at the roots. Hey, where's your better half?" Jackson asked.

Danny considered telling Jackson that Bolo and his friends were close by but he thought better of it. "Ms. Bolo stayed up north, in bed."

"Let's take a walk, son," Jackson said, handing Danny a beer and leading the way toward the back of the property.

They stopped under a Burr Oak tree next to the old well, a tree Danny had planted twenty years earlier. He handed over the envelope. Jackson opened it, pulled out the photos and studied them.

"Your friends look pretty clean-cut compared to you," he said.

Danny laughed. "Not really. They were sheared, too, for the pictures. You'd like them, Jackson. We've been friends since we were kids and we went to college together. We were passionate about everything in those days, and hopelessly naive. We got into some trouble, and haven't had frequent contact since. But lately, we've worked through some things."

"I need to ask you something, Danny, before I go ahead with this transaction. Whatever you're about to do, is it for a good reason? I try not to break the law for bad guys."

Danny almost laughed at the wonderful absurdity of Jackson's statement. "I'm relieved to hear that, and my friends would be too. I swear, we're not going to do anything you'd disapprove of. You might not think it was something worth doing but you wouldn't think it was wrong."

"Give me a hint, son. Something."

Danny thought about it. Jackson had respected his privacy to a degree few friendships would withstand, and if he needed to know this, this one thing that might explain why his old friend was suddenly going off the rails and involving him in the process…

"I guess what we're planning can best be described as an act of environmental protection."

"Armed environmental protection," Jackson said bluntly.

"Yes."

"So you want me to help you get yourself killed?"

"Jackson, you know we're tearing the shit out of this planet. We've talked about that for years, and you know my feelings about it. This thing we're planning, it's on the side of the planet, and the people and creatures who live here. We just want to do what we can to give the earth, and all of us, a fighting chance."

"Danny, it would do me in forever if something happened to you."

Danny looked him in the eye. "I'll be careful. We'll do what we need to and get out. I still see a long future in front of me."

"And you'll get back in touch with me someday," he stated.

"Yes," Danny said, his eyes tearing.

Jackson put out his hand. "Shake?"

Danny took the hand Jackson proffered, took it in both of his own and held it firmly. "You're like a father to me. I want you to know that. I will not in any way betray you."

Jackson's voice was gruff with emotion. "Well, okay then. I talked to the fella I know, and he said he could have this done in a few days, assuming the pictures meet his specs, which they appear to. He said he'll try to have birth certificates to go with them, but there's no guarantee on such short notice. If he can't come through, he'll give you a refund."

"What about the rifle, and the explosives?" Danny asked. "How much do I owe you?"

"I don't need any money from you, boy. I'm seventy-nine-years-old. What would I do with a bucket-load of money? What I do need is for you to be careful. Everything should be ready for you by Thursday. Best to come in the afternoon."

Danny pulled a small flip phone out of his pants pocket and handed it to Jackson. "It's a burn phone. If anything comes up, I'll call you on this, and you can use it to reach me, too. It's safer than your landlines but you should probably go outside to make or answer a call in case the house itself is bugged."

Jackson nodded. "I've used these a time or two. Is the number for the one you're using programmed in here?"

"It is. Just hold the number three button and it'll go straight to me," he said. "Jackson, I have plenty of money. I know all this will cost a fortune."

"Keep it, Danny. You're paying for the IDs, but the rest is on me. Just be careful. That's all I ask."

"I don't know how to thank you."

"I don't need you to," he said. "I've known you for eighteen years and you've never asked me for a thing. After Estrella died, you were here for me when my boys weren't and you've been here for me lots of other times. So I'm here for you now. Whatever the hell is important enough to make you get a Fed haircut and connect with people from your life again, well, it's important to me too."

Before Jackson went inside the house and Danny drove away, each promised the other as soon as things settled down again, on a full-moon night, they'd head out to the desert for another night of sitting on the truck bed, drinking Maker's Mark, shooting at beer cans, and talking until dawn.

Chapter 21

Tuesday morning, Anna got out of bed around 10:00. She was surprised to see Danny heading for the front door with keys in hand. "Where are you going?" She asked.

"To my bank, the Albuquerque branch. But it's going to be hot as hell today, so I can't take Bolo. I'm leaving her here with you," he said. "I may be a while."

Anna filled Mac in when he woke up, and they spent the morning together, both feeling at loose ends. They discussed what to do after Jackson came through with their IDs, and what to do if he didn't, but as the day wore on, neither of them could stop wondering what was taking Danny so long. By the time he finally returned at 3:00 in the afternoon, carrying a small gym bag in one hand, they were beside themselves with worry.

"Where the hell have you been?" Anna asked.

"I told you, the bank. But I did run another errand."

"I tried calling you a dozen times but you didn't answer."

"Yeah, sorry. I foolishly turned the burn phone off last night and left it in my bedroom. I need to check it to see if Jackson has been trying to reach me."

"Danny, don't ever do that again," Anna said sharply. "You scared us half to death."

"Hey, really, I'm sorry. I forgot the phone and I couldn't remember the number of yours or Mac's. I'll remember next time, I promise."

"Okay," she said, "Okay," her anger dissolving.

Danny set the gym bag down on the kitchen table. "This contains every dime I've saved during twenty years of working at Pinyon and living like a pauper. The bank manager was pretty upset I wouldn't take a cashier's check, but I insisted on cash. There are twenty-two ten-thousand-dollar bricks in here. Between your money, Anna, and what I have here, we should be able to live, at least at a subsistence level, for a long time."

Anna put her arms around him and held him hard. He hugged her back. Neither of them spoke. The amount of money he put on the table didn't matter. It was the act itself that touched her—his willingness to give everything he had.

"Anyway," he said, letting go of her slowly, "take a look through the kitchen window."

The cabin backed up to Skyline Road, a four-lane street running along the south side of the KOA property. Anna looked out the kitchen window and Mac nudged up beside her. They saw the traffic moving by, saw cars parked along the curb, saw a pale blue sky portending nothing.

"What are we supposed to be looking at?" Mac asked.

"The truck," Danny said, sounding as excited as a kid tearing open presents on Christmas morning. "The Chevy Silverado."

"The dark blue one?" Anna asked.

"Yep, that's our new ride. After I went to the bank, I bought an *Albuquerque Journal* and scanned the truck ads. I found one with an extended cab, so one of us can sit in the back seat instead of straddling the gear shift. I called the seller and drove out to his house to take a look. It's in great shape, with a lot fewer miles on it than mine has, and he was a nice guy. He happily accepted payment in cash and agreed to help me transfer my truck box. But the best part is, he signed an open title. When we get our driver's licenses, I can register the Chevy in Albuquerque under my new name."

"Where is your Ford?" Mac asked.

"It's here, back in the lot. Dave, the guy who sold me the new one, followed me back to town in the Chevy and parked it on the street outside. His wife followed him in their sedan so she could take him back home. Pretty cool, huh?"

"Very cool," Anna said, laughing at Danny's exuberance.

"I'm going to leave the Chevy on the street for now so the KOA office won't have any record of me having a second vehicle. We can keep an eye on it from the kitchen. On Thursday, I'll use my old truck to drive to Jackson's, so I don't scare him to death. After that, we can take it to a used car dealer and see what we can get for it."

Anna clapped her hands in applause. "Well done, Danny, well done."

"You're pretty good at this clandestine thing," Mac said. "Hey, I'm getting hungry. There must be a restaurant near here. How about a celebratory dinner tonight?"

"We can't leave the cabin with no one in it," Anna said. "Sorry, buddy. There is the camp store though."

An hour later, they polished off three microwavable burritos and half a dozen donuts, and started a fresh pot of coffee brewing. Sitting in the uncomfortable wooden chairs at the square kitchen table that folded down from the wall, they began reviewing the plans they had sketched out the day before.

At 2:00 in the morning, before they went to bed, Danny, who Anna noticed was looking drawn, almost gaunt, made a suggestion.

"Listen, guys, I'm used to spending almost all my free time alone, every night, every weekend, just me and Bolo. I don't mind giving up my isolationist lifestyle, but it may take a period of adjustment. Right now, I need to find my center again. So, I was wondering, what do you think of spending the next couple of days just hanging out together but not talking so much?"

"This has been exhausting," Anna said. "I'm an introvert too, Danny, not at the far end of the scale like you are, but I do think I'd feel more energized if I could just tune out and shut down for a while."

Mac piped in. "Hey, I'm a full-blown extrovert, but constant high-octane processing and problem solving is wearing even me down. I'm all for a break. I need a hell of a lot more sleep than I've been getting."

"What I'd really like," Danny said, "would be to go up into the mountains and hike for a day or two. Unfortunately, I don't think we can risk it. If anything went wrong at this point, like an accident, or a speeding ticket, it could bring everything to a dead stop."

"So, the cabin it is," Anna said, "once again. We do have sandwich food here, and there are restaurants and fast food places within walking distance. I'd like to skip the whole cooking meals thing, if that's okay?"

"Every man, or woman, for himself, or herself," Mac said. "Damn it, English is not a gender-neutral language."

For the next two days, they moved in and out of the cabin in orbits so small, they couldn't help but collide, but they were moving so slowly, each bump gently propelled them apart again. Mac went for short walks so he could smoke from the pipe cupped in his hand. When he returned, he slept for long hours without interruption. Anna bought men's swim shorts in the KOA gift shop, and wearing those and a t-shirt, went swimming in the pool twice a day and soaked in the hot tub at night. She also finished two paperback novels.

Danny spent most of his hours out of the house, walking Bolo on a leash along city streets and through quiet residential neighborhoods, or sitting at the outside picnic table reading the day's newspaper from cover to cover.

Thursday afternoon, as soon as Danny put on his boots and picked up his keys, Bolo glued herself to his side.

"It's still beastly hot outside," Anna said. "You should leave her here."

"I should but she clearly doesn't want me to. This won't take too long, and she likes going to Jackson's. He likes her, too. She'll be fine."

"Good luck, man," said Mac, clapping his hand on Danny's shoulder.

"Are you sure you don't want company?" Anna asked. "I don't know why but this scares me, Danny."

"You two stay and keep the home fires burning," he said. "I'll call you if I'm delayed at all."

By the time he turned onto the dirt road leading to Dry Gulch Ranch, it was almost 3:00. The temperature gauge on his dashboard read a hundred-and-three, and Bolo was panting hard. Danny had only driven a few hundred feet up the road when he heard an unfamiliar buzzing sound. He slowed to a crawl so he could look around the cab to find out where it was coming from, then brought the truck to a stop. He reached into his backpack. The noise was coming from his burn phone.

"Hello?" He asked.

"I'm about to be busted," Jackson said, sounding deadly serious.

"I'm about a third of the way up the drive," Danny said.

"Then it's too late for you to turn around. Toss your phone out the window. "And Danny, you know where to look." The line went dead.

Danny stared at the phone for a moment, then threw it as hard as he could out of his window. It landed behind a clump of sagebrush, out of sight. Hearing sirens in the distance, he grabbed Bolo's collar with one hand to keep her from getting knocked off the seat, and stepped on the gas. The worn shocks slammed into potholes and bounced the truck up and down. By the time he pulled into the driveway, he could hear the sirens close behind him, coming up fast.

As soon as he turned off the engine, he heard frantic barking from the barn, which meant the dogs were kenneled. He saw Jackson coming from the side of the house, hurrying toward him. His clothes were disheveled; his hair looked like a bad abstract painting; and he was holding a pistol in his right hand.

Before he could cross the parking lot to reach Danny, three state police cars converged on the hacienda, followed by a black van. The cops saw Jackson's gun and screeched their cars to a halt at an angle that would give them cover. Ducking down, they opened their doors and backed out of their cars. Every one of them took out a weapon and pointed it at the old man. One cop, squatting down behind his car with a bullhorn, shouted, "Drop the gun. Get down on the ground. Get down on the ground."

Danny suddenly noticed two of the cops were taking aim at his truck, at him in fact, and he froze. The guy with the bullhorn barked, "You in the truck, step out, and keep your hands in the air."

Danny told Bolo, "Stay." He got out of the truck. Holding his hands high, he used his hip to bump the door closed so Bolo couldn't escape.

The man with the bullhorn started shouting at Jackson again. "Drop the gun and get down on the ground or we will shoot," he said, in a tone that made it clear he meant business.

Jackson looked over at Danny with a contemplative expression, but Danny had no idea what the old man was thinking. Then Jackson smiled at him, a heartbreakingly sad smile, Danny thought, and lowered his weapon to the ground. As soon as he backed away from the gun, three uniformed officers charged him, knocked him down, pushed his face in the dirt, and cuffed him from behind. A man with an FBI jacket got out of the van, walked up to the pistol and bagged it, then handed it off to a colleague. The uniformed officers pulled Jackson roughly to his feet.

"Jewell Thomas Jackson," said the agent, "you are under arrest for conspiracy to transport and sell illegal firearms. You have the right to remain silent." He rattled on, giving the whole spiel as if reading from a phone book.

Jackson said, "I won't speak to you without my attorney present."

The agent smirked. In a loud voice he proclaimed, "We have a warrant to search all of the buildings on your property." He waved a legal-sized piece of paper in Jackson's face. Two uniforms half-led half-carried Jackson to an unmarked car. One of them opened the back door and the other pushed Jackson's head down so they could fit him into the back seat.

Once they had Jackson secured, two state cops ran over to Danny, grabbed him, flipped him around, shoved him against the truck and tied his arms behind his back with plastic cuffs. Bolo growled, a deep guttural threat. "Quiet," Danny ordered through the window. She whined once, then went silent.

One of the officers pulled Danny's wallet out of his back pocket, which he handed off to an agent, and the other one turned him around again so he was facing them.

"Mr. Shepard," the FBI man said, looking closely at Danny's driver's license, the one taken when his hair was still long and blonde.

"You don't look much like your picture."

"I grew up," Danny said.

"What exactly are you doing here?"

"Jackson is a friend."

"You should be more careful about who you hang out with," the man said.

"I worked here some years back on assignment from my employer. I got to know the family a little, and I stop by now and then."

"What is it you do for a living?"

"I'm a lancscaper in Las Cruces, but I'm on leave. My sister, who lives in Minnesota, was in a bad traffic accident and I'm driving east to help her out. I just thought I'd stop and say hello to the old man on my way. I don't know what's going on here, but I don't want any trouble." "Because you are at the scene of a probable crime, we have reasonable cause to search you and your truck."

"Okay," Danny said, "search away."

They patted him down, then one of them cut the plastic cuffs and told him he needed to remove his dog from the truck and keep her under control. Danny turned around and opened the passenger door and lifted Bolo into his arms. She squirmed to get free but he held her fast while they searched. They turned up nothing because there was nothing for them to find. Finally, they told him to put the dog back inside the vehicle.

The agent carried Danny's wallet to the black van, where Danny assumed they would run a background check. His license still had his Las Cruces address on it, and his wallet still held his Las Cruces library card, the card for Bolo's vet, and some Pinyon Landscaping business cards with his name on them. If they called the office, Eduardo would verify Danny's story and vouch for his character.

What his boss wouldn't do was volunteer any additional information about Danny. Eduardo, who had been pulled over by state police and border patrol dozens of times just because he was a brown skinned man crossing state lines, had little goodwill toward federal or state law enforcement.

Almost an hour passed with Jackson sitting in the police car, hands bound, sweating profusely. Danny stayed by his truck, roasting in the hot sun, while the cops and agents searched the hacienda and the barn. He finally asked one of the officers if he could give his dog some water so she didn't die from the heat. The man gave him permission. Danny reached in through the half-open window, popped open the glove compartment, and retrieved the thermos he always carried for her when traveling. He poured water into the cup-sized cap, and Bolo slurped it down eagerly.

The FBI agent who had taken his wallet finally returned it. "You can go, Mr. Shepard. We'll find you if we need you." The threat was implicit. Danny's heart was pounding but he tried to keep his expression impassive.

As he climbed back in the cab, he saw Jackson looking at him through the open window of the police car, grinning. When he turned the truck around to leave, Jackson winked at Danny, then yelled out of the open window to everyone in hearing distance. "You got nothing on me. Just my pistol, and I have a lawful purchase receipt and a permit to carry, you motherfuckers."

Leaving Jackson there in such a state, in the hands of people who fully intended to lock him away whether they found an arsenal or not, went against every instinct Danny had. Still, he forced himself to look away. By the time he reached the main road, he was sobbing so hard he had to pull over and wait until he could get his grief, and his rage, under control.

Danny pulled into a used car dealership near downtown Albuquerque. A salesman, in khaki pants, a short-sleeved shirt, and a bolo tie, stuck his head out of the office door and yelled he'd be with him shortly. Danny put Bolo on leash and slung his backpack over one shoulder. They got out of the truck to wait. When the salesman walked up to him, Danny asked what he would offer him for a cash sale. The man looked at the interior of the truck, checked the tires and the engine, then turned the key to listen to the motor.

He walked off, saying he had to consult with his boss in the sales office, then returned minutes later with a ridiculously low offer that Danny declined. The man went back inside for a few more minutes, then returned with a new offer, a better offer, but not by much. Danny accepted this time. He and Bolo waited in the cool office while the dealer prepared the paperwork. He signed the papers transferring ownership, took the cashiers check, and handed over the keys.

They were almost out the door when the man called out, "Hold up."

Danny, his heart pounding, turned around.

"You and your dog need a ride somewhere?"

Danny thanked him. "That's kind of you but a friend is meeting me at a bar not far from here." He turned toward the street and, with Bolo still leashed, hurried down the block. As soon as the dealership disappeared from view, he reached into his pack for the burn phone. He dug around for a few seconds before remembering he had tossed it.

He figured he was about eight miles from the KOA, a walkable distance, but even though it was going on 6:00 in the evening the temperature felt like at least a hundred degrees. A long walk on a cement sidewalk would burn and blister the pads on Bolo's feet.

He lifted her up, cradled her in his arms, and carried her back to the dealership.

"Could I use your phone for a local call? My dog is a little sick from the heat, so I'd like to call my friend to pick us up."

The man ushered him into an office and told him how to dial out. Danny pushed up the cuff of his shirt. He had written the number for Anna's burn phone on his wrist before leaving the KOA that morning, just in case.

Anna answered immediately.

"Hey, it's me."

"Are you okay?" She asked.

"Yes and no. Bolo and I would sure love to get a ride home."

"What happened? Did something go wrong?"

"Fourth and Broadway," Danny said, giving her the coordinates for a nearby intersection that would be out of the dealership's line of sight. "Over and out."

Ten minutes later, she drove up in the blue Chevy to find Danny sitting on a bus bench and Bolo curled up in the shade underneath it. She pulled over and pushed open the passenger door.

"Are you okay?" She asked.

Danny climbed into the truck and helped Bolo into the back seat, then reached back to pet her. "That was one intense afternoon, wasn't it, girl?" He said, rubbing her face and neck. "You were such a good dog."

Turning back to Anna, he explained. "I'm okay. It's a long story, but Jackson's been arrested, and I almost was. And I left empty handed."

"Oh, my God," Anna said breathlessly, pulling away from the curb.

"Where's Mac?"

"Watching the cabin. Where is your truck?"

"When I left the ranch, I thought someone might be following me. I didn't see anyone but I was kind of freaked out. I drove around for a long time so I could shake a tail, if there even was one, which there probably wasn't. Anyway, I wanted to get rid of the truck as fast as I could, so I sold it to the first dealer I came to. Goddamn it," he said. "I just realized we can't register this one, at least not under our new names because we don't have new names."

She drove him back to the KOA. Mac was standing in the room waiting for them, looking worried and expectant. Danny acknowledged him with a nod and went straight to the shower. He stood under cold water until he started to feel chilled, then dried off and put on a clean pair of jeans and a t-shirt. He joined them at the small kitchen table and told them the story of the bust.

"What will happen to Jackson?" Mac asked.

"I don't know," Danny said. "I'm worried about him. Really worried. I've never seen him in such bad shape. Maybe I can visit him in the jail tomorrow, or maybe they'll release him. They may not have found anything to hold him on, if he was telling the truth about having purchased the pistol legally."

"From the scene you described, they may be able to hold him on charges of threatening a peace officer with a loaded firearm," Mac said.

"*If* it was loaded," Danny said. "I'll try to find out more in the morning. He told the cops he had an attorney but I have no idea if he really does or not. I've never heard him mention one."

"My God," Anna said, "this is all unraveling." She got up out of her chair and started frantically pacing the small room. "I can't go back to Kate and Gracie, you've quit your job, Mac has put his at risk, and now your friend has been arrested. On top of that, we can't register the new truck, so if we get pulled over, we'll probably get busted. Fuck, it's all going wrong."

"Whoa there, Anna, take it easy," Mac said, as if talking to a spooked horse. He got up and put his hands on her shoulders. He slowly moved closer, until he could wrap his arms around her. He put his cheek against hers, and in a calming voice, said, "It's going to be okay, everything is going to be okay. This is not a good situation right now but all is not lost. We're going to be all right." He rubbed her back lightly, stroked her hair, and held her until she stopped shaking. Then he kissed her on the forehead and returned to his seat.

Danny watched them absently with a puzzled expression. There was something bothering him, something he was missing about what happened at Jackson's. It kept flashing in his periphery but he couldn't get a fix on it, like when the wind spins a glass mobile and the sun catches it for just an instant. Suddenly, he slammed his fist down on the table. "That's it," he said with a grim smile. "I need to go to the sporting goods store we passed on the way into town before it closes." He stood up and grabbed the truck keys off the table.

"I told you Jackson is a good man," he said on his way out the door. "He has our stuff, and he told me where to find it. Get everything ready to pack up while I'm gone, and I mean everything. We're back in business."

Mac and Anna quickly finished the packing. It was almost dark by the time Danny returned. He walked in without a word, set a shopping bag down on the kitchen table, and pulled out his purchases: a topographic map of Bernallilo County, a hand-held GPS and a high-powered flashlight.

"What's this stuff for?" Mac asked. "What are we doing now?"

"After we load the truck, we're going for a little drive, but I don't think we should check out of here until tomorrow," Danny said. "I still want to try to see Jackson in the morning, if they'll let me."

"Then why take everything out of here now?" Anna asked.

"In case we don't make it back here."

"You are freaking me out, Danny," she said.

"Trust me, Anna. Just trust me."

He studied the map and entered coordinates into the GPS while Mac and Anna loaded the new truck. The trick would be navigating from an unfamiliar point of entry with the truck lights off and the quarter moon barely breaking through a low layer of clouds. The GPS should get them to the spot he'd circled on the map. He wasn't totally sure it was the right spot but it was his best guess.

When the truck was loaded and ready to go, they all climbed inside. Danny wound his way through town, avoiding the freeway, taking surface streets past restaurant chains and cheap hotels, past suburbs, past farmland, until he reached the narrow dirt road separating the north side of Jackson's property from that of his neighbor, Hansen. Two miles later, he cut the headlights off and turned onto Jackson's open range.

He handed Mac the flashlight and asked him to point it straight ahead, or as close as he could get to straight by leaning out of the side window. "Watch for rocks or sudden drop-offs in the terrain."

Mac saw a pair of bright eyes and pointed them out.

"Coyote," Danny said.

When they reached the coordinates he had entered into the GPS, Danny stopped the truck and got out. He climbed up on the hood and stood, scanning in all directions, looking for anything he could recognize as familiar, but it was too dark to see more than a few yards in front of them. He took the flashlight from Mac and jumped down from the truck. His eyes followed the long beam as he walked in ever widening circles.

He stopped suddenly, holding the light steady. To his far right, he saw familiar dark shapes breaking the horizon. He knew where he was: staring at the skeletal remains of the sycamore trees that he and Jackson had visited every year for the past eighteen years, with their rifles and bottles of whiskey.

Danny shut off the light, got back in the truck and drove straight to the site. He turned off the engine. They were engulfed in total silence, and almost total darkness, except for a barely visible sliver of moon peeking out from the clouds.

"Wait here," he whispered, getting out of the truck, "and roll the windows up halfway so Bolo can't jump out."

"Why are you whispering?" Anna asked.

Danny chuckled, and in a slightly louder voice said, "I have no idea." He walked a few yards, stopped, and stomped his foot on the ground. He started walking again, in wider and wider circles, dragging his boot heel through the sand. Then he got down on both knees and began to sweep the dirt outward with his open hands, just as Jackson had done.

Mac's voice carried through the silence. "What the hell is he doing?"

"I don't know," Anna said, sounding nervous.

Danny stopped moving dirt around. He stood up, then bent over and reached down. He pulled the hinged, circular platform up with him as he rose. He stood the platform on edge, stepped aside, and gave it a shove backward. The fiberglass cover hit the ground with a soft thump.

He waved to Mac and Anna to come closer. Just before they reached the dark hole in the ground, he held up one hand to stop them.

"This is Jackson's fallout shelter," he said. "He showed it to me when I stayed with him on the way to Four Corners. Christ, it's hard to believe that was only a few weeks ago."

"It does seem like we were in Cabin #23 for months," Anna said.

"Years," Mac said, "years and years." He spoke in a slow drawl, as if the very thought of it exhausted him. They all laughed.

"I'm going to go down," Danny said. "I'll need to turn the lights on when I get to the bottom, so when I tell you to, when I tell you to," add "pull the cover back over the hole." I don't want any light to show through, in case the feds have some kind of aerial surveillance thing going on. If they find us here, we'll spend the rest of our lives in prison."

He climbed down the stairs into the darkness. "Okay," he said up to them. "I have my hand on the light switch. I'll knock when I'm ready to come back up."

As soon as everything went black, Danny flipped the switch. When his eyes adjusted to the sudden glare of fluorescent lights, he looked around the room. On the center of the table on the left wall, he saw a large manila envelope with his name sprawled across it. Inside he found three New Mexico driver's licenses bearing his and the others' photos, along with three matching birth certificates.

On the cement floor in front of the table, he saw six, sixty-pound cardboard boxes labeled C-4, and two smaller boxes filled with electric match blasting caps. Next to these, he noticed two wooden boxes with 'D' written on them in black magic marker. He found the crowbar Jackson kept on a peg on the wall and pried open one of the crates. Inside, he found a hundred and twenty round yellow dynamite sticks, each one eight inches long and a little more than an inch in diameter.

He turned off the lights and climbed up the ladder, then knocked on the hatch overhead. It opened immediately. Mac and Anna appeared, staring down at him.

Danny climbed a few more rungs and handed out the envelope.

"Driver's licenses and birth certificates. They're all there," he said. "He also left some explosives for us, more than we'll ever need, for now anyway. I want you to open the truck box, then use my sleeping bags and the Mexican blankets to create a thick layer of padding on the floor of it."

"Do you need help down there?" Anna asked.

"No, I'll bring up one box at a time. I'll start with the C-4. Just pray I don't slip."

"I'm praying, man," Mac said. "Praying with every ounce of faith I have left."

"Somehow, Mac, I don't find that real comforting," Danny said with a laugh.

He went back down into the darkness. Feeling his way, he lifted a box of C-4 and approached the ladder, which rose straight up the hole at a ninety-degree angle. Cradling the explosives in his right arm, he wrapped the fingers of his left around an upper rung and began to climb. At each step, he had to wedge one foot between the ladder and the cement wall to keep his body from careening backward when he let go of one rung so he could grab another.

"Slow going," he said when his head emerged from the hole, but no one was there to hear him. Mac and Anna were still readying the truck. One more agonizing step up one more rung, and he placed the box safely to the ground.

He went back down, carried a second box up to the surface. This time, he found Mac and Anna waiting for him. "Thank God for Pinyon," he said, handing his load off to Mac. "All those years of shoveling gravel and hefting cacti over my head just paid off."

"Are you coming up?" Anna asked.

"Not quite yet. There are four more boxes of C4 down there, but I think we should leave them for now because there are also two boxes of dynamite."

Anna and Mac stared at him, then at each other. Mac spoke first. "Dynamite? Really?"

"I know," Danny said. "It seems crazy, after Oakland."

"I'm not superstitious," Anna said, "but it does seem a little ominous."

"I know, I know," Danny said. "I don't like the thought of it either. It makes me feel sad and scared. I don't like handling the stuff but I did use it a few times at Pinyon, and it can do things C4 can't, like blow a hole in the side of a mountain."

He waited while Mac and Anna looked from him to each other and back to him. They were all waiting for someone to make a decision.

"Can't that stuff blow if you sneeze?" Mac asked.

Danny shrugged. "It looks like it's packed in the original containers, and it's not sweating. Anna, you're the chemist. You know all about this. What do you think?"

"There should be a date on the box," she said.

"I'll check. I'll be quick. I hate being closed up in the dark."

Danny took the flashlight and went back down. After a minute, he found the date, and climbed back up. "It's dated 18 January 2017."

"Almost brand new," Anna said. "It should be okay to transport, since dynamite isn't easily set off by shocks, or sneezes, until it starts to degrade."

"I think we should take it," Danny said.

"Okay, I guess," Mac said.

"Okay," Anna said. "But, Danny Shepard, if you blow us up, I'll never speak to you again."

Danny grinned at her in the darkness, then went back down into the bunker.

After he brought the two boxes of dynamite to the surface, he went down one last time. He emerged with an armful of blankets and a rifle slung over his shoulder. He grabbed the edge of the fiberglass cover, lifted it and let it fall back over the opening, then scuffed dirt back over the cover.

Each of them helped carry the explosives to the truck, setting the boxes on the open tailgate. Danny and Anna climbed up and together lowered the ordinance into the truck box. They stuffed the extra blankets from the shelter, most of their clothing, and the pillow Anna had brought with her from Portland, in and around the cargo, then closed and locked the lid.

Danny let Bolo out so she could run around for a few minutes. When he called her back to the truck, Mac opened the door to the back seat and she leaped inside. He climbed in after her, and she curled up with her head on his lap. Danny started the engine and Anna turned on the GPS.

"First thing tomorrow," Danny said, "we get this thing registered."

"Great," Mac said, "nothing like having the DMV nosing around a truck full of explosives."

"No big deal," Danny said. "All they'll do is check the VIN number and take our money. We'll drive out with the title and a shiny new license plate."

"Damn," Anna said. "I can't believe Jackson came through for us, only to end up sitting in a jail cell. I'm so sorry this happened, Danny. Do you think what he did for us is what got him in trouble?"

"It's possible, I guess, but I don't think so. He's been skirting the edge of disaster for a long time, and I think he knew this was coming. I just want to make sure he has a decent lawyer. If he doesn't, I'd like to use some of our cash to hire a skilled defense attorney. Any objection?"

No one said a word.

They drove off the rangeland and onto the paved road just as the first light from the rising sun appeared on the horizon, sending a thin stream of pale white light through a break in the clouds. Mac, who claimed he'd been dying to eat at a restaurant ever since they got to Albuquerque, suggested they stop at a Perkins on the outside of town for coffee and breakfast. Outside the diner, he dropped quarters into a vending machine to get the morning newspaper. While they waited for the waitress to come and take their orders, he skimmed the headlines.

"Ah man, ah Danny, oh no. Look at this," he said, pushing the paper across the table.

Danny looked at the headline and paled. He read the article out loud in a voice even he didn't recognize as his own. "An Albuquerque rancher, arrested yesterday on suspicion of gun trafficking, died in his cell at the Albuquerque City Jail last night, from an apparent heart attack. Jackson Elliott, the seventy-nine-year-old owner of a once prosperous cattle ranch south of town, had been arrested earlier in the day on charges of conspiracy to transport illegal firearms. The police spokesperson promised a full investigation into the circumstances of his death. A press conference is scheduled for 1 p.m. today."

Danny pushed the paper away and hid his face in his hands. He didn't want to be in the restaurant any longer. All he wanted was to be driving his old white truck across the desert on a moonlit night, with Jackson sitting on the seat next to him, grinning, his elbow sticking out of the open window and his gnarled hand holding onto the sill. Danny could almost feel the warm wind blowing through the cab, could almost see it tousling the old man's fine white hair, and for a moment, would have sworn he caught a whiff of clean sweat and mash whiskey.

He imagined them driving off-road, off endless miles of unbroken horizon, until they reached the middle of nowhere. He imagined them climbing up onto the bed of the truck, passing around a bottle of Maker's Mark whiskey, telling stories and tall talks into the wee hours. He imagined hearing howling in the distance, and Jackson starting to how the chorus of Don Edward's Coyote song. Hoo yip hoo yip hoo yip hooo.

Danny lifted his head. He was surprised to see Mac and Anna watching him. They met his gaze briefly, then looked away. Without a word, he got up from the table and walked back toward the restrooms. He dropped a quarter in the phone booth on the wall, dialed information, and asked for the number of Mike Hansen in Albuquerque. The operator asked if she could connect the call for him.

"Please," he said.

Mike answered the phone.

"Hi, I'm Danny Shepard. I don't know if you remember me from Estrella's funeral."

"I remember you," Mike said. "You must be calling about Jackson. I just now saw the article in the paper."

"Yeah, that's how I found out too. I'm not in the area, and won't be for a while, so I can't do this myself, but I wondered if you could get in touch with his sons. I don't have their numbers but I know he keeps them in a Rolodex on his desk."

"Sure, if the cops will let me into the house."

"I'm sure they will, if you explain. Or maybe they've already contacted the family. But just in case the boys don't know his wishes, he wants to be buried next to his wife. You remember the spot?"

"I do," Mike said.

"And, Mike, could you do him one more favor? His dogs are probably still in their kennels, hungry and alone, unless the cops have already called animal control. Could you see that someone takes care of them?"

"I know his dogs," Mike said. "I can take them. I'll go over there now. What a sad thing this is."

"It is Mike, it is. The saddest thing I know."

Chapter 22

On a wet and dark November night, in a dense stand of woods abutting a fast-moving river, Danny dug a hole large enough to contain the twenty-seven-gallon storage tote while Anna carried away the displaced dirt, bucket by bucket, and dumped it into the water below.

Together, they lowered the container of explosives, blasting caps, fuses and burn phones into the hole in the ground. Anna got down on her hands and knees and began spreading loose soil over the top of the container, mixing in dry leaves and pine needles to camouflage the freshly turned ground.

Reaching for Danny's outstretched hand, she pulled herself up. They brushed the dirt off their clothes and appraised their handiwork.

"If anyone walks through here tomorrow, they'll notice," Anna said.

"Hon, no one is going to walk through here in the next twenty-four hours. It's too late in the season for kayakers and the river is too high for anglers."

They looked in the direction of the bridge, less than thirty feet away. The thick ground fog had swallowed it whole. They listened for car traffic in the distance, but all they heard were the gurgling sounds of water rushing over the rocky bottom of the Umatilla River.

"You're right, I know. And God knows they don't service these bridges very often."

"No kidding," he said. "This one is what, a hundred years old, give or take a few? And they haven't inspected it since 2005. It's a wonder more trains don't derail."

He carried the shovel and bucket to the trunk of the beige Nissan and pulled out his wool-lined outdoor jacket. "It's getting cold. Did you remember to pack gloves?"

"Yes," she said, slipping her hand into his, "and my safety harness and my coat and my phone. And four rolls of duct tape."

"Don't forget to wipe the container for fingerprints when you pull it out again."

"I won't. We've gone over that a hundred times."

"I know I'm a pain in the ass, but I worry. One little mistake, and…"

"Danny, please. I can't bear to think about all the things that could go wrong, not right now. Let's just go home, okay?"

Nodding, he lowered the trunk and pressed down hard until the latch quietly clicked into place. He got in on the passenger side and Anna climbed in behind the wheel. She turned over the engine but didn't turn on the lights. They both warmed their hands in front of the heating vents while they talked.

"Not one vehicle has passed by here in the last hour," she said.

"Only locals use these back roads this time of year, and most of them are in bed by now. I doubt we'll see another car until we reach the freeway."

"I know your bridge is isolated, but I wish it had more tree cover, like this one does," she said.

"I do too. It would simplify things if I could hide the truck nearby. But as long as Mac is still okay with dropping me off and picking me up, I should be fine. You really don't think he was upset when you told him about our relationship?"

"He didn't seem upset, or even surprised. He said he was happy for us."

After a long silence, Anna whispered, "We're really going to do this, aren't we?"

"Yes, it appears we are."

"And you're sure, Danny? Completely and absolutely sure?"

"I don't see any other way to have an impact, hon. And you?"

She reached over and took his hand in hers. "If I had two lives, I'd live one of them with you, Danny. I would go to sleep every night with you beside me and, for the rest of my life, I would wake up every morning in your arms. We'd babysit for Kate when she needed us, and on some weekends, the four of us would take a drive up the coast or into the mountains, or the five of us, if Mac could get free."

"Sounds lovely," he said. "Perfect, in fact."

"It does, doesn't it?"

He reached over, pulled her close, and kissed her with such tenderness, she felt a shiver run up her spine.

They let go of each other at last and Anna turned on the headlights. She drove them out of the woods and onto the deserted two-lane road.

The next morning, she woke to the tinny ring of the travel alarm. She shut it off and turned over to wake Danny, but he was sleeping so soundly, she decided to go to the airport without him.

Bolo followed her out of the bedroom. The lab had turned nine that fall; her muzzle was almost white, and she had developed a limp in her back leg due to the onset of arthritis. They knew their lifestyle, coming and going at all hours of the day and night, leaving Bolo alone for far too many hours, was stressful for the little dog. A few days earlier, they had come home at four in the morning to find one of Danny's socks shredded on the floor, Bolo sleeping next to it.

Anna poured kibble into a bowl and watched Bolo wolf it down, then sent her outside while she dressed. She put on jeans, a warm flannel shirt and a heavy coat, stepped into her Birkenstocks, and went out the door.

Bolo was sitting on her haunches next to the car, eyeing her, waiting.

"Oh, honey, yes, I am going to take you with me."

After a twenty-minute drive to the Spokane Airport, Anna pulled up to the baggage claim area. She saw Mac standing there, a small backpack dangling from one hand. She parked the truck, got out and ran over to him, almost leaping into his arms.

"Your mustache is back," she said. "And your hair is growing out again."

"Good as new," he said cheerfully.

"Any other luggage?"

"Nope. Just my day pack." He saw Bolo looking at him through the passenger-side window.

"Hey, there's my girl," he said. He climbed inside and Bolo was all over him in an instant. Wagging her tail furiously, she pressed her face against his, pushed her wet nose against his neck, and tried to climb into his lap. Mac wrapped his arms around her, buried his face in her fur, and scratched her belly. Finally, he patted her rump and said, "Okay, in the back with you." She jumped over the seat, nosed the back of his neck and snuffled him, then nibbled his earlobe once before settling down on her haunches.

"God, it's good to be here with you, both of you," he said, reaching back to pet Bolo one more time. "How's Danny doing?"

"Good, he's good. He's excited about seeing you."

Mac nodded. "How are you?"

"Okay, I guess. This is harder than I thought it would be—emotionally harder I mean. For the past few months, I was able to shut it out some of the time, even think about other, more mundane things, like setting the table for dinner, or doing the laundry, or going to a park with Bolo. But now, it's not just a plan. It's a reality, and it's right in front of me all the time, every day, every minute."

"I have to admit, now that I'm here, I'm feeling a little nervous myself."

Even in the bright morning light, Anna could see his complexion pale. "You don't have to stay, Mac, you know that, don't you?"

"We settled that argument a long time ago, Anna. Let it rest." She bit her lip and nodded.

"Hey, I do have a favor to ask," he said excitedly. "I don't carry pot on planes, so one thing I would really, really like, would be for you to drive me straight to one of Washington's infamous pot stores so I can buy a whole lot of legal dope."

Anna laughed. "You've got it, Mac. I can't go in with you, though. They'll ask to see your driver's license, and there are a lot of cameras in those places."

"Not to worry, my dear, not to worry. I haven't had to use my new identity yet and I hope I never do. And if old Mac Caffrey is caught on film in a room full of marijuana? Trust me, no one will blink twice."

They pulled up to the gray, clapboard house at the end of a long dirt road.

"Is someone else here?" Mac asked in a hushed voice.

"Oh, the Nissan? No, it's ours. We bought it for cash, six hundred bucks, from a kid in Oregon. It's not registered to us and we'll wipe it down and leave it in a parking lot somewhere when we leave for good."

Mac looked relieved. "Wow, you weren't kidding about this place being remote. But you said the house was a fixer-upper, not that it was caving in on itself."

"It's not falling down yet, just leaning a little. The owner lives in Idaho and is trying to sell the ten acres. I called him and told him I was a writer looking for a remote place to stay for a few months while I finished my novel, a place with no Wi-Fi and no distractions. I sent him a cashier's check, so he's never seen me and he doesn't know about Danny. He is charging three times the going rental rate for this dump. He probably thinks I'm dealing drugs."

Danny, in jeans and a dark blue t-shirt, opened the front door and walked out to greet them. He hugged Mac, not the shoulder-to-shoulder hug most men give other men, but a bear hug, a full body embrace. "Good to see you, man."

"Great to see you too, Danny," Mac said warmly. "It's been way too long."

Inside, Danny showed him around the rental house, with its ugly gray linoleum floors and pockmarked walls and battered molding.

Since it only had one bedroom and one bath, the tour took less than a minute.

They sat down on metal folding chairs at a plastic folding table they had purchased at a Goodwill outlet. Anna set out three cold bottles of beer and a plate of wheat crackers, hummus, cheese, and microwaved chicken wings.

"Danny," Mac said, "when you told me you were going to take over the cooking, I thought you meant, I don't know, you were planning to cook?"

Danny laughed. "That was my intention but this place doesn't have a real kitchen. Yes, that is a stove behind you but it doesn't hold a steady temperature, and only one of the burners is still operational. Cooking is one of my long-term goals, though. I do still remember how real food tasted. Sometimes I even dream about it."

"How do you heat this place? It's fucking cold in here."

"Electric baseboard heaters, but the one in the bedroom is the only one working. It didn't matter much until the last few weeks when the weather started to turn. It's a good thing we'll only be here for a few more days."

Anna studied Mac's face. "You've lost weight, buddy. You look really good."

"I quit drinking," he said, glancing at the unopened bottle by his plate.

They all sat there in silence, unsure of where to take the conversation next.

"You two are starting to look a little like your old selves," Mac finally said, "letting your hair grow out."

"Yeah," Anna said, "but when we leave here, we'll have to get new haircuts and styles, maybe even new colors. It doesn't seem fun anymore though, like it did when we were all in Farmington. I look forward to the day when we can just be ourselves again, if such a day ever comes."

For another long, awkward moment, no one spoke.

"It feels strange," Anna said, "being together in this place. The three of us were so close when we dropped you off at your car in Albuquerque, Mac. But things feel off-key now. I think it's probably just the distance, the physical distance, but it makes me sad."

"Of course it's strange," Mac said. "I've gone back to my normal life while you two have been living out here in the middle of nowhere, staring into the abyss. I can only imagine how hard it's been. And I've never been around you as a couple."

"Do we make you uncomfortable?" Danny asked.

Mac was quiet for a moment before answering. "No, it feels right somehow, just different."

"Are you nervous about helping us?" Anna asked.

"You mean, am I totally freaked out by the knowledge we could be arrested any time, and in an instant, the world as I know it could be lost to me? The answer to that question would be yes."

"It's not too late to change your mind," Danny said kindly. "We have a car all ready for you. It's no Prius, but it's gassed up and ready to go and it will get you home in one piece. We would have no hard feelings, Mac, if you decide to do that. It's such a relief just to know Bolo will be going with you. She's getting old and this gypsy life has been hard on her."

Mac filled and lit the new pipe he'd bought at the pot store, took a hit, and exhaled slowly. "You're a good man, Danny Shepard. But like I told Anna on the way here, the option of changing my mind is off the table. Do I want to do this? No, I do not. But this isn't about what we want, is it? It's about what we must do."

Anna moved her chair next to Mac and leaned her head against his shoulder. "It's so good to see you again, buddy."

"You too, hon," he said, his voice breaking.

Danny reached over and put his hand on Mac's arm. "We've missed you, man. Welcome back."

"So what exactly are we up to here?" Mac asked.

Danny went into the back bedroom and returned with what looked like an arts and crafts project. He and Anna had taken a U.S. atlas, cut out sections of Wyoming, Montana, Idaho, Washington and Utah, and taped them together to make a contiguous map of all rail lines leading from the Powder River Basin to the Pacific Northwest. Danny spread it out on the kitchen table and pointed to the red and yellow lines they'd drawn with magic marker.

"The Powder River Basin is the heart of the U.S. coal industry, but because the industry's profits are declining, mining companies are desperately trying to open up overseas markets. Right now, four coal trains a day pass through Spokane, and, on average, one oil train. But if West Coast export terminals are built as planned, Burlington Northern Santa Fe Railroad predicts forty-five to sixty coal trains and twenty-two oil trains a day will roll through there."

Mac interrupted him. "All of those terminals are being hotly contested by local citizens, so they may never see the light of day."

"True," Anna said, "but we can't assume that public interest will win out over greed. The fossil fuel industry is spending a lot of money to force a different outcome. If they can get their product to places like China or India, there's no limit to how much money they'll make."

Danny ran his hands over the map. "The rail system serving the Powder River is immense but it's also vulnerable. All coal and oil travels over six hundred miles on just two lines, BNSF to the north and Union Pacific to the south. There is no redundancy until the lines reach Spokane and Eastern Oregon, where they branch out like the tentacles of a giant octopus."

Mac traced his own finger over the lines extending from Wyoming into the Pacific Northwest. "Wow. I see what you mean. Cut off the head and the body will die."

Anna punched his shoulder. "Yuck, that's a terrible image, Mac."

"Sorry," he said, grinning. "But that is your plan, isn't it?"

"We're going to take out a bridge here," Danny said, pointing to a section of the red line in western Montana, "and here," pointing to the yellow line west of Pendleton, Oregon. "We're going to blow them simultaneously. Amtrak won't be impacted, since they cut northwest of our targets, but all other rail traffic from the Powder River to the West Coast will be brought to a halt."

"Simultaneously? That means you'll have to split up," Mac said, sounding worried.

"Yeah, that's the downside," Danny said. "Each bridge is about two and a half hours from here, but in opposite directions, so the only other option would be to stagger the timing. But that would be even riskier since once one line goes down, federal, state and local law enforcement will go into a state of high alert."

"So you want me to do what?" Mac asked.

"We've already delivered the explosives to both sites," Anna said. "Mine has good tree cover, so I can park the car there and not be seen. Danny's bridge is on the side of mountain, over a deep gorge. He'll have cover once he climbs up, but an unoccupied truck sitting on the side of the road would stick out like a sore thumb. We need you to drop him off, then pick him up after he places the charges."

"What's the likelihood of collateral damage?" Mac asked.

"You mean people?" Anna said. "Next to none. Both bridges are rail only, no cars or pedestrians allowed. We've surveyed them dozens of times, day and night, and checked and rechecked freight schedules. Tonight, we have at least a three-hour window with no scheduled rail traffic at either site. That will give us enough time to place and set off the charges, and it will give the railroad companies enough time to stop all trains."

Mac nodded slowly. "How did you figure out how much explosive to use, or where to put the charges?"

"You're going to love this, Mac," Danny said. "Anna, before she left Portland to meet us at Four Corners, download the 1992 *Army Field Manual on Explosives and Demotions* onto a jump drive. Our country spends billions of dollars on the surveillance of U.S. citizens, and at the same time publishes online, for all to see, specific technical guidance on how to blow up a bridge."

"God help us," Mac said, raising his arms as if exhorting a higher power. "Our country is lost in the wilderness."

"Amen," Danny said.

"I have one more question," Mac said. "How long will it take them to repair the damage?"

"It depends," Anna said. "If we've planned it right, our charges will cut through the steel support beams, causing the trusses to collapse under their own weight. From what we've read in engineering books in the library, it could take months, maybe a year or more, to replace them, especially the one straddling a mountain gorge. However long it takes, we hope it's long enough for foreign buyers to realize the United States can't be trusted to meet their supply needs."

"Even if you blow these bridges to smithereens," Mac said, shaking his head, "I don't think a delay will be enough of a deterrent to tank the market, not after one incident. It would take repeated interruptions."

"We've got nothing but time," Anna said.

"Whoa, hold on a minute," Mac said. "I thought you two were going to retire to Aruba or somewhere when you finished up here."

"Not if nobody retires us," Danny said.

Mac pushed his chair back from the table as if to get some distance from them. "Fuck, man, why would you do that? When you take out these targets, you'll have done your duty. Even if you're lucky enough, we're lucky enough, to get away with it, the feds and the railroads companies are going to be kicking over every rock for a thousand miles, for a hundred thousand miles, to find us. You'll never pull it off a second time."

"But, Mac," Anna said, "what if every time they get ready to reopen a route, we close it again?"

Mac stood up and reached for the beer he had left untouched during lunch. He picked it up and twisted off the top, paused, then carried it to the kitchen sink and poured it out. He returned to the table and sat back down. "Theoretically, yes, continually disrupting rail shipments would probably put an end to the industry's West Coast wet dreams. But this is the twenty-first century. Satellites, remember? Radar? Surveillance? There are cameras on every street corner and in everyone's pocket. It's too fucking risky."

He picked up his pipe, rearranged the pot in its bowl for a better draw, set it down on the table again. Looking first at Anna, then at Danny, he said, "I can't bear the thought of losing either of you." Anna stood up and came around behind him, then leaned down and wrapped her arms around him.

"Ah, buddy. We're all getting old. Sooner or later, you will lose us, or we'll lose you. It's the circle of life. Danny and I are in agreement: if something is going to take us anyway, at least we can do some good on our way out. But you, Mac, you still have things to do, places to go, people to see. We will always find a way to stay in touch with you but we won't involve you again, I promise," she said, fighting back her tears.

Mac didn't argue, just pressed her hands against his chest. "Coming here, I felt so excited about seeing you both again. Now I just feel sad and lonely. You're moving on, going to a place where I've never been and will never go."

Anna started to speak but he interrupted her. "There's no need to try to make it different. It is what it is. We will play different parts in the unfolding of this planetary drama but we are still on the same team. We are still fighting the same fight."

"All for one, and one for all, and all for the earth," Anna whispered. "It's still the only thing worth fighting for, worth dying for, for without it, all is lost."

Danny folded the map and cleared the table. He returned with two decks of cards and a full bottle of Maker's Mark. He poured himself half a glass, then went to the sink and diluted it with water. He remembered Jackson accusing him of resorting to 'washy' drinks, and the memory made him smile.

Anna beat them at two games of three-handed pinochle. They joked and laughed and kept things light until long past dark. Then Danny said, "It's that time."

Mac and Anna squeezed out the front door past Bolo, who immediately began to whine. Danny walked her over to the couch and she jumped onto it at his command. He sat down next to her, rubbed her head and her ears, pressed his cheeks against her face. He whispered to her, "There, there. You are such a good girl, Bolo. I love you so much. I'm sorry we have to leave you alone again, but we'll be back, sweetie, we'll be back."

She stared at him, accusingly he thought, as he walked away.

Outside, they gathered around the Nissan. "She'll be all right," Danny said, more to himself than anyone else. "Everything will be all right."

"I keep picturing Erin," Mac said, "walking into the Vantage building. He thought it would be a piece of cake. What would he think if he saw us now, taking on something that could get us all killed?"

"You know how he'd feel, Mac," Anna said, taking his hand in hers. "He loved this earth. He would have been leading the charge."

Danny moved closer to them, completing the circle. Anna watched him reach into the pocket of his coat and pull out a leather pouch.

"Is that the one Estrella gave you all those years ago?" She asked.

"Yes," he said, carefully untying the drawstrings and letting the carved onyx bear fall into the palm of his hand.

Mac, in a low whisper, asked, "What is that?"

"It's a Zuni fetish given to me by Jackson's wife. I'm not exactly a woo-woo, new age kind of guy, but I can't help but think she saw this day coming. The bear is supposed to help keep me from being captured by enemies and increase my power. I've carried it with me all these years but never had reason to call on it until now." He pressed the carving to his lips, breathed hot breath over the cool stone, and inhaled deeply to breathe in its spirit in return. He held the air in his lungs for a long moment, then released it slowly. He carefully placed the token back in the pouch.

They embraced each other, not roughly, like soldiers about to go into battle. They embraced each other tenderly, sorrowfully, like old friends parting for what could well be the last time.

Danny and Mac climbed into the blue Chevy truck. Anna walked around to the driver's side window and put her hands on Danny's forearm. "You two be careful."

"You know we will," Danny said. "You too, hon."

She bit her lip, squeezed his hand, gave him a quick kiss and flashed Mac a quick smile. Then she turned her back and walked to the Nissan. They started their engines, and one after the other, drove off into the darkness.

Chapter 23

At 2:15 a.m. on the morning of 28 November, in a remote corner of western Montana, an explosion cut through the steel girders of a railroad bridge owned by Burlington Northern Pacific, dropping the entire span into a mountain chasm far above the Clark Fork River. At approximately the same time, in Eastern Oregon, a second explosion took out a Union Pacific Railroad truss bridge: its mangled frame plunged into the Umatilla River, where it lodged like a demon boat, all angles and sharp edges.

Martin Hadden, the agent in charge of the FBI office in Portland, Oregon, and Paul Summerland, the agent in charge of the FBI office in Missoula, Montana, issued a joint statement saying they were taking charge of the investigation into 'acts of terrorism'. They also confirmed that no trains were damaged in either incident and no bystanders were harmed. However, the statement read, "Only two major east-to-west rail routes are used to transport coal from the Powder River Basin to the Pacific Northwest, and both have been rendered impassible."

Four days after the incidents, eastern Washington's leading newspaper, *The Spokesman*, reported receiving a typewritten letter, mailed from Lincoln, Nebraska, on 30 November. The letter, which they published prior to informing the FBI of its existence, read as follows:

According to the online Oxford English Dictionary, terrorism is 'the unlawful use of violence and intimidation, especially against civilians, in the pursuit of political aims'. The 28 November bridge explosions were not acts of terrorism, since our intention was neither to achieve political aims nor to harm or intimidate civilians. Our intention was simply to buy the climate a little more time by stopping coal and oil in its tracks.

Kate pulled on a fleece jacket and turned up the thermostat. Most of December had been unseasonably warm, but the weekend before Christmas, a fast-moving cold front brought icy rain and the threat of snow to the region. She debated going upstairs to get Gracie a sweater to pull on over her short-sleeved pajama top, but her little girl appeared quite content sitting at the dining room table with a coloring book, a new box of crayons, and a cup of hot cocoa. Like most kids, she seemed oblivious to the cold.

Kate was surprised to hear a knock on the door. None of her friends ever dropped by without calling first.

She opened the door a crack to see a man standing there. He had a droopy mustache and shaggy white hair, but he was well dressed, in a wool sports coat, a dark turtleneck, pressed Dockers and brogans.

"Yes?" She asked.

"Kate?" He asked.

Curious, she opened the door a little wider, far enough to see a black dog sitting on its haunches by his side.

"Yes?"

She watched him remove a piece of paper from his coat pocket just as Gracie came to stand next to her.

"Hello," said Gracie to the stranger. Then she spotted the dog, and her greeting turned into squeals of delight.

Kate put one hand down to prevent her from bolting out of the door to reach the animal. The man smiled warmly at her excited child while handing Kate a two-inch by two-inch black-and-white photograph. She took it tentatively. She looked at it for a long time.

"My name is Mac," he said. "The boy on the left is Danny. The girl is, of course, your mother; Erin, your father, is next to her. I'm the one next to him. I'm his brother, your uncle. I'm sorry it took me so long to get here, Kate. I only found out about you recently, but I feel like I've been waiting for this moment for the past forty-three years."

She realized the man was watching her closely, studying the emotions playing across her face: mistrust, confusion, and finally, recognition. She turned her scrutiny to him. His eyes were kind and their color was the same green as her daughter's, the same as her father's, the same as her own.

Picking Gracie up in her arms, opening the door wide, she motioned for Mac Caffrey and his dog, Bolo, to come in from the cold.

THE END